The Girl With No Name

About the Author

Reine Andrieu was born in 1967. While she holds a degree in business administration, Reine soon found a new passion in the world of books and has been working as a librarian ever since.

REINE ANDRIEU

The Girl With No Name

Translated from the French
by Deniz Gulan

HODDER &
STOUGHTON

First published in the French language as *L'hiver de Solveig* by Librairie Générale Française in 2021

First published in Great Britain in 2021 by Hodder & Stoughton
An Hachette UK company

1

A CIP catalogue record for this title is available from the British Library

Paperback ISBN 9781529384215
eBook ISBN 9781529384222

Typeset in Plantin by Manipal Technologies Limited

Printed and bound in Great Britain by Clays Ltd, Elcograf S.p.A.

Hodder & … wable
and recy … ble
forests. … to
conform … in.

To my tribe.

"Truth does not do as much good in the world as the appearance of truth does evil."

François de la Rochefoucauld

FOREWORD

Mid-May 1946

My laces are undone. They must have come undone in the forest. I've been running. For a long time. I found this bench to sit on in the middle of a village square. I don't know where I am, but what does it matter anyway? I'm glad to sit down and rest a while. My socks are full of earth. I fell over several times in the forest. My legs and arms are covered in scratches. I think I even fell into a hole. I woke up freezing cold, at the bottom of a . . . yes, it must have been a big hole, not that deep but quite wide. I'm covered in dirt from head to toe. I'm all smelly and itchy. Especially my head. I haven't washed for days. For . . . for I don't know how long. I just can't remember. And when I touch my head, I can feel something sticky. My hands are red. Did I hurt my head? Maybe it was when I fell into the ditch . . . Some children walk past and stare at me looking puzzled. They even stop a little way off to get a better look at me. A slight breeze blows dust up from the ground. I'm lucky it's not raining. But I can see lots of big clouds. If it rains, I'll go inside the church. No harm can come to me in a church. It's late. It'll soon be dark. I sit on the bench and wait. What else can I do? I don't know this village or the people I can see in the distance. Two ladies are talking and looking straight at me. One is nodding as if to say 'yes' to the other. A man comes up to me. He's filthy and wearing a huge coat. He smells awful too. Worse than me. He asks me if I want to see something interesting, something I've never seen before. I shake my head. I want him to leave me alone. He tells me to look at him, saying he'll tell my parents if . . . He stops suddenly and bolts when he sees the two ladies in the distance walking in my direction. Soon they are right beside me.

"Hello. Are you waiting for your mummy?" asks one of them, bending down towards me.

"No."

"Or your daddy?"

"No."

The war has left many children orphaned. The lady sits down next to me.

"If you have no mummy or daddy, who looks after you then?" she asks.

I shrug. I wish I could answer. She asks if I live here in Bournelin. I shake my head. I tell her I've been running. She asks where. In the forest, I say. I show them my dirty socks. They don't seem to understand why I'm sat here on this bench.

"Where are your parents?"

"I don't know."

"What's your name?"

I rack my brain trying to remember.

"I don't know."

"How old are you?"

I try again, but my mind is blank.

"I don't know any more . . ."

They say I'm very young to be outside on my own at this time of day and ask me why I don't go home. They offer to walk back with me. I look at them in a daze, and this time it's me who doesn't understand. I tell them I don't know where home is.

"Don't you live with someone?" they ask.

I shake my head.

"Don't you know anyone in Bournelin?"

I shake my head.

"Where did you arrive from?"

I point to the street I had followed to the square.

"I came from the forest."

They look puzzled. "What do you mean 'from the forest'? There is no forest here, only fields . . . the forest is much further away."

Why do they keep asking me the same thing? It's perfectly simple.

"From the forest where I was running," I say with a shrug. "And I hurt myself too."

I show them my scratches. They ask what I was doing in the forest. Do they not understand anything?

"I WAS RUN-NING!"

"But you don't run like that for no reason!"

I look at them but find nothing to say. I shrug again. All I know is that I'm here. And I'm very thirsty. And hungry too.

I

Solveig, 12th September 2011

I haven't slept a wink. The images engraved in my mind were haunting me the whole night. I kept seeing those planes flying into the twin towers like a scene from an apocalyptic film . . . People jumping out of windows. Whether to escape the inferno in the crazy hope that some supernatural force or divine intervention would save them or to hasten their death, I couldn't tell. I don't know which is worse . . . Choice or chance. Just what goes through the mind of someone who sees a Boeing heading straight for the ninety-fifth floor, right there where they are sitting? Yesterday was the commemoration of the tenth anniversary of 9/11. The images we had all already seen a thousand times relentlessly invaded our screens once again. Disbelief grips me each time and the absurd nature of the images intrigues me. Who would have imagined that one day two planes would deliberately crash into twin skyscrapers, literally within minutes of each other? Two swipes of the sword. Two blows of the club. But what astounds me the most is what we don't see: the plan in the making, behind the scenes. That a human brain can conceive of such an idea, propagate it and have it endorsed by other human brains is beyond me. By human I mean biologically speaking, as there is nothing human in devising a plan of this nature. It's simply monstrous, heinous, egregious . . . But if you look closely, the expression of human violence has always been monstrous, it is putrefaction incarnate, stinking and lurking in a corner, regularly emerging to taunt humanity as if to say: "You see, I'm still here!" A dormant volcano that erupts when you least expect it. I'm thinking of the massacre of the Native Americans, religious wars, the victims of Stalin and Mao, and the Shoah of course . . . Unfortunately, the list just goes on and on.

I am what we call, with a hint of condescension, an old lady. That's how they refer to the Eiffel Tower and the Notre-Dame Cathedral in Paris. It makes me smile. Yes, I'm an old lady and proud of it. I'm happy to have made it this far. After all, aging means you have been lucky; lucky not to have died young. So how can you complain about that? Though it was inconceivable that I would have the misfortune to witness the event that happened ten years ago. The century I've lived through has been marked by bitter, violent, and barbaric events, all with one thing in common: they were all masterminded by fellow human beings. And for no reason other than a mere thirst for hegemony or expansionism, or in the name of religion, or other ideologies, which in my book do not justify the death of tens of millions of people. Isn't that what it's all about? And I continue to ask myself what lessons have been learned from all this, as humans keep repeating the same errors ad infinitum. Not *all* humans, I should add. Just a select few, those who decide for others. And those who find accomplices for their murderous delirium. As I said, this is nothing new. From the beginning of civilization man has always waged war on others. And he hasn't become more civilized since. Yes, he cultivated his land and raised his animals for food, but that is precisely when the trouble started. He wanted more than the others. And to dominate the others. For what? Just to satisfy an inflated ego? I'll just go ahead and say it: humans are either completely idiotic or crazy, or worst of all, full of hatred. I'm talking about so-called "civilized" human beings, of course, because the tribes who live in the remote corners of Africa or the Amazon are more civilized than the rest of us put together. They don't destroy other people or the environment. Hitler was insane or sick, so they say. Okay, fair enough. But he didn't act alone. The Nazi officials who carried out his orders weren't insane or sick. They were simply fuelled by hatred. The Armenian genocide. The Hutu and the Tutsi. Fuelled by hate.

I've got enough on my plate coping with my own demons without watching humanity shooting itself in the foot yet again. I'm seventy-five years old and have stumbled through life's trials and tribulations. I've been married and have two children who are grown up now. My husband and I were devoted to each other. We were in love even, though you're not meant to say that at our age are you? I can't stand society's obsession with youth . . . Can you still be in love when you're over seventy? I'll answer that. *Yes*! You can. Well we were at least. I know what you're thinking. Sorry to disappoint you but no, our relationship wasn't just based on the platonic tenderness that is supposed to keep old couples together and make sure they look after each other no matter what. My husband and I had more than that. We made love right until the end. In our own way and without shame. I won't dwell on it. I know it can make some people uncomfortable. Or make them laugh. Nothing wrong with laughing about it, that's not the problem, though it depends how and with whom. We used to laugh as we romped. Then as we got older, we learned to laugh at ourselves.

He was older than me and when he passed away in 2008 I thought I would die too. My children were immensely supportive, but his absence was unbearable at first. My way of filling the void was not to let a void take hold. My beloved is still there with me. I talk to him. My children graciously tease me, calling me Granny Bonkers, but if it helps me cope, then I don't see any harm in it. They think it'll stall the grieving process if I carry on. "Mum, you're just setting yourself up for more pain!" they say. But it's actually the opposite. You see by talking to him, I can process my loss. I don't ask him questions for example, to prove that I'm not crazy. But it terrifies me to think he is no longer there beside me. My children were distraught at first, but now they join in and sometimes even say a cheery "Hello, Dad!" when they get home. So as not to feel like they are speaking to the wall, they have hung a framed picture of him in the entrance hall and talk to his portrait.

I am so fortunate, he has been my rock all my life. I was on the brink and he appeared. That's how life is. It takes from you with one hand and gives with the other.

I live in Toulouse. I didn't grow up here though. I spent my childhood near Bordeaux. My parents and I lived in a magnificent manor house on the outskirts of a small market town called Lignon. My father, Armand Lenoir, was a doctor. His own father had invested in the metal industry and had made a fortune thanks to the rapid expansion of the railways. As a result, my father received a generous inheritance. My mother, Noemie, who came from a more modest background, managed the house and the staff. My brother was born three years after me. He was born sickly and weak so he immediately got all my mother's attention. This meant I was quickly left to my own devices, but it didn't bother me. I was an independent, carefree, and resourceful child. Although that didn't last long.

For the three years that I've been without my husband, I have managed to forge a different kind of life for myself, different, but not unpleasant shall we say. For starters, I adopted another cat. I love cats. I already had one called Amadeus. He is a big, handsome, lumbering tomcat; more interested in his food bowl than being stroked.

He looks like the cat I had when I was a child and he stands out because pearl grey is an unusual colour. Then, one day, as I was walking near my house, I saw a black kitten roaming around and looking famished. I took it in and named it Freddie after the singer of a rock band I love. My Freddie has a magnificent moustache too. When I'm feeling down, I put on a CD and sing along with my idol. The high notes are a bit difficult, but I let myself get carried away. It's a great tonic. His voice is superb, like velvet. I assume he is still alive, otherwise my spirits will take a nosedive again. This doesn't mean I don't enjoy listening to a fine rendition of a Beethoven symphony or a Schubert piano impromptu. I was brought up with the classics; you don't forget. And when my parents discovered jazz and swing, they were won over straight away, as was I. And to think that the Nazis described this music as degenerate! Because of course killing six million people in cold blood is a far nobler pastime . . .

2

Noemie, September 1940

I am a woman of principle. At least I was. I am a practising Catholic. My life and that of my family are lived according to specific codes of conduct. Such codes have an underlying moral philosophy based on good and evil, that no doubt stems from religion. My free will protects me from all excesses. But I must admit that in the last few weeks I have lost my footing somewhat and my carefree existence as a provincial bourgeois housewife—to call a spade a spade—has become dangerously precarious.

It all started a little over two months ago, one afternoon in early July. For several weeks, the German army hadn't given the French troops any respite. They invaded Belgium and Holland, and France's roads were overflowing with people trying to flee the shelling. Meanwhile German troops continued to advance. Even the Paris region suffered a terrible onslaught. We followed all this from home, near Bordeaux, which had been spared from the fighting, but the atmosphere was very morose. We all wondered what the outcome of this relentless enemy advance would be. The answer to our questions was not long in coming, as Marshal Pétain, newly appointed as President of the Council, announced in a quavering voice that the fighting had to cease. In other words, France should accept defeat. Anger and bitterness took centre stage in people's minds. Was France really so weak as to let itself be swallowed up by the Third Reich? Since the end of the Great War, the country was convinced it had the best army in the world. At least that was what the propaganda circulated at the beginning of the war would have us believe. Then Bordeaux, which became the provisional capital of France after the government's retreat, was bombed by the German air force just before the signing of the armistice. War now lingers on our doorstep, but I think we would have preferred to see it continue on our soil rather than witness our country capitulate in this way. The fighting is still in range. War is indeed here. We suffer the effects of it every day and in a variety of ways.

Since the armistice, we have had to live under the yoke of the invaders. The Germans control our country to the north of a line, whose trajectory appears random but has in fact been skilfully calculated, and the French institutions have no choice but to yield and submit to the will of the occupying power. How humiliating for a country whose national motto begins with the word "*liberté*"! Or former national motto, I should say, because since the government moved to Vichy, the official line is now "work, family, Fatherland". How wonderful.

The occupied zone is now living on borrowed time, in every sense of the word. On 1st July, the clock of the Saint-André cathedral in Bordeaux was put forward an hour to German time. Our watches too. This is ludicrous, given that Lignon has a border with the southern zone which remains on French time. So in the village of Polignac, over the border, just three miles from our home, people are living an hour behind us. How ridiculous! You can't even write or call between the two zones. I wonder how families who live on either side of the frontier communicate.

Many support The Old Marshal and believe that the armistice is a ruse and that he has something up his sleeve. But, in my humble opinion, if he really had something up his sleeve, he would have revealed it by now. Others support the Vichy regime and cheer on the invader with a big smile. They imagine that the armistice will rid France of Bolshevism when the left-wing Popular Front fails. But they don't understand a thing: it was Nazi Germany that signed a non-aggression pact with the Russians!

We own a large property in the Vaillant district; a manor house that Armand inherited from his family. It was late afternoon when two German military officers came to our door in their well-ironed green-grey uniforms to explain that we were under obligation to take in one of their soldiers. Our maid was out shopping to find what provisions she could, given the food shortages that were beginning to make life difficult, so it was I who opened the door. My two children, one and a half and four years old, were clinging to my skirt and my first thought was to push them gently behind me, so that they wouldn't witness the scene. I feared that Solveig, my eldest, would make one of her controversial re-marks, something she did regularly despite her young age. The German officers looked fairly young, maybe twenty-five or thirty years old. They were fluent in French, but the elder of the two had a strong accent. In that moment, I loathed their aggressive-sounding diction—it reminded me of the war we were in the process of losing and conjured up tangled images of defeat, deprivation, misfortune, confusion, enemies, hatred and death.

The public authorities may have no choice but to submit to our German occupiers, but we, the population, do have a choice. I'm talking about people like us, who don't support Pétain and prefer placing our hopes in a certain brigadier, a former member of the Raynaud cabinet who fled to London to lead the fight for France to the bitter end with whomever will follow him. It remains to be seen just how he will achieve this. All this is still very hypothetical. Marshal Pétain may be a hero of Verdun, but not everyone supports him, far from it . . . we certainly don't in our house. So, naturally, we didn't welcome this young Wehrmacht officer with open arms.

My husband, who is a doctor, was with a patient at the time. So they informed me that part of our house would be requisitioned to accommodate Sergeant Kohler. Nothing more, nothing less. I had no say in the matter. There was no "please," no "thank you" from the elder of the two officers. These were more or less his exact words as he pointed to his young colleague: "Your house has been chosen to accommodate *Feldwebel* Gunther Kohler of the Wehrmacht, here present."

I sought to appear confident so that they wouldn't think they were intimidating me. They can be so horribly hard and unpleasant that I had to make a huge effort to hide my emotional state. In reality, everyone fears them. They are often very brutal. And more importantly, they call all the shots in the occupied zone. So if they come knocking on your door, you have every reason to panic.

"For how long?" I asked.

"As long as it takes, Mrs Lenoir. We don't know that yet."

"I suppose we have no choice in the matter?"

"You suppose right, Mrs Lenoir."

Their obsequiousness fills me with horror. They smarmily use "Mrs this" or "Mrs that" in every sentence, as if to make the pill of their ghastly domination slightly less bitter to swallow. He handed me a typed sheet of paper that I didn't bother to read. I guessed it was a written requisition order. It wouldn't tell me anything I didn't already know.

"Come back tomorrow, I'll ask the maid to prepare the room," I said.

"No, you've misunderstood, it takes effect right away, Mrs Lenoir."

Seeing that I was obliged to comply, I moved aside with the children behind me to let them pass. I pointed out the stairs to Sergeant Kohler to show him the way to his new accommodation. The officer who had spoken to me had already left in the direction of the village. Before climbing the stairs, Kohler stopped for a few seconds to look at the entrance hall of our house. He observed every detail: the parquet floor, the wood panelling, the furniture, the ceiling, the windows, the doors, the stairs and the carpet covering them, and the framed pictures on the walls. He appeared to be assessing the standard of his new lodgings and looked like the cat who got the cream. This didn't surprise me, because, as I mentioned before, we live in a beautiful family home which is both spacious and comfortable. I haven't rubbed shoulders with many Germans before, but the few times I have, I worked out that the less you say, the less likely you are to get yourself in a quandary. So I took the soldier up to his room on the second floor and left him there. The children's rooms are on the first floor and though there is a spare bedroom there, I didn't want him sharing a landing with them. Our maid Ernestine's room is on the second floor. They will be neighbours. There is a room in the attic, but it has no washbasin. That's why I chose the room on the second floor, although I later came to regret it.

While the unwelcome addition to the household was settling in, I went to go and find Ernestine, who was back by now, and asked her to make up his bed and give him some towels. Luckily he had the presence of mind to go in the garden while she was preparing his room. Even though the bedrooms are large, the thought of him watching Ernestine hovering around the bed disconcerted me. I spied on him from the window, annoyed yet curious at the same time. He was smoking a cigarette and bore the self-confidence typical of all the Germans I had had the misfortune to come across. He was rather tall and lean, displaying his youthfulness in supple, almost graceful movements. What surprised me most was the colour of his eyes. They were unusually black. Not brown but black. The pupil seemed to take up all the space normally given to the iris. Though I hadn't looked him directly in the eye, I could sense something other than the steely cold stare which had pierced me when I had opened the door and been confronted with the metallic blue eyes of his commanding officer.

At that moment, I knew it would be complicated having the enemy living under our roof. In fact, I didn't know just how complicated it would be, but not for the reasons I had imagined.

When my husband had seen his last patient and I informed him of our new lodger, he frowned, but managed to remain calm. Armand never loses his composure. He doesn't get angry and unless you can detect certain subtle facial expressions, you have to be very perceptive to guess what's going on inside his head. He doesn't reveal his emotions. Unlike me. I panic easily and quickly, and have to get a strong grip on myself so that I don't let anything show. He asked me if I had made the necessary arrangements to accommodate the Kraut—or the uninvited guest or 'UG' as we would come to call him.

A strange period of cohabitation thus began. It was as if we had a permanent houseguest, one who we couldn't ask politely to leave, and his presence weighed heavily upon us. For the first few days, he was very discreet. He was polite and respectful and even made an effort with the children. But the fact remained he was still German, and our days of carefree games and idle chatting with the children were over, at least for a while.

Sergeant Kohler sometimes came back to the house accompanied by his German colleagues. These men came and went as they pleased, and thought nothing of occupying the vestibule for long periods, although their presence seemed to make him uncomfortable.

Armand and I are part of the Anti-German France, the France that refuses to give up its independence. We have an utter loathing for all citizens of the enemy nation. Each and every one of them. We see them as a single block, a mass entity that we must liberate ourselves from as soon as possible. So this intrusion into our daily life, into our home, inside our own four walls, was unbearable. We experienced it as a violation, an attack, an invasion. They were like a tick on an animal, sucking out all of the joie de vivre we were trying so hard to cultivate for the children's sake. Not to mention the comments from neighbours and patients, who, like us, loathed the enemy. My stomach was permanently in knots. I could feel my pent-up irritation rise if by chance I ran into one of the Germans lingering in our house, whether it be in the vestibule, on the stairs or on the UG's landing. Heartburn gnawed away at me constantly, and Armand had a hard time relieving it.

One day, in the late afternoon, I was busy in the garden. The park is beautiful in the summer. It is very green and the flowerbeds provide a splendid array of colours. I like to take care of them myself and I find tending to them therapeutic. We also have a gardener called Germain, who looks after the grounds. There is always a lot to do regardless of the season, between pruning, mowing, hedge trimming, maintaining the vegetable garden and so on. But the flowers are my domain. He knows that I like to take care of them, watering them, weeding them and dead-heading as their blooms fade. Towards the end of that particular day, I was trimming the wilted flowers from a climbing rose that was growing up one of the columns of our small garden pavilion. I noticed the UG, dressed in civilian clothes, approach and sit down. He obviously hadn't noticed me there. I discreetly moved away. Such was my rejection of all that he represented, I could not bear to be physically near him.

Nevertheless, that day I loitered, surprised to see him in the pavilion. He had been living with us for a month by then and my curiosity began to get the better of me. I was torn between feelings of repulsion and a strange attraction towards him. Since he has been living in our home, his compatriots' selfish behaviour aside, I have no complaints about him. On the contrary, he is pleasant and generous. He regularly brings us food, tobacco and other rationed commodities that we can no longer find at the market or in the shops, and he is kind to the children when he bumps into them in the hallway. What's more, he praises Cosima's cooking and is extremely courteous to Ernestine, who isn't exactly gracious to him in return.

As I watched, he took a book out of his trouser pocket and began to read. It was an extremely hot day, and the heat had released a heady mix of fragrances from the flowerbeds. The weather was perfect, and the heavily scented air was a reminder that, despite the war, nature was unperturbed by man's hatred and insanity.

It was this solace that, like me, the young German officer seemed to be seeking. When you took out of the equation our different allegiances in this conflict, as people we were essentially not so different. He was there to wage war, to defend the interests of his nation, but the man I was observing looked so ordinary. He had left behind in his room all of the trappings of a German soldier. Watching him sat there, I could see no trace of his leader's deadly ideology.

I deduced that war has this unfortunate consequence of distorting relationships. In normal times, this man, more or less of the same social standing as Armand and I, would have been a welcome guest in our house. We could have discussed politics, news, literature, music, and much more. But the current situation prevented it. For some reason, I couldn't take my eyes off Gunther Kohler. He was immersed in his reading, completely relaxed on the bench, his legs stretched out and crossed, his slender hands holding the book at arm's length. Suddenly, a bird flew away right next to me and I uttered a cry of surprise that betrayed my presence. He immediately looked up from his book and spotted me.

"Mrs Lenoir, I didn't know you were there . . ."

"Oh . . . well, I just arrived," I lied quickly.

My location meant that this was impossible, but I didn't know what else to say. He grinned at the pains I was taking to explain myself. I smiled back, somewhat embarrassed.

"Have I passed the exam?" he asked with a crooked smile.

I didn't know how to reply and decided to be honest with him.

"It's not easy, Mr Kohler, you know, when your country has been occupied."

"Especially with the occupier living under your own roof?"

I looked down at the ground before responding.

"Exactly. Do you have any idea how it feels?" I asked boldly. I moved closer to him.

"Of course I do, it's not easy for me either."

It was the first time that we had spoken to one another in this way, far removed from the usual daily domestic subjects of bed linen, meals, the plumbing in the bathroom or the door that wouldn't close properly.

We were both embarrassed, he not knowing whether to continue reading and me hesitating between pursuing the conversation or going back into the house. In the end, he was the one who broke the silence.

"I have been wanting to thank you and your husband for a long time, Mrs Lenoir."

"For what?"

"For having me to stay in your house."

"It's not like we had a choice is it?" I couldn't resist saying.

"Evidently. But I feel at home in your house. And although our relationship is not exactly friendly—or limited to the basic pleasantries, shall we say—I'm well treated, the food is good, the house is comfortable. So, I believe I owe you some gratitude."

His reverence angered me. Yet, when he mentioned our lukewarm relations, I felt ashamed. I bowed my head.

His black eyes were focused on me. I could see a kindness, a goodness in them that merely reinforced my shame and crushed my resistance. All my revulsion and resentment, the brave stance I had thought was necessary when confronted with the enemy, melted like the wings of Icarus flying too close to the sun. To avoid giving myself away, I pretended there was something that required my attention back at the manor and headed indoors.

Over the next few days, I found myself inventing reasons to bump into him during his routine comings and goings. I had some task which took me to the second floor or I happened to be in the hallway when he arrived. I would have some urgent work to complete in the garden so I could be near the pavilion where he sat and read after a day at the barracks. We would exchange a few words. If Armand or Ernestine were in the vicinity, I didn't stay long. I didn't want them to surprise our tête-à-têtes.

Gradually we began to occasionally meet at the end of the day in the small pavilion to talk. Armand was busy at the surgery and Ernestine was occupied with the children. Despite his youth, Gunther was very cultured, and talking to him did me good. We never lacked for topics of conversation. Each new meeting reinforced our budding friendship. The pleasure we got from these secret encounters was so delightful that I would look forward to this stolen moment together all day. He had felt the same, as I learnt later. Luckily our only witnesses were the wisteria, the roses or the hellebore. At least, that's what we thought . . . One evening, we had to muffle our roars of laughter as we tried to sing together. He couldn't keep up with the rhythm of the song and soon the melody got lost in a mishmash of words. It suddenly hit me that I should be prudent and avoid frequenting him in this part of the garden, where though we couldn't be seen, our laughter could attract curious ears. We parted that evening with a sparkle in our eyes and joy in our hearts. In such troubled times, it is rare for frivolity to supplant seriousness, so when the opportunity arises, you must make the most of it. These moments were like a burst of pure oxygen, a breath of fresh air in the claustrophobically morose atmosphere. For a few fleeting seconds the war and its adversities seemed far away. There was even a glimmer of hope.

One evening, I decided to take him a piece of the cake that Ernestine had managed to bake with a few scarce ingredients. Gunther usually had his meal on a tray in his room. From time to time he brought us a chicken or charcuterie and at other times he provided vegetables. We gladly accepted everything. We gave him food, water and lodging, which we indeed felt merited the odd contribution. While Ernestine was bathing the children and Armand was seeing his last patient, I took the piece of cake up to Gunther. He was touched by my gesture and asked me in for a moment. For the sake of propriety, he took care to leave the door ajar. On the lower floor we could hear the children playing in the bathtub. A little embarrassed by my intrusion into his intimacy, he pretended he wanted to show me something. He had pinned some pictures on the wall and now he pointed to a portrait of an attractive young blonde woman.

"My fiancée," he explained. "She lives in Cologne. I haven't seen her for almost a year now."

"She's pretty," I said without thinking.

I had felt obliged to say something that would please him. Yet at the same time, I felt a pang of jealousy at the thought of Gunther with this young German woman whom I didn't even know.

"Her name is Hannah," he replied simply.

I was surprised by her first name, which sounded Jewish to my ear. As I scrutinized the photograph, I wondered how a German soldier in love with a young Jewish woman must feel in a country subjected to the Nuremberg laws which prohibited mixed marriages. Although I may have been mistaken about her being Jewish. I was annoyed at the tenderness with which he gazed at her face.

"But it's hard to remember after a year . . . It's a long time . . ." he went on with difficulty.

"I understand," I said. "But you must have had a few French girlfriends since you've been here?"

I regretted this stupid question as soon as the words were out of my mouth. It was meant to be tongue-in-cheek and playful, but it simply revealed my uneasiness. Besides, I didn't even wish to know whether Gunther had seen any other women while he was in France. He sensed my awkwardness and smiled at me. Silence reigned while he considered his reply.

"You are well aware, Mrs Lenoir, that we German soldiers are not much liked over here. Most French girls refuse to get involved with us, which is understandable."

Then he chuckled. "Though not all of them by any means; some of my friends have even fallen in love! I haven't had that opportunity but I haven't been looking for it either."

He uttered those last words in a low voice, his eyes glued to the portrait of his fiancée.

We were stood next to each other in front of the photograph. He looked down. He seemed confused and undecided. My arm brushed against his and I could feel myself becoming increasingly confused. We were both lost in thought and I was ready to bet that he too was recollecting our recent complicity. I decided to put an end to our conversation before he noticed my turmoil.

"Goodnight, Gunther."

He looked surprised to see me leave.

"Thank you for the cake, Mrs Lenoir."

"Noemie, please!" I whispered.

"Goodnight, Noemie."

Before I stepped out the door, he spoke again.

"I sometimes hear you and your daughter playing piano. You play really well and your daughter is good for her age."

"These days we don't really have any desire to play."

"I understand." He lowered his gaze. "I'm a musician too. Didn't I tell you? My favourite instrument is the cello, but I also play some piano."

I smiled.

"Goodnight, Gunther."

On my way down I ran into my husband who was on his way up.

"What were you doing on the second floor?"

I could hardly lie about being there.

"Did the UG want something?"

"Of course not . . . Should he so much as dare to ask me for something!" I stammered, feigning anger to hide my embarrassment. "I was putting some linen in Ernestine's room."

"Can't she do it herself?" he asked.

"Yes, but that's how we arranged things. It's really not important . . ."

I didn't sleep well that night.

I dreamt about my childhood.

I was at the dining table in my great-aunt's house. She was angry because I had spilled my bowl of *café au lait*. No matter how many times I said I didn't do it on purpose, she kept scolding me. In my dream she had her two fists on the table in front of me as I held my head in my hands. I was crying, so dismayed was I at the mess I had made.

I lost my parents to the Spanish flu in 1919 when I was only four years old. As most of my relatives died in the epidemic, I was raised by my mother's aunt, one of the only surviving members of the family. This brave and courageous woman did everything she could to compensate for the fact I had no parents. She had no children herself. Perhaps that was one of the reasons she was maladroit in showing me any affection. She rarely kissed me, and when she did, the gesture was awkward and fumbling. When she deemed my behaviour to be inappropriate for a little girl of my age, she didn't beat about the bush and promised me God's fury if I did it again. One day, I got the hem of my dress and my knees very dirty while playing in a muddy part of the yard. So annoyed was she, that she opened both arms and looked up to the sky, asking the heavens in complete seriousness who would want to marry someone so slovenly. I was seven years old at the time, and the idea of marriage was completely abstract to me. I was more curious to see if the heavens would answer her—I was worried that I would be punished by whomever was up there in the sky.

As time went by, I realized that she was doing her best to educate me in her own way, abiding by the social etiquette and religious precepts that were appropriate for our station in life. For this reason, she was often stricter than necessary in her quest to bring up a 'proper young lady'. Deprived of my parents and a stable and reassuring family environment, I donned this role gladly, as an abandoned kitten attaches itself to a charitable owner.

I first met Armand at the home of some friends of my aunt's. He was studying medicine at the time in Bordeaux. This handsome young man captured my teenage imagination, me a love-sick teenager, whose head was often stuck in sugary sweet romance novels. From then on, I imagined all sorts of scenarios in which I would try to see him again, but failed to carry out any of them. However, fate stepped in and I met him again at a funeral. His father had died and my aunt, who by this time was old and fragile, had asked me to go with her to pay her respects—a proposition that I had eagerly accepted. My aunt was somewhat surprised at my enthusiasm and I'm sure she thought I was woefully deprived of a social life if I jumped at the chance of attending a funeral. She understood later on, of course. Armand and I saw each other several times whenever he returned to Lignon and the family estate. I was sixteen years old and he was twenty-one. When we met, we would walk through the vineyards or along the stream that runs through the village. He used to tell me all about his life in Bordeaux and his studies, which he was passionate about. I would recount the various books I was reading, the content of which I had to modify, so as not to appear dull or stupid. The more we saw each other, the bolder he became, though we never went any further than a few chaste kisses, which for me was already the height of eroticism. We courted for two years. Then my aunt died, slipping away peacefully one icy morning during the harsh winter. I was saddened by this loss and now found myself alone. Armand decided the time was right to propose. His studies were nearly over and he was finally ready to set up his surgery at the manor. Everything fell smoothly into place. His mother, who by now was widowed, would live with us too. Or should I say, we would live with her. That's how I became Mrs Armand Lenoir, delighted at having the protection of my beloved and a roof over my head. My mother-in-law welcomed me graciously into their lives, in memory of my aunt whom she had been very fond of.

But our life with her didn't last long and ended in terrible tragedy. One evening, the poor woman was hit by a train entering Lignon station. We had both been waiting for Armand who was returning from Bordeaux for the last time—his medical degree was finally complete and he was ready to embark on his new profession. While she was searching for a handkerchief in her bag, her red lipstick fell out and rolled along the platform. She automatically reached out to pick it up, not realizing how close she was to the edge. She lost her balance and fell onto the rails just as the train approached and ground, screeching, to a halt. I watched the scene in helpless horror. As soon as he got off the train, Armand tried to resuscitate her, but to no avail. The blow proved fatal. This was how my life as Armand's wife began. The accident plunged both of us into a deep melancholy and our life as newlyweds was inevitably tinged with sadness. My husband was slow to regain the smile and lightness that had won me over during our courtship. We didn't have the heart to do anything remotely entertaining and our lovemaking in the beginning was somewhat of a disappointment. And as my education had given me a rather bland view of what a couple should be, I didn't question what Armand had offered me: a quiet life, quickly filled by the arrival of a first child, then a second. Though deep down I used to long for the carefree light-heartedness of our early years. Armand's sadness eventually turned into a kind of coldness towards me. I consoled myself by observing other couples who by force of habit had ended up with the same sort of marriage as ours.

Unable to sleep that night, I realized just how bored I was with my life. However, the current context prevented any familiarity with someone like Gunther. Right then and there I decided I would avoid running into him from now on. It wouldn't be difficult; his schedule ran like clockwork. My decision made, I finally fell asleep although I still couldn't erase his face from my mind.

The next day, Gunther went to the pavilion in the late afternoon. I saw from afar that he was looking around the garden. Was he looking for me? Then he lingered a while in the hallway before going up to his room. When I heard his footsteps on the stairs, they seemed heavier than usual. I felt like I had a lead weight on my chest. I closed my eyes and told myself that I had done the right thing and that it would be the same every other day. And so it was.

However, soon afterwards, something happened that put an end to my good intentions. One morning it was raining heavily when Gunther came home wounded but conscious, aided by two German soldiers. His head and chest were bleeding. They explained to me in their guttural French that a metal beam had fallen on him in a dilapidated hangar where they had been picking up equipment. I called out to my husband to drop what he was doing as I could see that this was an emergency. I occasionally assist my husband in urgent situations like this one when he needs another pair of hands. He quickly and efficiently sent the other two Germans on their way. Gunther was losing blood and needed treatment fast.

"Lie down," he ordered. "And you, put on some overalls and take off his jacket and shirt."

I followed my husband's instructions. Gunther didn't stop staring at me the whole time, and tried to catch my eye. I stopped myself from looking at him and satisfying his silent expectations, and concentrated on doing what was necessary. When I opened his shirt and saw the wound, I nearly fainted. Blood gushed out of the gash in his chest. I had seen a lot of injuries before, of course, especially since the war began. Did it have this effect on me because it was him? My husband was none the wiser and busied himself with Gunther's head while I made a swab of compresses for his chest.

Gunther winced when Armand cleaned the wound.

"I'm going to stitch you up," he announced. "Be warned, I don't have any more painkillers or anaesthetics. Your colleagues took the lot, so I have no more pain relief to offer you."

"Go ahead doctor, I'm ready."

He screamed out in pain when Armand stuck the needle into his scalp. He waved his arms in the air searching for an imaginary lifeline. One of his hands found my arm and he grabbed it. He dug his fingers into my flesh with such force I could feel his torment. It even crossed my mind that maybe my husband was making him suffer unduly. But I knew Armand. He hadn't chosen this profession by chance. He had always been driven by a real desire to help people. Everyone, without exception. I finally looked at Gunther who was gazing at me beseechingly. His tears of pain moved me. He realized that he was hurting my arm and reluctantly let me go. I held his hand with both of mine to comfort him, like I would have done with any other patient. He closed his eyes. Armand noticed my gesture and stole a glance at me while still focused on the needle. I dropped Gunther's hand, which seemed to surprise him, and he opened his eyes. This time it was he who grabbed my hand. Armand took this to be a sign of desperation, but I knew what it meant. I knew that my life would never be the same again. I knew that the man convalescing under our roof was the embodiment of this transformation and that he would bring me suffering and joy in equal measure.

When Armand had finished, I helped him with the bandages. Dizzy with pain, Gunther found it difficult to get up. Armand and I helped him to his room. I placed him on his bed as best I could to avoid his wounds. Armand brought Gunther some tablets and then went downstairs to greet the other patients as the waiting room was slowly filling up. I helped Gunther swallow his medication and was about to leave when he grabbed my hand and kissed it. I didn't know what to do and kept my head down, still not daring to look him in the eye.

"Thank you, Noemie," he managed to whisper.

I blinked to acknowledge what he had said and pulled my hand away sharply. I stepped outside and was about to close the door but then felt guilty for being so cold towards this injured man who meant well. I leaned around the door again.

"Will you be all right? If you need anything, just call. I'll leave the door ajar."

"Noemie, what's the matter? Have I done something wrong?"

"No, Gunther, no."

Both my head and my body were saying no.

"It's not you, Gunther, it's me."

I left.

What I had feared would happen soon came to pass. On the first day I sent the maid up to Gunther to take him his meals, his medicine and anything else he needed. Ernestine is from Toulouse. Her family moved to Lignon about ten years ago. When she came back downstairs, she couldn't stop ranting in her local dialect about Gunther who was having trouble eating, washing and getting dressed on his own.

"Good God, these Krauts are delicate little flowers, they whinge and complain like littluns! You couldn't put that one on the front line!"

I pretended to agree with her, telling myself that someone would have to help the poor man with his daily hygiene, which he simply couldn't do himself with his wounds and bandages.

I spoke to Armand about it and he told me in no uncertain terms that we could not expect a nurse to do it as they had far too much on their plate at the clinic.

"Could you take care of it please."

I nodded. Unbeknown to him, my husband's request would turn out to be my salvation as well as my downfall.

3
Justin, end of May 1946

"Justin! You're the youngest here aren't you? Come here, I've got a job for you!" That's pretty much how I was assigned little Angela's file. As I was young, they thought I was the most suitable person to handle a little girl's case.

The child had been found in the square by two women searching for a soul to save. A lost little girl who doesn't know who she is or where she lives, raises a lot of questions. Questions the spinsters had asked themselves as well as the little girl, but the child had had no answers. She simply couldn't remember.

I'll go back to the beginning. Two weeks ago, on 15th May to be precise, two ladies arrived at Bournelin police station with a little girl. "Justin! You're the youngest here", etc. When I got to the reception desk to see what all the fuss was about, I found two sanctimonious-looking matrons of a certain age, each holding the hand of a little blonde girl. Her eyes were as big as saucers as she looked around her in amazement, clearly wondering what she was doing there. She was covered in scratches that had left bloody marks all over her skin. They hadn't been able to get her to reveal who she was but you could see that something untoward had happened to her. The two women kept up their bleating: "All she does is repeat that her socks are dirty! She doesn't even know where she lives, the poor thing . . . could she be touched in the head?" Hearing this, the little girl looked daggers at them. And quite right too! The child was obviously anything but stupid. You could tell, from her gaze, her appearance, the way she carried herself and the few words she had managed to utter. I thanked the spinsters, grabbed the girl's dirty hand and guided her into a quiet office. I sat down next to her and opened the window, as the smell was overwhelming. She didn't appear to be afraid; she just seemed lost. I offered her a glass of water and she gulped down two in a row. I tried to make small talk to glean some more information. When she didn't reply I decided to question her.

"You said you were running in the forest . . . Which forest do you mean?"

"I don't know."

"Did you see anyone?"

"No, I don't think so. I ran. I fell over."

"Did you hurt yourself?"

She looked down at her scratches.

"Those scratches, did you get them while you were running?"

"Yes, I did."

"And did you hurt yourself when you fell?" I asked again.

"I fell down a hole. I fell asleep and then an animal woke me up."

"An animal?"

"Yes, I think it was a rabbit or a fox."

"Rabbit or fox, couldn't you tell the difference?!" I laughed, making a weak attempt at a joke to try and lighten the atmosphere and put her at ease. I didn't succeed.

"I can't remember. Maybe I dreamed it. But then I got up and ran again. To the square, where those ladies found me."

I looked at her feet and started to take off her shoes. Her feet were bruised and covered in blisters. She must have walked for miles.

"Do your feet hurt?"

She pouted as if to say she didn't know that either. I knew I had to get her examined by a doctor quickly. She might have suffered other, less visible injuries from the fall.

An hour later, Dr Bertin gave me a quick diagnosis.

"This little girl has suffered trauma. She fell, that much is obvious, and you can see the mark of the impact on her temple. But I'm not sure if that's what caused her amnesia. Because she has amnesia, did you understand that, Justin?"

"Yes, of course . . . But are you sure she didn't take a serious blow to the head?"

"First, give her something to eat, the child is starving, aren't you little one?"

She nodded. I went to go and look for some food. Not an easy task. Even though the war is over, rationing is still the norm. But I knew whose door to knock on. The boss always has a few treats in his drawer. I don't know how he does it, but he manages to get tobacco for his pipe, as well as all kinds of sweets. I took a plain biscuit and an apple. The little girl stared at them greedily while the doctor looked at me, astonished.

"Since we don't know when she last had a meal, she needs to eat slowly, in small, spaced doses. A head injury cannot be ruled out even if she doesn't display all the symptoms. The fall caused her to briefly lose consciousness, hence her confusion about the animal she saw. Its presence could have pulled her out of the concussion or maybe it was just a vision . . . But this little one is in good physical health, I think, apart from the superficial wounds that we'll treat right away and of course the exhaustion from malnourishment. Her main problem is psychological and directly related to whatever she went through in the hours before she arrived here. Hours or days, how can we know? She has most likely been terrorized, but by what or by whom is anyone's guess."

"How long do you think it will take for her memory to come back?" I asked then.

"My dear Justin, how long is a piece of string? It could take an hour, a day, a week, a month . . ." the doctor said with a shrug, incapable of giving me the answer I sought.

"But what am I going to do with her?" I asked the doctor—and myself—in a low voice.

"We should see whether the sisters can take her at the orphanage. But don't let her stew there for too long. They're not very welcoming, so I've heard. You'll have to gain her trust and question her every day to see if she remembers anything."

"And how do I do that? I don't know how to do that sort of thing! I have other fish to fry. We're in the middle of that investigation into the fake Resistance."

"I'll go and talk to your chief. I'll ask him to give you time to take care of her. The war is over, Justin. The crooks can wait. She can't."

"You know, doctor, it was to catch those bastards who discredited the Resistance and stole from the villagers that made me want to join the police force in the first place."

The doctor shrugged again.

"You may be able to do both . . . But take care of her, Justin, it's important. If you need me, I'm here. This is an interesting case for me too."

He walked towards the door, stealing a last look at the girl.

"One more thing, doctor! How old do you think she is? Can you guess her age?"

"I'd say she's about ten years old."

At this point, I began to wish I wasn't the youngest member of the local force. Why is this happening to me? Just when our team are in the process of cracking down on a fake resistance movement created—incidentally—just after the Allied landings. They had to have known that the locals would be willing to supply them with provisions. These criminals looted the local farms for their own personal consumption. And they didn't just target the chicken coops and vegetable gardens, they got the poor people to hand over their jewellery and hunting rifles, all in the name of the Resistance, which desperately needed supplies, money and weapons. If the villagers didn't comply, they were beaten up. A gang of criminals has been identified and the police are about to make the arrests. They just have to corroborate a few witness statements to prove that the suspects definitely have no links with the real Resistance. It's a matter of days now . . .

I had vowed to myself that I would not be taken to Germany as a forced labourer. So to avoid being conscripted into the Compulsory Work Service, known as the STO, decreed by the Vichy government, I joined the local Resistance in 1943. It wasn't just to hide, as I had been active underground for more than a year already, but my mother had just passed away and I no longer had any family ties to hold me back. My father, who died shortly after I was born from his injuries sustained in the Great War, was not there to warn me or urge caution. Thanks to my experience in the field, I soon became group leader. However, from 1944 onwards, many fraudulent underground movements formed by ill-intentioned thugs muddied the waters. The French people were afraid and no longer knew who to trust. They were willing to help the genuine resistance fighters, but not to deprive themselves for a cause which could turn out to be dishonest. I swore that I would have these criminals, who preached fake patriotism at the eleventh hour, hung drawn and quartered. And I would have the law on my side.

I should have been a schoolteacher, like my best friend Eliette. However, the disillusionment brought on by the war took away any desire I might have had to face a class of young souls in the making. What is left to tell them that isn't lies or at best untruths? That adults must be obeyed? Not at any price. That you have to work hard at your lessons to become a good person? If it's just to get slaughtered in the next war, what's the point? I came across many uneducated young men in the Resistance who were worth far more than many sons of so-called important figures in society whose heads were crammed full of knowledge. Teach children to be *good* citizens? Collaborators and other scoundrels who distinguished themselves during the war also went through the education system and undoubtedly learned to be *good* citizens . . . For what may I ask? And as for teaching grammar and arithmetic, I wouldn't be very good at it. So, gradually, even before the war ended, I realized that teaching wasn't for me. I would have felt like an impostor. My late mother's brother, who was in the police force, encouraged me to join too. I'm not saying the police played an entirely innocent role during the war. There were some rotten turncoats in its ranks who displayed extraordinary zeal without being asked. But my uncle's arguments convinced me: "We need men like you, Justin, intelligent, with your head screwed on. We didn't come off particularly well during the war, it's complicated, but I think you'll see it's a rewarding job, one that makes you feel useful." I haven't ever regretted my decision. And now this case falls into my lap: a young, mysterious orphan with no memory.

How am I going to find any trace of the child's parents if she doesn't even know who she is? I sit down beside her and ask her if she can bring herself to trust me, and for some reason she says "yes", her big dark eyes looking into mine. Here we are, the two of us, in this anonymous room in a provincial police station, with no idea what to do next. We stare at each other as if looking for answers. Then, unconsciously, our eyes make a pact. I can feel myself succumb. I feel my heart open up wide to absorb this little girl and her distress.

This little girl with her angel face, her fine, delicate features and her skin covered in scratches from the branches and undergrowth as she ran frantically through the forest. This distressed little girl has decided to place her trust in me, Justin Mayol, an ordinary policeman.

From that moment on, this was more than a mission for me: I promised myself to be worthy of the trust she had placed in me. In this job when you find yourself in such a situation, you resemble a dog with a bone . . . I swear that I'm going to snoop, sniff, scratch, dig around, and do whatever it takes to find what I'm looking for. Like I did to uncover those fake resistance fighters. The trouble is that I don't yet know where to start, other than finding a way into her nebulous memory to discover what happened to her. I feel like I'm looking for a needle in a haystack during the harvest.

My chief informed me that he had notified the convent orphanage on the outskirts of town. Throughout the war, the sisters have taken in children with no parents, or who lost their parents in the turmoil. On hearing the word "orphanage", Angela—that's what we call her now—choked back her tears.

"Do you know what an orphanage is, little one?"

She nodded.

"I'm going to take you there for the night, but tomorrow morning I'll come and get you so we can find out where your parents are, okay?"

"Yes."

"You do have parents, don't you?"

"I don't know. I think so."

"But you don't know where they are?"

"No, I don't know where they are."

"Did you understand what the doctor said? You've lost your memory. It's probably just temporary, but we're going to try to help you get it back. And with what you tell us, we can start looking for your parents. Are you sure you don't remember your last name?"

I randomly said a few local names, hoping that one of them might sound like or remind her of her own. Faure? Martin? Simon? Fournier? Morin? The little girl just stared at me blankly. Nothing seemed to resonate with her. I decided to give her a pencil in case she wanted to write anything down. Our name is probably the word we write the most in our lives. But once again, nothing. Her little hand gripped the pencil, the lead poised over the paper, but she didn't write a thing.

"Don't worry. It will come back." I smiled at her. "You're going to come with me to the orphanage. You'll be well taken care of there. After a good night's sleep, I'm sure you'll start to remember."

I secretly hoped that the atmosphere at the orphanage would be as nice as I had portrayed it. The sisters are not exactly good at dealing with fragile children who have already suffered trauma at such a young age. I heard that some of the sisters are extremely strict, unnecessarily so. Not to mention the harsh living conditions: the girls sleep in large dormitories and are subjected to prison-like discipline. They are forbidden from speaking during mealtimes, and the slightest misdemeanour, even something as trivial as dropping a fork, is punished. The children wash in ice cold water in winter and many of them suffer from frostbite. Dr Bertin told me that he had had to treat a child whose hands were one mass of sores from the cold. Her frostbite had become badly infected and the poor child was in agony. Those who run the orphanage consider kindness and affection to be a sign of weakness that could diminish their authority. I'm not sure Angela will survive there.

The next day when I arrived at the orphanage, she rushed to come and see me. I took that as a bad sign. I had to get her out of there fast. However, the next day and over the days that followed, I began to realize that Angela's memories were more deeply buried than I had first thought.

It has now been almost two weeks since Angela was found. We are very slowly starting to make progress. She with her memories and me with my investigation. Even the tiniest of details which resurface are the beginning of a lead for me. I snoop, scratch, sniff, and dig around, as I promised I would. I don't lose hope. I'll get to the bottom of what happened sooner or later. I'm also glad now that I was assigned this case. What I considered to be a curse a fortnight ago was actually a blessing in disguise. This child is a godsend. The doctor was right: the fraudulent resistance fighters will have to wait or be brought to justice by my colleagues. It won't affect the war. Angela's situation, on the other hand, is serious. But I'm powerless at this point. I'm angry and frustrated but I must let things run their course.

4

Angela, 3rd June 1946

Thank goodness I've got Justin, as those spiteful old hags at the orphanage are driving me mad. I've only been here two weeks and they're already getting on my nerves. We're not allowed to do anything. We can't even read. Justin got me a book as I love to read, but they confiscate it in the evenings, saying it's not good to read before bed, as it can give you bad thoughts. What rubbish! I have always read, I can tell. Holding a book feels familiar to me. I don't think it gives me bad thoughts. It's the opposite—if anything I would say it actually gives me good ideas. It's like the whole world is in the same room as me. I discover so much and it makes me think. Justin said I must come from a "good family" judging by my education and my habits. The other girls at the orphanage are a bit dim. I feel sorry for some of them as they witnessed their parents die in the war, but others are half-wits. They do everything the sisters say, even if it's stupid. I can't be like them. So I asked Justin to bring me another book which I hid under my bunk. I ask the sisters for the first book from time to time so they won't get suspicious. I've learnt to make them think I obey, while I do the forbidden things in secret. I made a pact with my bunk mates. To stop them from saying anything, I make their beds for them. On even days, I do Laurette's, and on odd days, I do Marceline's. Since I arrived here, I have been trying to remember my name. I often pick up a pen, like Justin told me to do, hoping that I'll remember something. Like a reflex, Justin says. But my mind is still blank. Justin can see it upsets me, so one day he came in and said they'd found a name for me, till I remember my real one. He asks me if I have a favourite name and when I say no, he asks if they can call me Angela as I have a face like an angel.

I agree, as it's a nice name.

The police have begun to look for the forest. It's not easy because the town is surrounded by fields. Then after the fields there are woods all around. I can't remember which direction I came from. The only memories I have start in the street leading into the village square. Before that, I can't recall anything, except running into the forest. The policemen took dogs with them. The idea was that the dogs would sniff the clothes I wore the day I was found, so they could track my scent. But the sisters burned the clothes I was wearing the day I arrived, so it was impossible. What idiots! The dogs were unable to find the forest I ran through. For several days they wandered all over the woods surrounding the village, without finding a thing. There was no way of knowing where I came out.

Justin also investigated reports of missing persons in the area, to see if a ten-year-old girl had been reported missing. On a map, he marked out a thirty-mile radius around Bournelin and asked the local authorities and the police force to investigate. If a girl had disappeared, the police would have been alerted. But no, nothing. Justin was tearing his hair out. I couldn't have walked more than thirty miles though . . .

Justin then had another idea: maybe I had been kidnapped for a ransom. I could have been snatched and held somewhere in the area, as my parents are probably rich. Then he realized if that had been the case there would have been missing person posters all over France. He keeps repeating that it just doesn't make sense. I don't understand what doesn't make sense, but I can see he's out of his mind. If only a tiny little glimmer of memory would come back, just a tiny weeny bit, then I could try and piece the rest together. What if my whole family has disappeared? What if my whole family is lost in the woods . . . If so, who would have reported them missing? The neighbours? The family? Or no one? I tell Justin my idea.

"But you wouldn't have made it that far on foot, Angela . . . I mean there have been no reports of missing persons within thirty miles of here."

"Maybe it's because people didn't notice that my family was missing . . ."

"I doubt it. You seem to come from a well-established family, socially speaking. You must have had people around you: domestic staff, neighbours, perhaps even important figures like the mayor, the doctor, the parish priest . . . How should I know? You went to school, your teacher would have noticed if you were missing and alerted your parents."

Justin shook his head and looked down at his feet.

"No, if your family had disappeared, it would have been reported."

"And what about if someone hurt us?" I asked.

I don't dare say what I'm thinking, then I change my mind, as the police have said that "no stone must be left unturned". I must give Justin all the help I can.

"I mean a murderer. There really are murderers out there. It's not just in storybooks . . ."

"Don't talk nonsense, Angela. And if this was so, your family's disappearance would have been noticed."

"We could make the circle you drew on the map bigger?" I suggested.

"The chief doesn't think it's necessary—it's too far away . . ."

"Good, then I have no more ideas," I say, feeling miserable.

I really like Justin. And I think he likes me too. He's so nice to me. Occasionally, he takes me to his house so he can say things he can't say at the police station. Sometimes Eliette is there. She's the same age as Justin: twenty-four. They went to school together. They seem to like each other very much, in a friendly way. Even though I'm a little girl, I know the difference between love kisses and friendly kisses. I don't really like Eliette. When she's around, Justin laughs with her and ignores me. Although she squints a bit, she's got a pretty face. But she looks a bit like a peasant and her clothes must be ten years old. I know that's not a nice thing to say, as we've just come out of the war and it's been hard for everyone. I think she likes Justin more than he likes her. Justin is handsome. He looks like a big child, with a soft face, no beard, and dark chocolate eyes, like a film star. I haven't been to the cinema very often, but I know what actors look like. I've seen pictures in magazines. I don't think Eliette and Justin are well matched.

It makes me sad to think that I might have parents somewhere. They must be worried about me. I can't stop thinking about it. Even at night. I rack my brains trying to catch a glimpse of my old life.

Things are horrible at the orphanage. I sleep there each night and I stay every morning to attend school. Justin wants me to stay on at school for several reasons. He doesn't want me hanging around the police station all day because it's pointless until we have more clues about my parents. And then the doctor said that it could stir things up in my head. I also think Justin doesn't want to have me under his feet all day long.

I have a lot of nightmares, but I hardly ever remember them in the morning. I wake up sweating and feel terrible with a pain in my chest that's really tight. The sisters tell me off because I wet my bed sometimes and the other girls make fun of me. I don't care, I'm not the only one. When it happens, they make us wash our dirty sheets. I've never done it before and wet sheets are so heavy. As I'm not strong enough to lift them, the sisters shout at me and make me write lines as a punishment. I don't see how this will stop me wetting the bed, it'll probably make it worse: the more scared I get, the more I need to wee.

Plus they make me wear those horrible old orphanage clothes which are either too big or too small. They are usually stained, with holes in or just plain ugly. I look awful in them. They force me to wear jumpers that itch too. Luckily, it's June, so I can take them off during the day. When I first got there, covered in scratches from the forest, the wool rubbing on my skin was unbearable and made me cry.

"My, you're a delicate little thing, aren't you?" they would say without sympathy.

"It hurts, I prefer to be cold than wear this!"

"And who will pay the doctor if you get ill?!"

"No one, Dr Bertin will look after me. Please, is there anything less itchy I can wear?"

"No there isn't and you are going to have to make do like everyone else. You're not the mistress of the manor here, you know!"

And the swines left me with the itchy jumpers. So Dr Bertin covered my worst scratches with gauze, to help them heal better.

I wish Justin would let me stay with him, but he can't. He would have to adopt me but as we don't know if I have any parents, it's not possible. He says it's too early and that we don't have a choice. We have to wait till I get my memory back. Dr Bertin takes good care of me. He comes to the police station two or three times a week to talk to me, to see if it helps me remember anything.

There is a detail that puzzles them both though: my reaction to closed doors. I can't bear it if a door is shut completely. I start shaking all over and get anxious and curl up in a ball to protect myself. And I start crying and can't stop. The first evening at the orphanage, when Sister Raymonde, the nastiest one of them all—"Sister Pigswill" as I call her—closed the dormitory door, I got scared and I started trembling and panicking . . . The other girls went to tell her and I was punished.

"Scared of the dark at ten years old, whatever next? Just calm down. We can't take everyone's whims into account here."

When Sister Pigswill had gone, I bravely went and opened the door slightly. Just a little, which was enough to reassure me. The horrible old witch doesn't understand a thing, it's not the dark, it's the door! It's the same in Justin's office. If he closes his door completely, it happens to me again. The doctor says it's because of the trauma I suffered. I must have been locked inside something. But who would do that? My parents? What if my parents had done it? Some parents really do torture their children . . . I've read about it in books.

Who am I? I feel like a boat floating in the middle of an ocean which is much too big. I can't get my bearings. A tiny boat that doesn't know which way to go.

5

Gunther, November 1940

How stupid can you get? Instead of being a war casualty, I'm a casualty of my own carelessness. A wooden beam fell on me in a dilapidated hangar, wounding me badly and causing a disabling chest injury. It's absolute agony if I laugh, sneeze, or cough. I am extremely lucky to be living with one of the village doctors, Armand Lenoir. And I have another consolation: Noemie. Noemie Lenoir.

I arrived in the Bordeaux region five months ago just after our two countries signed the armistice which split France into two: one zone is occupied by our troops and the other is known as the free zone. The role of our unit since then has been to monitor the free passage from one zone to the other near the small town of Lignon, about twenty-five miles from Bordeaux. Life is calm and quite pleasant here.

I have noticed a striking contradiction since my arrival. On the one hand there is an abundance of wealth, particularly for us Germans. The exchange rate is very favourable, one Reichsmark being worth twenty francs, almost twice its true value, meaning we can more or less buy what we want. On the other hand, there is much poverty and destitution as a direct consequence of the war. Yesterday I was able to buy luxuries such as chocolate, coffee and clothes. Not just for me though. I'm going to send a parcel to my family in Cologne, as my mother wrote to me telling me that everything is in short supply on the other side of the Rhine too. Some French people are living rather well. I guess it largely depends on their pre-war situation and where they obtain their food supplies. As always, if you've got money, it makes life a lot easier.

Another big divide which is just as striking is the attitude of the French towards us. On the one hand you've got those who have come to terms with losing the war. They are kind to us, sometimes ingratiatingly so, and it makes us cringe. They venerate the Marshal and are delighted the war has ended. When we see them in the street, they smile or call out to us. Others, however, loathe us and are scornful and openly antagonistic. Especially since Marshal Pétain and the Führer decided that the French would collaborate with us. The Lenoir family belong to this latter category. I can understand why they don't like us, as the Reich has taken over the local government, the police stations, and the town halls, and the German flag is flying everywhere. Or the Nazi flag, I should say. And some of us are actually lodging in their homes, like I am with the Lenoirs. A lot of us are in this situation. It works well for some, but for others it's more complicated. It depends a lot on the host's political opinions and what they make of Pétain's choice to end the fighting. As for the Lenoirs, I know that they don't agree with the Marshal. Their welcome was icy. I feel like I have to keep apologizing for being there. Our chief of staff has instructed us to behave correctly with the local population and to aid them as much as we can, which is what I'm trying to do. But it's not easy to be polite and helpful when you're faced with a wall of overt hostility. In the beginning, I was very circumspect and kept my head down as much as possible even though I would have loved to converse with them and hear their opinions on the war. No anger. No bitterness. Just a normal adult conversation. I would have liked to participate in their family life too. I miss my family terribly. The Lenoirs have two adorable children I would be keen to get to know. Their daughter is especially bright, a remarkable girl, very endearing. She expresses herself surprisingly well for her age. Though I soon realized that any *rapprochement* is out of the question. Any discussions about the war would quickly turn sour. I understand, of course, for it's easier for the victor to talk about it than those who have to accept defeat. I couldn't possibly intrude into their private lives. They keep themselves to themselves, and I do the same. Even though I'm technically entitled to treat their home as my own, I would feel uncomfortable doing so and prefer to abide by their rules. Certain rooms in their house are out of bounds to me and conversation is limited to the essentials. I'm allowed to request a towel or a book, but not to discuss the pros and cons of the Third Reich or Vichy policies. I must not make mention of the aberration of our cohabiting arrangement either. To keep the peace, I give way and obey my hosts' implicit wishes.

I often wonder what my reaction would be if the shoe were on the other foot. How would I cope watching my country being swallowed up by another, with the invading power showing utter contempt for my culture, my traditions, and my freedom? Without being able to react or express any disapproval? It would be unbearable, of course, and this helps me comprehend their behaviour when I hear their derogatory remarks.

One day I noticed a change in Mrs Lenoir's attitude. While I was reading in the pavilion one afternoon she appeared out of nowhere. I wondered whether she was spying on me. She was visibly embarrassed. We exchanged a few words. From that day on, we started to become better acquainted. We got into the habit of meeting there, to talk, out of sight. I think she hides this from her husband and staff, as she would be ashamed if they saw her giving me any attention. One day, shortly after our first "meeting", she was very disagreeable with me in front of her husband. I inferred that she was afraid he might find out about our relationship, which though I would not go as far as to call a friendship, is certainly becoming more amicable. They refer to me as the "UG" behind my back. I know this because I heard them talking one night when I was supposed to be out. I racked my brains for a while trying to figure out what it meant. Then I understood: Uninvited Guest. It wasn't that hard when I put myself in their shoes. I felt hurt at the time but I had to face facts. For them, I would never be anything other than an intruder in their house. I wondered if Noemie, Mrs Lenoir, was merely attempting to pull the wool over her husband's eyes or if she genuinely meant the things she said. I later understood that the hostility she displayed towards me in front of her family and staff increasingly bore little resemblance to her true feelings.

Since I've been here, I've been thinking about Hannah a lot. Several soldiers in my unit are involved with French girls. Sometimes these have turned into genuine love affairs. Two people with no commitments. There's nothing wrong with that. But the situation is often untenable in public. I sometimes wonder what will happen to these romances as the war progresses and I'm not particularly optimistic. Unless such couples move to another country less directly affected by the conflict. I also realize that I may soon be in the same boat, except that I'm not free, I'm engaged to Hannah. And I'm falling in love with someone else. I haven't seen my fiancée for a year now. I received a few letters and sent some in reply, but the spark is slowly fading. I can feel it. She assures me of her love and says she is waiting for me. But I just don't know anymore.

One day I showed Noemie Hannah's picture. I think I wanted her to know there is someone out there who loves me for who I am and not *in spite* of who I am. I suppose I was trying to make myself more attractive in her eyes, and I also wanted to see her reaction. She frowned as if surprised. I think this was because of Hannah's name. Noemie must have guessed she was Jewish and wondered about our relationship.

My soldier comrades tease me about Noemie. They think she's Jewish because of her dark hair, dark eyes, and olive complexion. I'll spare you the details about her nose and their other inane clichés. Have they put two and two together? I'm careful not to tell them about my Jewish roots on my maternal grandparents' side. This technically makes me what the Nazis call a "*Mischling*", literally a Jewish half-breed. My father is Aryan. My parents married in 1913, when mixed marriages were commonplace. Today, my parents are atheist. This doesn't change anything for the Nazis though, as they don't see a simple conversion to Christianity as enough to wash away the disgrace and shame of our origins. As for Hannah, our parents have known each other since we were children. Her parents are both Jewish, but her family isn't religious either. We grew up together. When we were teenagers, our feelings for each other intensified. We never imagined that we would ever have to live apart, or that anyone else—let alone someone else's spouse—would ever encroach on our happiness.

This crossbreeding makes us *Mischlinge* outcasts, disliked by the Jewish community because we don't participate in its rituals, and hated by the Nazis for our Jewish blood. My parents were both teachers at the University of Cologne. In April 1933, my mother was dismissed under the "Law for the Restoration of the Professional Civil Service", which, under the "Aryan Clause", permitted non-Aryan civil servants to be expelled from German public institutions. From then on, only my father was able to continue his work as a civil servant. My mother, resenting this relegation, continued to teach at home and gave private lessons. As for me, I was a cellist before joining the Wehrmacht. After my music studies, described as "brilliant" by my teachers at the conservatory, I joined the Gürzenich Orchestra in Cologne. I don't know by what miracle my father managed to get me into this prestigious institution, but I think it was my German ancestry on his side of the family that undoubtedly opened doors for me.

Hannah wanted to go into medical research. Hopefully, if all has gone to plan, she should be completing her studies by now. But her Jewish background will mean she will never be able to work in that capacity. At most, she might get to be a general practitioner, or whatever else the Nazis deem most appropriate for her.

I spent my childhood in a nice part of Cologne. Though we weren't wealthy, we led a comfortable existence. Our house had a small garden. I was an only child and received all the care and attention a child could dream of. My mother was a great admirer of France and French culture, which she passed on to me. She would read me stories in French and it took me weeks to understand them and learn them by heart. I cherished these special moments when I had her all to myself. Later, we would have poetry competitions in French. The winner was whoever could come up with the most beautiful sentences, turns of phrase, metaphors and other stylistic figures of speech. It was such fun. And then Hitler came to power and the repression began, as he deprived us of more and more freedoms. We had to live with pervasive hatred which then gradually turned to fear. The atmosphere became execrable. We sought refuge in music. Our whole family were musicians. We each had our own instrument: my mother played the violin, my father played the piano and I had the cello. I remember the three of us in the living room, trying to master Schubert's Trio for Piano and Strings. It was sheer delight! How we laughed as we worked on the long piece that lasted almost ten minutes. It was a temporary respite from the horrors that were happening in the world outside. We were in our own little cocoon and the music helped to instil in us a feeling of strength and serenity.

I enlisted in the Wehrmacht and chose not to mention my Jewish ancestry. Though Jews cannot enter the army, *Mischlinge* are in theory tolerated. I did not therefore commit any crime. The army recruiters apparently didn't pick up on my omission, otherwise they would never have made me a sergeant. I think that being a musician in the Cologne orchestra dispelled any suspicions. I want to serve my country and I feel German not Jewish. Some *Mischlinge* I know have even Aryanized themselves, lying about their origins so they would not be assimilated into the community so hated by the Nazis. But none of this makes any sense. I am already one hundred per cent German, so why should I justify myself? How can you be one hundred and twenty, one hundred and fifty, two hundred per cent German? My mother advised me not to enlist.

"You don't know what the next step is, my boy . . . These people are capable of anything since *Kristallnacht*. Your father and I know how brave you are, you have nothing to prove!"

"But I want to serve my country, Mother!"

"And the day they ask you to persecute or kill Jews like they did that night two years ago, what will you do?"

"I'll cross that bridge when I come to it . . ."

"I know that you love your country. I do too; but we have everything to fear from this authoritarian regime which is based solely on the hatred of one community and the glorification of another! The war will be fought on two fronts: enemy countries on the one and Jews on the other. In both cases, it won't be pretty! I'm telling you!"

I joined up regardless. Today, a year on, I'm just an ordinary German soldier, like the others. I defend my country against enemies. I don't quite understand the sense of it all though. Many young soldiers are dying in battle to satisfy the hegemonic and vindictive desire of one man. Hitler wants National Socialism to dominate the world, both in the East and in the West. He wants to create a world devoid of what he calls the "Jewish democracies", which for him are France, England, Holland and so on. There haven't been any free elections in my country since 1933 and opposition parties are banned. He wants absolute power, no obstacles in his path. Thank goodness I'm not out there fighting on the front. I'm a sergeant and for the time being I'm stationed at the Lignon barracks. But until when? If they send me to the front, what will I do? I don't want to kill in the name of a war that isn't mine. My mother was right. Third Reich politics don't deserve defending. Today, serving my country equates to serving this despicable regime. I'm becoming increasingly sceptical. I wish I could talk to Noemie about it, but I don't dare.

She now takes care of dressing my wounds and my personal hygiene when my bandages prevent me from doing it myself. I think Ernestine refused to do it. I don't like that girl. She's nosy. I think she rummaged through my belongings while I was out as some of my things had clearly been moved. We're on the same floor and sometimes I can feel her spying on me. I need to watch out for that one.

For the first few days after my accident, I felt like a prisoner. I was trapped not just in my room, but inside my body and mind too. I would spend the day on my back, or sitting at best, and it drove me insane. The slightest movement was excruciatingly painful. I must know every bump, stain, and detail on that damn ceiling as I spent so much time looking at it. I hated being out of action and was so frustrated I could feel the anger mounting. But worst of all was the mental anguish. I was being tortured by my feelings, new feelings I was trying to repress.

Then there was that night, eight days ago. For three weeks Noemie had been coming up to my room at regular intervals to look after me, when something happened that changed everything. Last Thursday it must have been around eight o'clock in the evening when Noemie came to see me. This wasn't her usual time as she had already dealt with my dressings earlier in the day and collected my evening meal tray. The children were in bed and Mr Lenoir was seeing his last patients. I could hear Ernestine moving around in her room which adjoined mine. When the door opened, I was thoroughly absorbed in my novel. Noemie didn't knock—she later confessed it was because Ernestine would have heard. It was obvious she was visiting me on the sly. It wasn't the doctor's wife or my nurse who opened the door. It was Noemie, the woman I was already secretly in love with. The compassionate and sincere way she looked after me, her contradictory nature, and her bold gaze made me feel alive. She has an odd way of blinking her eyes when she looks at someone, as if her entire attention is focused on you and nothing else matters, making you feel unique.

I don't really know what my reaction was when she entered my room that night. My gut feeling was that she had come to see *me*, Gunther, not the wounded soldier. At least that was the hopeful thought that crossed my mind when she opened the door. The kind of sentiment that leaps to attention unexpectedly and which you hope won't be proved wrong, leaving your heart in limbo. I put my book down, curious as to what would happen next. I told myself not to get carried away, not to court disappointment. She seemed overcome by emotion and spoke in hushed tones.

"Excuse me, I forgot to knock. I seemed to remember that I hadn't closed the shutters."

"The shutters?"

"Yes, for the blackout."

Disappointed, I turned to look at the window to see if she was telling the truth. I could see the moon rising outside. My heart sank.

As she walked across the room to close the shutters, I followed her with my eyes, wondering what this was all about. After all, there's nothing odd about wanting to check that all is in order before nightfall. Yet there was something in her demeanour that I couldn't put my finger on. Something unspoken I could sense. After closing the shutters, she turned around, with her back to the window and her hands behind her. She didn't move, and just gazed at an imaginary point in the centre of the room. I indicated the space next to me on the bed, inviting her to sit beside me. My heart was pounding. She sat down rather clumsily, knocking my book to the floor. As she leaned over to pick it up, I stopped her and cupped her face with my hands. She closed her eyes and leaned towards me. But my chest injury prevented me from moving any closer. At that moment, we were both startled by a loud noise—it sounded like a heavy object had crashed onto the floor in Ernestine's room. We then heard the door to Ernestine's room open. I cursed the girl under my breath for disturbing us. We sat motionless for a few minutes, listening out for the slightest movement on the landing. When the danger seemed to have passed, Noemie came to her senses and stood up. She faced the mantelpiece and held onto it. I could sense her agitation. Suddenly she turned towards me. I held my hand out to her from the bed. Throwing caution to the wind, she came back, sat down again and leaned towards me. Her elbow brushed against my wound and I winced in pain. Embarrassed, she began to apologize, but I cut her short. Instead, I reached for her face and her words melted on my lips. I can't describe how happy I felt to feel her mouth on mine. Just as I was expecting her to retreat at the last second, in an ultimate refusal to do the unthinkable, she kissed me eagerly, abandoning all thought of retreat or resistance. I wished time would stand still, that my wounds would miraculously disappear, and that she would slip into my bed. But the stolen moment had to end. She quietly rose and wished me good night. Her eyes seemed to say, "What will become of us?", as she left the room on tip toe. I couldn't sleep that night, torn between elation and anxiety.

Over the next few days, life resumed its course, but this time it was interspersed with tenderness and fond kisses. That was all my injuries would allow. Noemie refrained from dropping in more often and from prolonging her visits more than necessary. We lived in our own little bubble in which our longing for each other grew stronger every day. Feelings of despondency were followed by euphoria and vice versa. We had to be prudent and very quiet, except when we knew exactly what Ernestine was doing downstairs, and how long she would be occupied. The days went by. My wounds were healing quickly and our caresses became bolder. I would soon be able to go outside. We were in no hurry, however. Our secret rendezvous in my room, though brief, more than fulfilled us.

I am relating all this in detail, not to boast of my romantic exploits, but to be able to remember them. I want these events to be as indelibly imprinted on my brain as they are on every living cell of my body, in the depths of my flesh, until the day I die.

6

Germain, November 1940

I have just finished the pruning. The park looks magnificent. It's a lot of work, but very satisfying to see the garden transformed by my hard graft. And my expert knowledge too of course. I'm pretty good at my job. I was trained by my father, who was trained by his father before him and so on and so on. People often come to me for advice, which just goes to show. In my family, we have the greatest respect for everything that grows: trees, shrubs, flowers, and crops of all kinds. At my parents' home, and now at the Lenoirs', I look after a vegetable patch. It's a necessity at the moment. Even potatoes are hard to find now. So, when Mr Lenoir asked me at the beginning of the war if I could cultivate a vegetable garden on his land, I was happy to oblige. And I must say that the lady of the house is delighted to have her own vegetables grown right here. At the moment we have leeks, carrots, parsnips, and celery. Oh, and I nearly forgot the potato harvest, which was rather good this year and made some excellent soups! Not to mention the fruit trees in the park that are laden with pears and apples. The other day, Cosima, the Lenoirs' cook, made stewed apples and she gave me a jar. It's delicious—she adds a hint of cinnamon and vanilla and it tastes like heaven on earth. Cosima is Italian. She arrived in France with her parents just before the Great War, when she was eight or nine years old and never managed to lose her Italian accent. Cosima learned to cook from her mother. Like me learning how to garden from my father. She is an excellent cook too. The Lenoir family are lucky to have her.

But my favourite of the lot is Ernestine, the maid. For other reasons, of course. She may not be the sharpest crayon in the box, but she's kind and devoted. When she comes to fetch vegetables for Cosima, I flirt with her. And sometimes I take her to the potting shed. She's never against the idea. And then we have a quick roll in the hay, as it were, and it feels like the most natural thing in the world. It's damn good and she appears to like it too, otherwise she'd send me packing and I wouldn't push it. I admit there are no grand gestures, tenderness, or suchlike. Having a shag between the hoes, the axe and the rakes is not exactly romantic and sometimes it's downright dangerous . . . The other day, we were going at it with such force that we knocked over all the seed trays I'd prepared for the next season. It was my own stupid fault as I had stood them on the workbench and Ernestine's bouncing buttocks tipped them over on to the floor. I had to plant them all over again from scratch! It's an arrangement that suits us both. One day, we'll do things properly, you know like stroking, kissing, all that romantic stuff. Maybe even on a bed. Even though Ernestine is a bit of a rough diamond, I think deep down she has a heart. I think we all do. I didn't get a lot of love from my mother. There were four of us, all boys, so, by golly, we've taken more slaps than hugs in our time . . . Except maybe my little brother Étienne. Although he's the youngest, he's my hero. He got himself an education too. Even though I'm good at what I do, I regret not doing my studies. I didn't have the brains, and especially not the concentration. Right from when he was very young, you could put Etienne anywhere where people were talking and he would just sit still and listen and note it all down in his head. He's like a walking encyclopaedia. You ask him what the capital of China is and he reels off the answer instantly.

While I have trouble locating China on a map! Each to his own. For me, it's plants. But don't get me wrong, I wasn't a dunce at school. I was good at arithmetic. It comes in handy for the gardening because it's all about numbers. So many seeds per metre of furrow, spaced so many centimetres apart, so much water in summer, so much water in autumn, this quantity of compost for such and such a surface area, and so on, not to mention when I'm having to convert hectares into acres or centimetres. This is more important to me than knowing where China is.

As for Etienne, he's now a professor of natural history. Though at the moment he's pretty into politics. He doesn't like the turn the war is taking and wants to "do something", as he says, with some other comrades who are equally committed. For now it's just the beginning, it's not that organized. But I have faith in them. I know Etienne; things will soon materialize once he's worked out the *why* and the *how*. What bothers him though, is that so far it seems only communist organizations are involved in clandestine activities locally. So he's not sure whether to get involved or not. He has nothing against the Communist Party but finds that with them there's not an awful lot of room to manoeuvre. And to add insult to injury, there's the non-aggression pact signed at the start of the war. The Russians are technically German allies now, which makes the Communist Party's position rather ambiguous. In any case, things are starting to move. You can sense the conspiracy in the air in certain parts of town.

I'm just watching from the sidelines for the moment. Besides, I'm extremely busy at the Lenoirs' place. They are providing me with quite enough amusement. Where do I start? Okay, let's begin with the police commissioner. A few days ago, a well-dressed gentleman in a three-piece suit and shiny shoes came to see Mr Lenoir. It was Bach, the local police commissioner. I personally don't trust the man. I'm sure he's just like the chief of police and all the other high-ups: at Pétain's beck and call. And when you consider that Pétain shook Hitler's hand last month, it doesn't look good. I get the impression that Lenoir is leaning the wrong way in this war. Or not in the same direction as me in any case. Who knows what Bach wanted from him that day, but I doubt it was medicine for his heartburn. That lot are all corrupt. They believe that the die is cast and that the Germans are going to swallow up France. My blood boils when I think how the Krauts have even banned 11th November from being a public holiday! I presume that date leaves a bitter taste in their mouth. It angers me to see Mr Lenoir getting involved with these people. I thought he was more patriotic and more committed to freedom and everything that makes France what it is! And besides, he's a good boss and kind to his staff. He gives us a regular pay rise, he's understanding when we get into difficulties and he even pays us when we're off sick. Sometimes I think that Mr Lenoir is a one-man Popular Front! So I naively imagined that the occupation would stick in his throat, like it does mine, as we can no longer do as we please. What's more, as a doctor, he has to take orders from the Wehrmacht and treat any sick or wounded Germans who come to his door. In his position, I would kick over the traces!

To top it all, the Lenoirs had to welcome a German soldier into their home. And this is my second source of amusement: the Fritz. Or should I say the Fritz and the lady of the house because there's something brewing there, that's for sure! They think I don't see them, but I can be very discreet too. At first, she was rather cool towards him. Then little by little, I started to see them in the garden pavilion chatting together. I was at some distance so I couldn't hear what they were saying, but from their attitude and their faces, I could see that they were having a good time. In fact, one day they annoyed me by singing a Charles Trenet song. The Kraut looked all happy singing away and this made me angry because Trenet is my idol! Even though we're a modest family, we have a gramophone at home and almost all his records. At the end of July, a newspaper announced his death in a plane crash, giving no further details. I was overwhelmed by grief. Inconsolable in fact. But a few days later, he came back to life. The newspaper had got it wrong . . . I was so relieved and literally dancing for joy. What on earth possessed the idiots to go and announce his death? It can't be much fun reading about your own death in the newspaper when you're still alive and kicking. I hope the editor gets fired.

Anyway, to come back to Mrs Lenoir and her Fritz, I didn't see them for several weeks after that. He had been wounded, according to Ernestine. It's handy having a spy in the house. Her room is right next to his. She doesn't miss a thing, she's a cheeky one. Apparently, according to her, there's something going on. I didn't know whether to believe her or not because she's a bit of a gossip is Ernestine. She likes to make up stories and embroider the truth to make herself more interesting. Just like her brother Joël. They are as bad as each other with their tall tales. They have the gift of the gab those two—together they could sell an accordion to an undertaker! I was actually able to check whether Ernestine was telling the truth a few days ago. It was the Fritz's first outing since his accident. He was on crutches because he didn't seem to have fully recovered from his injuries. The lady of the house was by his side to help him walk. He was pale before, but now he looks like the living dead! They went out into the garden and took the central pathway that leads to the pavilion. But instead of stopping in the pavilion, they went and sat on a bench, hidden from view between two bushes. Hidden from all but me, that is, because I happened to be nearby and had a perfect view. As soon as they thought they were alone, they started to embrace. At first, it made me laugh. They looked so sweet. Nothing like me and Ernestine and our wild rutting! You could sense their tenderness and their affection for each other. You could even call it love, the real thing with a capital L. I almost felt jealous! Then I came back down to earth and realized that the lady of the house was carrying on with a Fritz! Devout as she is, I could hardly have imagined her taking a lover. Much less under her own roof and a Kraut of all people! Bravo, Noemie, full marks all round! You could have knocked me over with a feather when I saw them. She's not the only one, of course. I know of several girls in town who are quite willing to sell themselves out to the Krauts, but Mrs Lenoir, well, I'll be buggered, if you'll pardon the expression.

I can see that I'll have to be wary of my employers from now on. If they come and talk to me, as they are wont to do, I must be prudent. Especially when it comes to Etienne and his new activities.

7
Armand, December 1940

What strange times we live in! When the Great War ended, I was eight years old and hoped that we would never have to experience such atrocities again. But humans are clearly foolish enough to repeat their mistakes. So what did thousands of men die for if they just start all over again twenty years later? The icing on the cake this time is that it feels like we're in Germany. The Krauts got their revenge. To think that the June armistice was signed in the same railway carriage as that of November 1918! Hitler likes to provoke. All posters and signs in the streets and shops are now in German, except when they announce a public execution. Then they take the trouble to translate it. And if any billboards or announcements put up by the German authorities are sabotaged, such acts are punishable by death, so it's wise not to meddle with them. The mayor of Bordeaux, Adrien Marquet, who worked briefly in the first Pétain government as interior minister, has since been advocating close collaboration with the Nazis. He is not sympathetic to Pétain's National Revolution, but in my eyes, his policies don't differ that much from those of the old Marshal. It all comes down to the same thing. Since 1st July, Bordeaux shopkeepers and traders have been forced to accept German currency at an outrageous exchange rate. And Pétain's lot don't care! The locals had to hand in their firearms to the German *Kommandantur*, established in the Château de Lignon. The new German authorities have banned all motorized leisure travel, put in place strict blackout regulations, and decreed that all formal administrative documents must be written in German. As if that wasn't all bad enough, they then introduced "meat-free" days: butcher shops must stay closed three days a week. But perhaps the most despicable of all is that in October, Jews had to fill out a mandatory census form. What on earth do the Nazis intend to do with it? They have already passed that appalling law forbidding Jews from working in certain professions. Teachers, university professors, journalists, and policemen have all been affected and the list goes on and on. What exactly are they planning? It doesn't make any sense. This situation is surreal.

And there's no way of sidestepping an order, otherwise they threaten you in their craggy, guttural attempts at French. The other day I "forgot" to hand over the list of painkillers and narcotics in my possession to the *Kommandantur*, and I thought they were going to shoot me on the spot. I sense that things are going to get very tough. I envy those who live in the southern zone, the so-called "free zone", though the word "free" seems like an exaggeration to me in a country under enemy rule. In town you can see more and more visible signs of opposition. It may be subtle but it's still visible in the chalk graffiti, the "V" for victory, the sabotaged propaganda posters, and the small political leaflets. All of this proves how fed up a certain category of French people are, those who won't be cowered by the enemy. When I come across any such signs, they give me encouragement. And their actions incite me to do the same!

I think my wife, Noemie, is close to breaking point. We have been ordered to take in a German soldier. Unfortunately for me, he had to go and get himself injured which meant I had to treat him. My Hippocratic oath is a burden on such occasions, and I would gladly take it back. I stitched the Fritz up with no anaesthetic, pretending I had run out. My goodness, it felt good! It's not very Christian of me, but religious dogmas have gone out of the window recently. I didn't turn the other cheek, it was more a case of "an eye for an eye, a tooth for a tooth". This whole situation is sadly lacking in humanity. Noemie had to dress the UG's wounds and take care of his hygiene, the poor woman. I can only imagine her repulsion. When I asked her to do it, she rolled her eyes but didn't make any fuss. Noemie never makes a fuss; she is the perfect docile wife. I can't complain about her. So many men have a hard time with their wives. Noemie runs the house beautifully. She also helps me out when I need it. She takes care of our staff and the children. Our youngest, Valentin, is difficult and in poor health. He needs more attention than Solveig who is older and more resourceful. Noemie and Valentin have a close bond but I sometimes wonder if it is a bit extreme. Having said that, he is not even two years old, so it could be normal. Besides, he's a boy. As we know, boys and their mothers always have a special relationship. Solveig is an independent little girl. She is only four and a half years old but extremely clever. She is very quick-witted and makes us laugh with her outspoken remarks.

The four of us would have been so happy if it weren't for this despicable war. Though to be honest, we've come off rather well: we have no children at the front, Germain, our gardener, grows the vegetables that comprise a large part of our diet and our living conditions are comfortable. And we are not Jewish . . . It seems like an outrageous thing to say, but it's the sad reality and the direct consequence of our dear Marshal's pact with that scoundrel Hitler. Innocent citizens are worried sick because they are Jewish or of Jewish descent. I see these people in my surgery. They don't understand what's happening to them. I feel helpless as a doctor as there is nothing I can do to allay their fears. Especially given the ominous news from Germany. Over on the other side of the Rhine, the Jews are already total outcasts. Chances are high that they will become outcasts here too. What's happened to our national sovereignty? On what grounds are we forced to bow to such a heinous and repugnant regime? I am naturally of a calm disposition, but this war has triggered in me a form of violence that gnaws away at me and I can't rid myself of it. My patients and my family are increasingly on the receiving end, and I despise myself. Sometimes I'm rude to Noemie, and she puts up with it, but I can see that she suffers.

I had a visit from my friend Gabriel Bach. He is a non-practising Jew and, until recently, the local police commissioner. Then out of the blue came the Jewish status laws and he was directly in the firing line. He was dismissed last month, as were most of the Jewish civil servants in leadership positions. He is extremely worried about his family and their fate. He asked if he could count on me if things got serious. We talked over cigars, alone in the living room.

"Armand, if they persecute my family, will you help me?"

"Of course, Gabriel. But 'persecute'? That's a strong word. What do you think is going to happen?"

"I don't know exactly. In my opinion, dismissing Jewish officials is just the start. They won't stop there. I have a feeling that things are going to get ugly for us. I don't know if I should keep a low profile or, on the contrary, get involved in the sort of underground resistance groups that de Gaulle is orchestrating. Or both. The Jew with two faces. I'll have to learn the art of dissimulation. I'm not particularly good at it."

He laughed nervously as he flicked his cigar ash into the ashtray. I tried to reassure him.

"One thing is for sure: you can count on me at any time. As for the organizations you mentioned, rebellion is in the air, you can sense it in town. I don't know who's pulling the strings. Unless they are acting in isolation, of course. I hear that some men have gone to London to form intervention groups and coordinate actions here on the ground. I can't go to London but I'm keen to support these movements any way I can—through my profession, I mean. I think it might be useful for them to have a medical doctor they can rely on to treat the wounded, unofficially speaking. But I don't know how to make contact. People are very discreet and with good reason. Some say the Communist Party is behind the actions; others deny it, arguing that the Communists' hands are tied by the German-Soviet pact. If you get any information on this, please tell me. We have to be extremely careful: the Krauts get very upset if you throw a spanner in the works. And when they're upset, they're quick to retaliate."

"And what do *you* think about this clandestine activity? It feels like a David and Goliath situation, don't you think?" he asked.

"Probably, but it's worth a try, isn't it? You just said yourself that you wanted to get involved."

"It's dangerous, very dangerous even," replied Bach.

"That goes without saying, but we can't sit back and do nothing, it's worth fighting for isn't it? Can you imagine if the entire French population revolted against the invader? He would be forced to leave the country with his tail between his legs."

"Are you not forgetting that many French people support the Marshal?" Bach pointed out.

"Only because they want to be on the winning side . . . If the population begins to see that there is another way out, perhaps they'll switch allegiances? They'll realize that Pétain was wrong to concede defeat so quickly. Do you remember back in June when we thought he was bluffing? It was wishful thinking, but at that point it was clear just how many people thought we should continue the fight and seek victory at any cost."

I in turn knocked the ash from my cigar into the ashtray before continuing.

"And people are hungry. They'll soon get tired of the Germans confiscating everything."

"I guess you're right . . ." conceded Bach. "I admit that I don't know what to think right now, between the fate of the Jews and the occupation of our country. I don't know where my priorities lie."

"Your priority is to protect yourself, Gabriel. Protect yourself and your family. Will you dine with us? From the delicious smells coming from the kitchen, I'd say that Cosima has prepared a feast."

8
Noemie, April 1941

What was going to happen happened. Gunther and I succumbed to our feelings for each other last October, our mutual attraction for one another blossoming during the many hours I spent caring for him during his forced convalescence. A few weeks after the accident, Armand deemed Gunther fit enough to go outside using crutches. The stairs posed a problem though.

"Will you help him down?" Armand asked me without a second thought.

I pulled a face, then obeyed sullenly. After all, I have always been a subservient wife, so it would come as no surprise to him to see me agree to yet another of his wishes, however unpleasant it might seem. Deep down, however, I rejoiced at the task he had entrusted me with. Was he really so blind or naïve as to throw me into the arms of another man, the man I had been tending to with such devotion for over a month? Did he deem Gunther's nationality sufficient reason for me to despise him? I felt reassured in any case that I was good at concealing my emotions. If he hadn't noticed anything up to now, that was a good sign. But what if he was manipulating me, only to catch me later on during one of my intimate encounters with Gunther? My imagination was running wild and I couldn't contain it. And this has changed little since. I am always on the lookout for the slightest remark, a change of tone, a look, or a gesture that would imply he knows.

Despite these fears, Gunther and I try to see each other in secret as much as possible. I fantasize about spending a whole night with him, without worrying about being caught. That will probably never happen. I am afraid of what will happen to us. It's getting harder and harder to suppress our desire for each other. I think I'm discovering real passion for the first time in my life. I've never felt such ardour for my husband. And the strength of my sentiments overwhelms me. I never imagined that two people could crave each other to this extent, yearning to be caressed, kissed, *possessed* by the other. Sometimes it scares me. I feel like I can't control myself any longer. The other day, I was rummaging around in the potting shed looking for the seeds that Germain had set aside for me to plant. He had gone out to run an errand for Armand who wanted him to find some live hens so we could have eggs every day. I was wondering how Germain would go about finding hens at the present time. Anything edible is scarce, or at best overpriced. But Germain knows all the surrounding farms and he always manages to find a way. Armand is aware of this, which is why he asked him. While I was busy in the potting shed, I saw Gunther approaching. I was astonished because he rarely ventures into this part of the garden. We then stood there like two fools in the shed, pondering what the other was doing. Gunther, as the guest, clearly decided he should be the first to come clean.

"I've done something stupid. I knocked over a large pot of flowers in the alley over there. I was hoping to find something here which I could use to scoop up the earth and put it back."

He pointed vaguely in the direction of the alleyway. I began to hunt for a suitable garden implement. He did the same. There were shovels and spades of all different shapes and sizes stood in a corner. We were ostensibly busy searching, but our thoughts were stubbornly fixated on just one fact: we were both alone in this small shed and away from prying eyes. The nearby church bell chimed four times, startling us both. We laughed at our surprise. We were so awkward that the slightest noise, no matter how familiar, made us uncomfortable. Gunther walked to the door and looked outside. Then he came back to me. I knew what he was going to do and I was ready. Petrified at the thought of the gardener catching us, but ready. My whole body clamoured for him and was already reaching out to him. He wrapped his big, lithe arms around me and we devoured each other with hungry kisses. After weeks of temptation and feeling starved of the other's company, we threw ourselves into the madness of our love with no thought for Germain who could walk in on us at any moment. His hands undressed me frantically, our lips still glued together. His clumsiness seemed to make him nervous. Or was it his nervousness making him clumsy? I grabbed at his uniform that he was still wearing and hadn't taken the time to change out of when he got home. I thought how crumpled it would be after our frolicking. I threw his jacket and then his shirt onto the earthy ground. When the skin of his torso met my bare chest, we were already in seventh heaven, oblivious to the risks we were taking. Then we spotted the long low sideboard against the wall. He lifted me up and sat me on it, spreading my legs as he prepared to enter me. I gripped his pelvis with my legs to pull him closer to me and feel the powerful thrusting of his hips. After weeks of torment, we were unable to hold ourselves back, and buried our faces in each other's shoulders to smother our cries of ecstasy. Despite the chill in the early April air, we were soon drenched in sweat. We couldn't have been more out of breath if we'd run around the entire estate. We were both panting like thirsty dogs. After this surge of emotion, we came to our senses and picked up our scattered clothes hurriedly.

Shortly afterwards we heard footsteps on the gravel path. Through a skylight, Gunther spied Germain coming down the boxwood alley and pulling a wheelbarrow loaded with a wire cage full of chicks. I was overwhelmed by panic. We wouldn't get out without being seen. Germain would come to the shed to put the cage under cover, while he prepared the future henhouse. As we both hastily dressed, Gunther and I looked for a place to hide, but there was nowhere two people could conceal themselves. Suddenly there was a screeching noise, followed by swearing. Gunther looked through the window again and breathed a sigh of relief. Someone up there must be watching over us. God had decided not to punish me. Germain had knocked over the wheelbarrow containing the cage, tipping it over and releasing the chicks which had all spilled out into the park. The gardener was now running after them as best he could, trying in vain to catch them. Despite the comic nature of the scene, which we would gladly have continued to watch, we seized the chance to flee. We decided that Gunther would go first and take the path back to the manor. Then I would go and help Germain recover the chicks. I would also inform him that it was I who had knocked over the flowers in the alley.

Once Gunther was out of sight, I went up to Germain who looked surprised to see me. He looked at me in a peculiar way, but I didn't give him time to observe me any further as I began to chase after the chicks. I had brought some of the seeds from the potting shed that Germain uses in the nesting boxes to feed the birds here in the winter. My idea was to tempt the chicks back with food, and it worked. We managed to draw them into a corner and catch them.

When Germain and I had locked up all the birds, we laughed about what had just happened. He told me that there were four females and one male chick. We could even think about breeding them! I congratulated him on his find, which would fill our plates for a good while.

"Now all you need is a chicken coop," I teased.

"Now that I have the birds, that's just what I need! I'll do it tomorrow. Just four stakes, a piece of wire mesh and a few planks should do it."

"Don't forget the perch, and most importantly the nesting area! They must be comfortable and happy to lay well!"

"Don't worry, Mrs Lenoir, I've thought of everything."

"I have total faith in you, Germain! I was joking, you know. By the way, I stupidly knocked over a bowl of flowers in the alley earlier on, and they spilled all over the ground. I wanted to put the flowers and soil back but couldn't find a suitable tool to do it."

As I said this, I pictured me and Gunther in our not very earnest quest for a shovel.

"Don't worry, I'll take care of it. In fact, I'm on my way there now. Anyway, it's a little late to start building a chicken coop."

Then he pointed to a sheltered spot behind some trees. "I was thinking of installing it there."

"That's a good idea," I replied. "Not too far from the house to collect the eggs and it doesn't detract from the garden."

In the evening, I found an excuse to go up to the second floor to make sure Gunther had got back to his room safely. I stayed in the doorway to talk to him. He blew me a kiss from where he was standing. Then I went back down to join Armand.

Over the past few days, we have become accustomed to listening to Radio-Londres. All other sources of news here, be it radio or newspapers, just spread false claims or, worse, propaganda. When we discovered Radio-Londres, we realized to what extent the population was being fed pure lies. First, we listen to *Honour and Country* with Maurice Schumann, Charles de Gaulle's spokesman for Free France. This is followed by *The French speak to the French.* These programmes raise our spirits and give us news other than the official line spouted by the Vichy government. Technically, the war is over in France. The country is under occupation, our soldiers are still prisoners in the stalags, but fighting on our soil has ceased. Radio-Londres reports on the Allies' progress. It also keeps us informed of the various resistance movements operating in the country. And things are happening, yes, all over France, little by little! Clandestine information networks are sprouting up and they in turn communicate with the Free France movement in London. Armand pays close attention to everything that is said. I think he would like to take part, though he hasn't said as much to me. Naturally the Germans ban us from listening to this radio station. The only one we are allowed to listen to is Radio-Paris. It goes without saying that it is the mouthpiece of the Vichy collaborators, censure and propaganda being the order of the day. The Germans try and interfere with the Radio-Londres broadcasts to stop us receiving them, but we still manage to tune in. I love the opening credits: three short notes followed by a long one, like Beethoven's Fifth Symphony. "Pom-pom-pom-poooom." In morse code, this means "V", as in "V" for victory. It might seem silly, but just hearing that sound galvanizes us! The wireless is in a small room adjacent to the lounge. This is where Armand sits to read on a Sunday. It's a smallish room, but very bright and comfortable, simply furnished with a small sofa and a large armchair. The wireless stands on a desk placed against the wall, enhanced by a big mirror. When we get settled in there every evening at eight o'clock, we are careful to close the doors to the lounge and the hallway. Armand searches for the frequency and off we go. We listen to every word and it bucks us up. We have to keep the volume low as we do of course have a German living in our house. Sometimes, during the day, we listen to Radio-Paris which is widely broadcast and easy to pick up, as the Germans have gone to great lengths to ensure it is easily available to the local populace. We put it on to assess how public opinion is being manipulated but also for the high quality of its music. Sometimes

I wonder what the artists who perform on this radio think. Are they pro-German? Collaborators? Or do they simply do their job without worrying about politics? What choice do they have?

The key phrase at the moment, so as not to arouse suspicion, is "I don't get involved in politics". People make me laugh. *Everyone* is involved in politics. Even the average person on the street. Even if you don't react to what's going on, you're still *involved.* Even standing aside and not reacting to what's going on is a political act, because it means you're condoning the collaboration. What do those who claim they don't get involved in politics actually mean? That they are not taking sides? Or that their actions won't offend either side? The person who denounces his neighbour for engaging in black market activities for instance is participating in a political act. He is supporting the collaboration because he knows the regime prohibits this. He who profits from the black market is supporting the collaboration as well, because although it is prohibited, the regime has provoked it through food scarcity and thus upset the balance between supply and demand. And he who looks on and remains silent also condones the collaboration by tacitly accepting the situation. And, ironically, the collaborators themselves benefit most of all from the black market. It is they who still have some money and influence . . . In reality, only the deaf, dumb and blind can genuinely boast that they are "not involved in politics".

As regards the musicians who perform on Radio-Paris, I'm poorly placed to judge. Everything is more complicated in wartime. After listening to Radio-Londres we immediately put the frequency back to Radio-Paris in case the Germans should decide to come in here for some reason and turn on the radio. That way they'll instantly hear which station we tune in to and whose side we're on. In theory at least.

9

Justin, 10th June 1946

It's been three weeks now since Angela arrived in the village and the investigation has stalled. I did ask the Bordeaux police for assistance, but apart from borrowing their dogs to search the forest the other day, I don't expect to receive any more help from them. They appear to have a lot on their plate. I know that the war ended fairly recently and that they have a huge amount to do reorganizing the administration, but still . . . They don't really seem to care if there's one more orphan out there. I tried to use the family's disappearance as leverage, but they said a family doesn't just disappear like that and things would soon get back to normal.

So Angela is here, waiting for us to find something and for her memory to come back. She often comes home with me. I try to make a fuss of her as it's not like she's going to get much affection at the orphanage. Eliette tries to help sometimes, but says she has a "bad feeling" about the girl. Eliette is my oldest friend. We grew up together and ever since we were small we've been inseparable and told each other everything. She means the world to me. She's the only person who truly knows me. In fact, I think she knows me better than I know myself. She has been working as a primary school teacher since the war ended. She says Angela doesn't like her. I refute this but she doesn't believe me. She thinks that Angela is judging her. It's true that Angela is not like other little girls. She has an astonishingly critical mind for a child her age. The other day, Eliette and I even fell out over her.

"That child is sly!"

"What rubbish!"

"I'm telling you she hates me and wants to come between us."

"That's a bit over the top isn't it?! How could a ten-year-old come between us?"

"You've bitten off more than you can chew, believe me!"

"But Eliette, she's unhappy! Do you have any idea what the child is going through? She can't even remember her own name! She's got no one, and doesn't know where her family is, or whether they're alive or dead!"

"Don't be so dramatic! Of course we're going to find her parents. She needs to make an effort though. I get the impression that she's wallowing in her sadness, so she can spend more time with you."

I could feel myself losing my temper.

"Are you crazy or what? This little girl has amnesia, do you even know what that means?"

"Yes, thank you, I'm no stupider than you. But you? You've fallen hook, line and sinker! You're completely under that child's spell!"

I hate these conversations and they always leave me feeling terrible. I don't want Angela to have to suffer any more than Eliette in all this. It's true, Angela does take up a big part of my life, but what's the alternative?

As for the investigation, the fragments of memory that Angela has regained are sadly not enough for us to make any headway. Dr Bertin says that if she has experienced a traumatic event, she could have retreated into amnesia as a survival mechanism to protect herself and this could last indefinitely. She remembers things like the colour of her bedroom and the unusual grey cat they had, but no names. One odd thing though is that she cannot bear for doors to be closed when she is in a room, implying she was locked up somewhere. Is this the source of her trauma? Questions like these keep going round in my head.

Yesterday there was a development, however. Poinseuil police station, just over thirteen miles away, informed us they had finally caught a pervert who had been on the rampage in the area for two months. Colleagues in Poinseuil told me that among his various offences, he had broken into the home of an elderly lady and tied her to a chair. He had undressed himself and then masturbated in front of her while singing a bawdy song. Though scared witless, the victim escaped with no injuries. The problem is that he also did this to children, hanging around schools in another town not far away. Not only did he fondle himself in their presence, but he also committed other indecent acts. My colleagues sent me the official transcript from the interrogation. I will only quote part of it here, as they grilled him for quite some time.

"So, you think it's funny to expose yourself in front of everyone do you, you filthy little perv! On the evening of 10th May, what were you doing at Mrs Renaud's house?"

"I don't know . . . Who's Mrs Renaud?"

"I'll refresh your memory then. Mrs Renaud is the old lady you tied up and who was then forced to watch you perform your filthy antics!"

"A lady . . . Okay, but which one? And they're not filthy antics! As if you never do it yourself!"

"Doing it in public is against the law, do you hear me? It's illegal and you're looking at a prison sentence. Do you understand that?"

"Mrs Renaud, was she the widow?"

"Go on!"

"Poor old thing, it must have been a while since she last saw a dick!"

"Spare us your disgusting remarks! Have some respect for your victims at least!"

"But I didn't even touch her! Well, just to tie her up. But I didn't touch her private parts. I swear I didn't! Although perhaps she would have liked it . . . ha ha."

I don't know how my colleagues in Poinseuil stopped themselves from beating the living daylights out of the swine at that point. When he asked "which one?" he wasn't taunting them; he had indeed inflicted the same treatment on other women, mostly elderly and living on their own.

"And the children in Montjoly Park? Tell us about them!"

"Ah! The children, that's different. That's much more exciting than an old widow."

"Shut it or—"

"It's up to you, do you want me to talk or not?"

"What did you do in front of the children?"

"The same as I did with the old women, but I didn't tie them up. They were curious."

"No they weren't curious you sick pervert, they were scared shitless at the sight of you! How many of them were there?"

"Three or four."

"Be precise!"

"Three."

"Did you touch them?"

"Not at first, no. But then I thought it was a pity as they were there, so I asked a little girl to do me a favour."

"What exactly did you ask her to do?"

"Hold my cock."

At that point I stopped reading, not wanting to know what happened next. I wouldn't want to be in his shoes faced with my Poinseuil colleagues. It can't have been easy interrogating someone who shows such contempt for his victims—not to mention the sheer effrontery of the man! The transcript didn't mention the asides, but I could read between the lines.

"They didn't try to escape?"

"They didn't dare. I informed them that if they ran off I would tell their parents they spent the money for the church collection plate on sweets."

"Is that true?"

"Is what true?"

"The sweets story?"

"I don't know! But all little 'uns do it, so I guess they did too!"

"Let's get back to the little girl you mentioned. What did she do?"

"She was crying."

"Did she obey you?"

"Well, yes, because I think she was scared of me and at the idea of being scolded by her parents."

"What did she look like?"

"Pretty."

"Describe her, for God's sake!"

"She was . . . I don't know!"

"Damn it, if she held your penis, you must have seen the colour of her hair or her eyes!"

"Not dark."

"What, her eyes?"

"Her hair. Her eyes, I don't remember."

"Long?"

"Her eyes?"

"Her hair, you bastard!"

"Yes, sort of."

"Age?"

"How the heck would I know! Not that young or old . . ."

"What did the other children do when you assaulted the girl?"

"I didn't assault her! She just did what I told her!"

"But you still committed an act of violence. My word! You have no idea do you?! Children are generally afraid of adults, in case that fact had escaped you! Especially scum like you! Where were the other children while this was going on?"

"They were still watching, but from a distance. They wanted to go but were waiting for her."

"And then what happened next?"

"Then . . . I don't know."

"Go on! You know very well what you did next!"

"All right. All right. I just asked her to . . ."

"What? What did you ask her to do?"

"Well, she was right there beside me, wasn't she. It was exciting like. So I took her head in my hands and . . ."

I looked up, fearing I wouldn't be able to stomach the rest. I imagined my little Angela in the hands of this depraved monster and felt nauseous. God, please don't let it be her . . . Please God don't let it be her. But even if it's not her, some other little girl has been subjected to this horrendous ordeal. That man is a dangerous sexual predator. I read to the end and the rest of the document confirmed my worst fears. Poor child. I hope with all my heart that this louse will rot in hell for his despicable acts. I imagined him wearing a big brown dirty overcoat, which hid his nakedness beneath. His hair was probably long and dirty, his fingernails too. The whole situation was too dire for words. This repulsive human being embodied the worst of man's depravity. His vile intentions made me want to vomit. I went to the telephone intending to call Poinseuil and find out if they had the name of the victim.

"Gauthier, it's Mayol in Bournelin."

"Ah, Mayol! Did you read the transcript?"

"Yes, I did! It's appalling. Do you know the name of the little girl involved?"

"No, all three children ran away when he released her."

"And nobody knows who she is?"

"No, they don't. No parent has come forward with a blonde child to file a complaint. We interviewed the only eyewitness who came to tell us everything but he was too far away to identify the children. That's how we found out that the guy was in the area. We then compared his statement with what his other victims, the elderly ladies, told us. I'm sorry, Mayol."

I was lost for words and sat down on the edge of a desk.

"And couldn't your witness have stepped in and prevented the worst of it?"

"He said he was scared of the man's reaction, which is understandable."

"No, when it comes to children's safety, I'm afraid it's not 'understandable', as you say."

"He could have been armed . . ."

"Perverts are never armed! They use sex as a weapon."

"Yes, *we* know that, of course, but the eyewitness didn't."

Silence. My thoughts were all over the place.

"Damn it, so the little blonde girl just ran back home, and got on with her life as if nothing had happened?" I went on presently. "Her parents must have noticed a change in her behaviour surely?"

"No nothing, I'm telling you . . ."

"I don't get it, the children must have come from somewhere nearby, a school perhaps? Couldn't we question all of the children from the local schools? And show them a picture of him? Eventually one of the children will recognize the bastard!"

"And how exactly do we explain that to the children? 'We're going to show you a man and you tell us if you think he's a bad man'?" I could hear the irony in my colleague's voice over the phone. "It's not possible, Mayol, it would cause too many tongues to wag. This affair is sordid enough as it is. The town really needs to forget all about this incident. Especially now that we've arrested the culprit. They're just children, they'll get over it."

"I hope you're kidding, Gauthier?"

"Why would I joke?" he replied.

"Did someone ask you to cover this up? Let me guess . . . the mayor . . . or the priest?"

"Aren't you taking things a bit far, Mayol? . . . Anyway, the guy's going to be sentenced, and pretty harshly from what I can gather!"

"Based on the old women's testimonies? What's he going to get? Six months in jail, a year? That's what you call being sentenced *harshly*?"

"One of the 'old women', as you put it, could have been your mother!"

"And so what? You don't think there's a difference between showing your arse to an old lady and raping a little girl?"

"It wasn't quite rape now, was it . . ."

In a rage, I jumped up from the desk I had been leaning on.

"Putting your penis into a little girl's mouth isn't rape in your book?" I shouted down the phone.

"What I meant was there was no violence as such; the girl is intact . . . At least, according to the witness . . ."

"Damn it, Gauthier, I've been looking after a child for the last three weeks who's lost her memory. She is 'intact' as you put it. Physically, there's nothing wrong with her. She still has all her body parts. Not a scratch on her. But believe me, in that small child's head it's total chaos! All because she has suffered psychological trauma. So I'm not going to let you lecture me with your amateur psychology—let's leave the subject to the experts. A child is not just a bag of flesh and bones, comrade, it's also a human with a brain, a human with feelings and a fragile human at that! Nobody protected that poor child in Montjoly Park when she needed it the most. And you're telling me that it doesn't matter because she's 'intact'?"

"I didn't say that . . . Calm down, Mayol . . . But I have orders, can you understand that?"

"And what about a moral code, do you have one of those?" I went on, still shouting. "Does it not occur to you to challenge those who want to hush it up, those who don't want to see their precious little town tainted?"

There was no response on the other end of the line.

"What did they promise you for your silence? A promotion?" I asked, calmer now.

"Nothing, I assure you . . ."

"Gosh, I can tell from your voice that you don't believe a word of what you just said! What's one girl's life in exchange for a juicy opportunity to climb the ranks, eh?"

Gauthier didn't reply.

"Do you at least have a picture of the man so I can ask Angela if she recognizes him? And if she *is* the victim, I promise you there will be trouble!"

"You'll get it tomorrow," he said meekly.

"Make sure I do!"

I hung up in a state of fury such that I had never experienced before. Sweat was pouring down my brow and my shirt was covered in wet patches. Since they can't find that little girl, I will have to show the picture to Angela as soon as I receive it. If this guy is indeed the person who harmed her, I am worried about how she might react. Would she go into shock again? And if she was the victim, why didn't her parents report her missing? It doesn't make any sense.

For the past few days, I've been obsessed with another idea, an idea which has not yet fully taken shape and flutters around in my head like a butterfly. Sometimes it surfaces briefly, interrupting whatever I am doing, only to get lost again in the meanders of my brain. Then all of a sudden the idea took root in my mind, as if the butterfly had finally decided to settle. I was overcome with anxiety as I spoke my thoughts aloud. "He'll come looking for her."

"Who will come looking for her?" asked my chief who had entered my office at that moment.

"The kidnapper. If the flasher is ruled out, which we will know soon enough once Angela sees the photograph, we will have to consider that the entire family was in fact kidnapped. And if the family is being held captive somewhere and Angela has escaped, there is a strong chance that the attacker will start looking for the little girl. He has no way of knowing that she has amnesia."

I had my chief's full attention now. He nodded, his pipe clamped between his lips.

"We have to protect the girl. Your theory makes sense. He is probably trying to track her down as we speak to prevent her from talking."

Then he paused.

"But it's been almost three weeks. If she hadn't lost her memory, she would have led us to him by now, don't you think? The more time passes, the more he must think that she's dead. The police aren't looking for him."

"Unless the kidnapper didn't realize right away that she was missing. In which case he may be looking for her while trying to remain in hiding himself . . . That takes time . . ." I mused.

"That's a lot of ifs and buts . . ."

"In any case, we mustn't take any chances if there's the slightest risk of Angela coming to harm."

"You're right, she needs to be kept safe," he agreed.

10

Gunther, November 1941

I've been with the Lenoir family for over a year now. Life is running its course. I must have been born under a lucky star as these past months have been marked by events that could have meant I was sent to fight in the Balkans, North Africa, or even worse, Russia. But fortunately they have kept me in Lignon. If my commanders knew I was a *Mischling*, they would have already packed me off to the Eastern Front by now. Nevertheless the situation is changing, and for the worse, and it is the Jews who are suffering in particular. My mother wrote to me that in Germany Jews are being rounded up and deported to camps in Eastern Europe. What happens next, no one knows. Well I certainly don't. Yet I miss my country. I haven't had any further news from Hannah. My mother couldn't tell me if her family were worried about these roundups. They had lost touch after Hannah's parents moved to another part of the city to hide. What on earth is going on in my country? I sometimes think I'm safer here in the lion's den than back in Germany with my loved ones.

Things are not just changing for the Jews, though, they're changing for us too. Since we opened the Eastern Front and tore up the pact with the Soviet Union last June, French communists have been engaged in silent and deadly clandestine guerrilla warfare. For several months now, small groups have been carrying out terrorist attacks. What's more, they're not just communists: French citizens hostile to the Vichy regime have joined their ranks. They sabotage our infrastructure and strategic routes, bridges and railways, cut off the electricity supply, put sugar in our fuel tanks, and devise all sorts of ploys to harm us. They do their utmost to obstruct our actions and our communication systems. They don't accept that we won the war and have taken over their country. Their sole aim is to drive us out. I suppose we'd do the same in their shoes. I admit they are very brave, because if they're caught, the Gestapo interrogate them in an attempt to dismantle their whole network. And the Gestapo don't go in for half measures, resorting to torture if they have to. These terrorists always know our next course of action as well as our whereabouts. We have to be particularly vigilant at the border between the two zones, as they go to great lengths to circulate information. The other day, a very innocent looking young girl arrived by bike at the checkpoint. She showed us her ID card, her *Ausweis*. We searched her bag, as we do with everyone and found a book.

"Do you read a lot?" asked the soldier I was on duty with that day.

When she didn't answer, he took the book in his hands to feel the weight of it. He then passed it to me so that I could weigh it in turn.

"Don't you think this book feels rather heavy?" he said to me, keeping his eyes on the girl.

I didn't know what to answer. The book was indeed heavy, but I thought that this could be simply due to its large size. Meanwhile, the young girl had gone as white as a ghost. I realized what my colleague was hinting at though and I had no desire to confront this girl, guilty of nothing more than being a patriot. I was happy to close my eyes to her misdemeanour to avoid seeing her distress and I would have gladly given my right arm for a diversion which would have thwarted the soldier's plans. Instead, he grabbed the book and opened it. As I expected, only the first pages were intact.

The rest had been hollowed out and inside was a handgun no less. He stared at the poor girl who was now shaking like a leaf as she looked down at her feet.

"What a pity to sacrifice a book for such a vile purpose, Miss! A book should be respected!" remarked my colleague snidely.

"You deserve to be punished, don't you, for damaging this book?" he went on with a smirk.

He unceremoniously grabbed her by the arm, pulling her off her bicycle, which fell to the ground. Then he dragged her to the van where the other soldiers were quietly smoking so that she could be taken to the *Kommandantur* building and undergo a proper interrogation there. I don't know what happened to her after that, but I can guess at her fate. The fact that she was a woman, and a young one at that, wouldn't have changed anything for them. A terrorist is a terrorist, full stop. But the resistance groups are very competent and their networks are impossible to trace. They are extremely well organized. Each agent only possesses the information he or she needs to know to carry out their own mission. The problem is that when the Gestapo don't get any useful information out of a prisoner they get angry and the physical abuse and cruelty can be merciless. Before the war, I had no idea how inventive men could be at torturing their fellow men if they feel it's worth it. I have witnessed spine chilling scenes designed to "make people talk". Fingernails being torn out, cigarette burns on the face, electric shocks to the genitals, and a host of other barbaric acts . . . I had no idea it was possible to subject human beings to such agony. Being at war and shooting someone in the heat of battle is one thing. That's what a soldier is there for: to kill the enemy. It is another matter altogether to act in cold blood, consciously inflicting immense pain on a man—or a woman—no matter how much of an enemy he or she is deemed to be. Luckily, once again, that's not my domain. That's for the Gestapo to deal with. Having said that, if I see dubious activities, or behaviour that appears inconsistent with the collaboration, I naturally step in. I weakened when we arrested that girl partly because of her youth and the utter waste of a young life dedicated to the wrong cause. Nevertheless, I am a German soldier and even if I don't adhere to the ideology of the Reich, at least as far as the Jews are concerned, I must obey orders. I am a bit like a dog who has learned not to bite but who leaps at the chance of a juicy bone.

Up to now, the damage resulting from this kind of French patriotic resistance has been mainly material. But at the end of October, some terrorists killed two German officers in broad daylight; one attack occurred in Nantes and the other in Bordeaux. The reprisals were immediate so that they wouldn't think of doing it again. I was appalled when I heard that about fifty prisoners from the Souge camp in Bordeaux had been shot dead without any trial whatsoever. Most of them were communists. It's a simple equation: fifty French lives for two German lives. It's not even accurate to refer to those prisoners as "terrorists", as not all of them had committed criminal acts. So there you go, shot to be made an example of, and so young too. I understand that such incidents can shock the enemy ranks. The situation is growing increasingly tense. There has been an escalation in violence and the tension is rising on both sides. I can feel it when I walk around Lignon. These unjust and uncalled for executions have made us very unpopular here. However there are still many who occupy the middle ground. French business owners, for example, support Pétain and accept our presence, even seeing it as advantageous for them as they rely on orders from the German army to operate.

The German army constructs buildings as well as communication and transportation infrastructure, so having

German troops stationed on French soil keeps the economy ticking along. The same goes for us soldiers; our purchasing power means we can buy, sometimes at very favourable prices, products such as food or other commodities that are scarce. Some traders have cottoned on that they can make good money out of this. Rationing and food cards don't come into it. Either you've got money and can buy just about anything you want, or you go hungry. Sordid logic but it's as simple as that.

My mission is to secure food supplies for the German troops stationed here, in addition to the army rations. Since the armistice agreement stipulates that the French state must provide for the German troops, I comb the countryside looking for potential suppliers and pass on the information to my commanders who produce the requisition orders. It's basically forced sales. I visit farms likely to supply all kinds of foodstuffs: vegetables, cereals, wine, rabbits, chickens, eggs, pigs and so on. The high-ups noticed that I am at ease with the locals, as I speak their language, but it's also because I know how to handle them. All I do is show them understanding and we often end up talking about this and that; sometimes even about the war itself. I like going into the countryside to meet these people and immerse myself in their rustic way of life—they are often friendly and welcoming. It is a breath of fresh air compared to the barracks. I don't really look like the typical Aryan, which probably works in my favour. If I don't wear my uniform, people don't immediately realize I'm German. My age is on my side too. Many of the smallholders have children the same age as me who fought in the war before the armistice and are still being held prisoner. Obviously, you get those who grumble about a portion of their harvest or crop production being seized by the occupier. They would prefer to give it to the locals and they hand it over to us very reluctantly. Others comply with no complaints.

My official role is thus limited to this mission which suits me very well. I wouldn't be much good at anything else. I won't earn the Iron Cross, but I don't mind. I prefer to keep a low profile and not attract the attention of my superiors. My biggest fear is that they discover I am a *Mischling*. This would result in my immediate dismissal, which wasn't the case when the war first broke out.

I haven't been back to Germany at all since I've been in Lignon. I travelled around France for a few weeks, doing errands for the Wehrmacht, but that's all and that's fine by me. I have no desire to change my posting. Firstly, I have a dislike of gunfire, and secondly, I need to be near Noemie in Lignon. For most of us soldiers, life here is a piece of cake. It's almost like living in a holiday resort. The area is incredibly attractive, with lots of good food and wine. We eat well and don't want for anything. Even the first frosts of autumn don't bother us, as we are lodged in well-heated houses and have a good supply of warm clothes. I suspect that our brothers in arms on the Eastern Front can't say the same. Most importantly of all, our lives aren't in danger—you can't put a price on that. Except when you come face to face with an angry, armed French objector, or if like me, you underestimate the viciousness of certain wooden beams! This piece of crap has left me with awful scars and pains in my chest which still bother me, especially when I sneeze or laugh. Sometimes I chuckle and then wince in discomfort, and when Noemie sees this, she laughs in turn to see me being such a weakling.

The day before yesterday, they asked me to visit the *Kommandantur* in Bordeaux next week to evaluate the food procurement arrangements for the troops based there. At first, I thought I would take a train in the morning and return in the evening, enjoying a few hours of freedom alone in Bordeaux. Then I had the idea of asking Noemie to meet me in the city so that we could finally spend time together away from prying eyes. It would be delightful to be with her in Bordeaux, like a normal couple, without fear of being seen! But it won't be easy for her to get away from the manor for a whole day. She will have to find a jolly good reason for doing so.

I haven't yet told her that I'm half Jewish. You can never be too careful. We don't talk about the war when we're together. We have a tacit agreement that it's the only subject not on the table during our conversations. After all, I don't know who their friends are, and one slip of the tongue could have dire consequences. I can imagine the scene at a dinner party when their friends discover that a "Jewish Nazi" is living under their roof. At first, they might joke about it, but what then? What they forget or perhaps don't realize is that their enemies are also capable of challenging the regime and that not all Germans are participating in this war equally. As German soldiers, of course, we have an obligation of loyalty to our country. But not all German soldiers are convinced Nazis, devoted to Hitler's cause.

I often wonder, and I suppose it's similar for soldiers of all nationalities, how far I am willing to go for my country while remaining faithful to my own convictions and my conscience. Would I be capable of being part of a firing squad like the one which gunned down fifty people in Souge to set an example? Would I be capable of torturing a young Frenchman? Would I be capable of participating in the persecution of Jews as they are doing in Austria and Poland? It is highly likely that we will soon be called upon to seal the fate of the Jews in France. What will I do then? My mother was probably right to warn me. The same is true among civilians: many people in Germany, Poland and most likely Italy, are refusing to accept the presence of the occupying forces and are organizing resistance movements, like the ones here in France. Ultimately, all of us are not so very different.

To silence these doubts, I try to take one day at a time, enjoying those precious moments when Noemie and I are together and the simple happiness of being in love and being loved in return.

11

Noemie, December 1941

A lot has happened in the course of this war. The Japanese attacked the American base at Pearl Harbour in the Pacific, in retaliation for the American blockade that prevented them from moving into Southeast Asia and notably Indochina and the Dutch West Indies, which are now colonies of nations under German rule. The Americans suffered devastating human and material losses. But this led Roosevelt to decide to send American troops into this war on the side of the Allies, so in some ways these events were a blessing. This has all given us renewed hope that things will get better.

At the same time, daily life is getting harder. We have to queue for hours to get basic necessities like butter, flour and so on, and that's when they haven't run out altogether. Fortunately, the hens and the vegetable garden make up for the food shortages in the shops. I'm almost ashamed sometimes, but at least we don't use the black market. Well, not unless absolutely necessary, such as when we are obliged to invite the crème de la crème of Lignon society, if only to return the invitations. Armand's status as a doctor means we occasionally have to entertain the town's notables. Personally I could do without them, but that's how it is. And it isn't the done thing to serve swede at such gatherings!

My love for Gunther makes me do the craziest things. For almost a year and a half now we have been carrying on our affair in the shadows. We just can't take it any longer, all this sneaking around and snatching hurried moments together.

So, two weeks ago I lied to Armand so that I could join Gunther in Bordeaux. Visits to ailing old aunts are usually the perfect alibi in novels to pull the wool over your husband's eyes, but personally I don't have an aunt, let alone an ailing one. I had to come up with something original that was consistent with my role as the docile, loving and somewhat frivolous wife. And so I proceeded thus. A few days before, I sought out Armand's caresses, pretending I was craving affection. Normally Armand is the one who takes the initiative in the bedroom. So a couple of times, I took charge, or should I say gave very clear "signals". We've been married for a few years now and I know that a husband who is satisfied, by which I mean a satisfaction of his carnal needs, is more inclined to acquiesce and let his wife have her way. At least, that's how mine is. This was the first step. Then the rest fell naturally into place. One evening, the four of us were in the kitchen and we were getting ready to sit down to dinner. The ruckus the children were making was getting on my nerves, and I must have looked weary and exhausted which prompted Armand to ask me if there was anything wrong.

"I'm *tired*! *Tired* of the children who won't do as they're told, *tired* of Ernestine who does as she pleases and spends more time in Germain's shed than in the laundry room, *tired* of that UG who is poisoning our very existence within our own four walls . . . *Tired* of this war that never ends! I can't take it anymore!"

I then began to sob quietly to complete the performance. I could tell he was thinking about what I had just said. All of it had in actual fact been the truth, and this helped to ease my conscience. He was visibly moved by my distress. I prayed to myself that he would come up with a suggestion himself for my nervous fatigue.

"Take a day off . . . I don't know . . . Go and get some fresh air somewhere . . ."

"What about the children?"

"I thought we paid Ernestine to take care of them? She should be with *them,* not Germain!"

"I don't know . . . Where do you want me to go?"

"What would make you happy? The city or the countryside?"

I pretended to consider his question carefully.

"The city . . . the bustle of the city, people, the shops, even if there's not much left in them . . . . Yes, to tell you the truth, I'd love to go to Bordeaux. I haven't been there once since the beginning of the war and I miss the hustle and bustle."

For authenticity's sake, I then pretended to be disenchanted.

"No I can't go, I've got nothing decent to wear! I'll look like a farmer's wife. Forget it!"

I started sobbing again.

"You're fine the way you are," Armand told me then, putting his arm around me. "And a trip to the city will be the perfect occasion to get some fabric coupons and renew your wardrobe."

"You're probably right. I guess most French women are in the same position as me, whether they live in the town or the country . . ."

"But do bear in mind one thing: in Bordeaux there are three times as many Germans as anywhere else in France! So if you're sick of seeing the Fritz, Bordeaux isn't the place to go . . ."

"What do you mean, three times as many? Why is that?"

"Because of the city's location. It's strategically important."

We sat down at the table and Armand poured the wine.

"That's why the army, the air force and the navy moved there," he went on. "Bordeaux is near the sea and they are building a huge submarine base in Bacalan, to control the South Atlantic and intercept ships arriving from the United

States. And Bordeaux is not far from the Spanish border, which they now control. A lot of people are trying to escape to England via Spain."

"Pffff! That's just our luck . . ."

"But I don't think their presence will prevent you from having a stroll around town," he concluded, kissing my forehead.

That's how I let my husband convince me that I needed a change of scenery and should visit Bordeaux for the day. Gunther and I met at the Saint-Jean train station on a cold November morning. He had already completed his errands by the time I arrived so we had the rest of the day to ourselves. The city was grey and the weather was very windy and damp. I was wearing my warmest coat but even with the collar turned up I couldn't escape from the icy wind. Our much-anticipated rendezvous started off rather dismally. I had taken care to put on a veiled hat to conceal my face in case I ran into anyone I knew. After all, Lignon wasn't that far away.

Although I was looking forward to spending an entire day alone with Gunther, the whole thing left a slightly bitter taste in my mouth. We had developed a very strong attachment, but sometimes I wondered whether I should just end it all, for the sake of my husband. My Christian upbringing was playing havoc with my conscience and the idea of living in sin polluted my every deed. Even my actions which could be defined as "good", I now saw as a cheap attempt at redemption. I despised myself. I wasn't the person my nearest and dearest believed me to be. I was lying to everyone, including myself. But Gunther's love made me feel desirable, modern and happy. I was a woman who was mocking convention and enjoying her new existence. I now felt a zest for life after years in a marriage which seemed soporific in comparison. But now I was living a double life and the pressure of the contradiction was exhausting. Not to mention that Gunther was German; a soldier fighting for the German Reich whose politics sickened and appalled me. Even though we avoided talking about the war, it was present in our conversations regardless.

Walking along, we paused in front of a bookshop. We looked in the window and a book caught our eye. Actually, it wasn't so much the book as the drawings on either side of it: two large sketches of Hitler on one side and Mussolini on the other, perfectly recognizable despite the simplistic style. In the middle, on a display stand, was Victor Hugo's *Les Misérables*. I looked at Gunther out of the corner of my eye to gauge his reaction. Although he was in profile, I saw the corners of his lips curl up.

"Come on," he said as he ushered me inside.

"What are you doing? I hope you're not going to give that bookseller any trouble?"

"I want to buy you a present."

"But I can't get accept anything from you! How would I explain a gift to Armand?"

"Say that you bought it yourself! Okay, in that case you can give *me* a present. I want a memento of you."

We went in and as soon as he noticed Gunther's uniform, the bookseller looked visibly shaken. I could see the anxiety in his eyes. We browsed through the shelves and Gunther found what he was looking for: an anthology of French poetry. The most beautiful poems by French-speaking authors were compiled in a small, elegant volume.

"Will you dedicate it to me?" he asked.

"Of course, I'll just write, 'To Gunther, my German lover with whom I had a passionate affair in my family home'," I said, smirking.

He didn't find it funny.

"So our romance means nothing to you then?"

"Of course it does, Gunther . . . But it's not exactly wise, is it?"

"You could just put our initials?" he suggested.

"Yes, if you want," I replied curtly.

As the bookseller took the money I heard Gunther murmur to him: "Between you and me, you should take those out of your window. It might get you into trouble."

The man didn't answer, or even look at Gunther, as if just seeing a German would contaminate him with goodness knows what kind of awful disease. As for me, I felt ashamed. It's true that the shopkeeper was risking everything by displaying such pictures, but what ashamed me more than anything, was being seen walking arm in arm with the enemy. I could feel the bookseller's contemptuous gaze—it was clear where his loyalties lay. Gunther tucked the package under his arm as we left. I tried to forget about this awful encounter so as not to spoil our day. Gunther leaned over and kissed me as a thank you for the gift. He noticed my turmoil but didn't say anything. A short while later, as we were walking along one of the streets near Saint-Jean station, we passed a local woman who was very heavily made-up. She certainly wasn't a woman of loose morals, just a very pretty young lady who was a little too dolled up. Gunther scrutinized her with disgust. I caught his eye and couldn't help but question him about his reaction.

"But did you see her make-up? Why does she have to hide behind all that warpaint?" he retorted.

"It's nothing outrageous, Gunther. Women are like that here, they're vivacious, that's all. She was probably trying to distract herself from her unhappiness by getting made up. I don't see any harm in it."

"In our country, women don't wear so much make-up. It's cheap."

"So she shouldn't wear make-up, she shouldn't work, and above all she should stay at home and look after her children and obey her husband's every whim?" I hissed. "'*Kinder, Küche, Kirche*'—isn't that what you say? What a life for your women! Those are your Führer's ideals, Gunther, I hope they're not yours!"

"And in your home it's so very different?"

I leapt in front of him and looked him straight in the eye.

"As far as I'm aware, my husband doesn't keep me under lock and key! Otherwise I wouldn't be standing here with you now, thirty miles away from the house, would I! And if I wanted to work, I could. In fact, I do, I help him out at the surgery. As for make-up, I wear as much as I like."

"But you apply it in a way that looks natural and pretty," he said to appease me. He tried to take my hand but the gesture enraged me further and I pulled away.

I remembered one of our conversations a few days ago, during which he told me that back in Germany people thought the French didn't wash and that their houses were dirty and untidy too. I had retorted indignantly that *they* were the ones with the problem, being so obsessed with hygiene. I could see how spotless Gunther kept his room at home. Everything had its own place and the slightest speck of dust would never linger more than half a day. He scrubbed his washbasin daily and insisted that Ernestine change his bedsheets twice a week. Poor Ernestine was fed up.

"What does the Kraut *do* in his sheets?" she used to moan every time it was "sheet day". For a moment, I worried that she might be alluding to something of a more sordid nature that involved me.

As for his personal hygiene and his clothes, Gunther was as meticulous and painstaking as a cat. One day, when I mocked him for this, he told me that the military authorities had ordered them to ensure they were always immaculately turned out and that their lodgings were the same. I then realized that our two nations would never see eye to eye. There was a large gulf between us, starting with their obsession with cleanliness and ending with the sadistic violence they used against their fellow human beings, both of which were pathologically abnormal.

We continued walking around Bordeaux in silence. I couldn't shake off the silent fury that his remarks about the pretty French girl had unleashed in me. Then, if looks could kill, a couple walking in the opposite direction gave me a disgusted sidelong glance.

"Have you ever wondered how it makes me feel to be seen on the arm of a German soldier? That's not 'cheap' in your eyes? Have you not noticed how people look at me?"

"Noemie, please! Of course I do. There's nothing we can do about it, you know that."

There was a pause before he stopped walking and forced me to look at him.

"Darling, please, let's make peace," he pleaded softly.

"Let's make peace." He made it sound so simple. A few little words that could change the world. I started to chuckle at the madcap idea of our respective leaders asking themselves the same question in a whisper as Gunther had just done. I couldn't stop laughing and it cheered me up no end. Then I told Gunther the reason for my mirth and he joined in, imitating Hitler purring into Churchill's ear: "Darling, let's make peace, shall we?"

The rest of the day was tinged by a much-needed recklessness in the refuge of a hotel room. It was impossible for us to have any intimacy at home. Our lovemaking was slow and drawn out, with gentle caresses and untold affection. As we laid naked on the bed, our skin still warm from where our bodies had been intertwined, Gunther lit a cigarette.

"After the war, I'm going to take you back to Germany, or somewhere else . . . Far away from that husband of yours who doesn't really love you."

"But in Germany you've got Hannah. Besides, I don't want to go and live in your country. Right now, that place is too belligerent, too hostile for me."

"I haven't heard from Hannah in ages. I don't even know if she's still alive."

"And what about the children?"

"They'll come with us."

"I don't know if I would have the courage to leave Armand. He hasn't done anything wrong. He just doesn't understand me, that's all."

"And me, do you love me?"

"Yes, of course I do."

"If you can't face living in Germany, we could go to South America? What do you think? Argentina? We could learn to tango . . . I've always dreamed of learning to tango."

Whirls of smoke wafted up to the ceiling. I took the cigarette from Gunther's fingers, inhaled and passed it back to him.

"Argentina? Why not."

"Or Canada . . ."

I would have given anything to prolong that moment, a unique moment that belonged only to us, away from the rest of the world, where nothing but our pleasure and our well-being mattered. For one whole afternoon, it was like the war had ended. We imagined ourselves living elsewhere, together, in peace. But presently we had to come back to reality and return to Lignon to resume our lives and our nonsensical co-habitation.

Getting out of the house for a few hours had done me a world of good. I can't breathe at the manor. I live in permanent fear, cowed by a deep-rooted, uncontrollable anxiety which never leaves me. It's not purely the fear of being caught with my lover. I have other concerns too.

Armand, for instance. He has joined the underground resistance movement. Until two days ago, I had an inkling but wasn't completely sure. I often hear him whispering away in the entrance hall with people whom I believed at first to be patients. But these so-called patients never enter the waiting room like the others. That was the first red flag for me. And sometimes you hear the doorbell ring and when you open up, there's no one there. And then he has had this troubled look about him recently and he is strangely aggressive, so I caught on that something was awry. And two days ago, he came into the living room looking very worried. It was early afternoon at a time when he would normally have been with his patients. I was finishing up the account ledgers. I could tell there was something on his mind and looked at him to show that I was all ears.

"Noemie, I have a favour to ask of you."

"A favour? What kind of favour?"

He frowned in concentration.

"I need you to cycle to Polignac to deliver a letter."

"Polignac? In the free zone?"

His request surprised me, because I would need an *Ausweis* to go to the free zone and I didn't possess one.

He hesitated again.

"I'll get you an *Ausweis*," he went on, as if he could read my thoughts.

"You don't get an *Ausweis* just like that, at the drop of a hat! What is all this about, Armand?"

"I think you know."

"How long have you been doing this?"

"About six months. Hadn't you guessed?"

"A little . . . I had a feeling that something was going on but I wasn't sure. And since you didn't say anything, I naively thought everything was normal. Why didn't you tell me sooner?"

"To protect you. The less you know, the better. Right now, I have no choice but to involve you. It's a matter of extreme urgency."

I stared at my husband, impressed by his dedication to this shadowy cause.

"You know what you're risking, Noemie? Have you heard how the Gestapo treat so-called 'terrorists'?"

"Yes, Armand, I have."

"Are you still willing to do it?"

"If it's really important then yes, I'm willing. I trust you."

"Okay, listen carefully; you'll cycle to Polignac. When you arrive, you'll go inside the church, light a candle and come out again. You'll see a beggar who will say, 'A coin for a poor pauper,' and you will reply, 'I don't have any coins left, I put them in the church collection box.' They will reply, 'God bless you.' This will mean the coast is clear for you. Next, you need to make for the town hall. You'll walk around it and just behind the greengrocer's nearby, you'll find a stock of empty gas canisters stacked in crates. You need to slip this document between the tenth and eleventh row of crates starting from the right—take note—and you should find a letter there that you will retrieve and bring back with you."

Then he showed me the envelope he had been holding all along, which I hadn't noticed.

"What about the *Ausweis*?"

"Here you are."

I was taken aback to see he had organized everything in advance, without even asking me if I would do it. I opened the *Ausweis* which was in both German and French.

"What's my official reason for crossing the border? They'll ask me at the checkpoint," I asked.

"You will say that you have to pick up some supplies I ordered from the pharmacy. If they ask why I have ordered from him, you'll say he has far more stock than the chemist in

Lignon. And you will indeed pay a visit to the only pharmacy in the village to pick up my order which should be ready for you. Inside the package there will be pliers, staples, suture threads and some specific medical items in case they search you on your way back to see if you were lying. Here is the list. Now do you think you can do it?"

"I suppose so. I'm not very comfortable with this kind of thing, but when it comes to our country's future, what choice do I have?"

"For now it's the only way to combat the occupying forces. Several underground resistance networks have sprung up, all with the same aim: to drive the Germans out. Be extremely careful, Noemie, you must try to act naturally and be discreet. You *must* get this envelope through. You're going to take an empty briefcase in your saddlebag to put the medical supplies in on the way back. Before you get to the border, you will hide the envelope in your bodice. You will only take it out and put it in the briefcase once you're on the other side, so it'll be within easy reach at the last minute."

"Won't the Germans be surprised to see an empty briefcase?"

"You will say that it's to put the medical supplies in, which is true."

"What planning! It must be important if everything is organized down to the last detail."

"It is all extremely important. You must be very careful. If something feels wrong or isn't just as I've described, go directly to the pharmacy. No church, no crates. Understood?"

"I think so. I suppose you can't tell me anymore, such as why I have to do this?"

"No, each person involved only knows what he or she has to do. It's a question of safety. So that if we get caught, the Germans can't trace the network all the way back up."

"Yes, of course . . . When do I have to go?"

"Right now."

I was speechless. At least I wouldn't have the time to mull it over and weigh up the pros and cons. I grabbed the incriminating document.

Meanwhile, Armand went to get the briefcase that would suit our purposes. I went up to my room to hide the envelope under my clothes. Lately, coal has been in short supply, so we only heat a few rooms on the ground floor. This December has been bitterly cold, so I have taken to wearing many layers to keep warm. I mustn't hide the envelope under all these layers otherwise I won't be able to get to it without undressing completely. So I decided to tuck it in between my jumper and bodice. On top of that, I have my woollen jacket and my coat. That way the letter will be well hidden but accessible. The waistband of my skirt should hold it in place too. Once I was safely kitted out, I went downstairs.

Armand joined me in the hall. He kissed me awkwardly as he is not accustomed to such gestures, and I left the room with my stomach in knots. I got my bicycle out of the shed behind the house, where we also store logs. Then I mounted my bicycle and pedalled off, thinking to myself that I might not be back for some time. I then tried to banish these gloomy thoughts and think about something else, deciding it was better to concentrate on the task at hand and prepare myself mentally. I longed to cycle off into the countryside just to feel the wind blowing through my hair, the chill of the air whipping past my nostrils, and my legs burning from the effort. I should like to cycle along with no cares in the world other than watching a hare scurry away, or birds of prey circling over the fields looking for a rabbit or a field mouse, the trees stripped of their leaves and waiting for spring to banish winter. I imagined life on the farms I rode past, logs on the fire, hot chocolate on the table, the hullaballoo of the children's teatime. As I pedalled towards the border, reality caught up with me. At the checkpoint, I stopped in front of the German border guard and showed him my *Ausweis*. His broken French and guttural accent terrified me.

"Why are you going to the free zone, Frau Lenoir?"

"I have to pick up some pharmaceutical products for my husband who is a doctor in Lignon."

"You can't get them in the occupied zone?"

"The pharmacy in Polignac is the best stocked pharmacy in the area."

I showed him the list that Armand had given me. He opened the saddlebag and took out the briefcase. He opened it without asking my permission and told me it was empty.

"It's to put the medical supplies in once I've bought them," I explained.

"Show me the money."

"What money?"

"The money you'll spend."

I froze. Armand hadn't mentioned anything about money, though logically any order would require payment. I quickly improvised. I could feel the sweat pooling under my armpits.

"My husband has an account with the pharmacist," I replied. "He pays it every three months."

I don't know what came over me then, but I didn't stop there.

"He'll probably give me the invoice today."

I desperately hoped that he wouldn't be at the checkpoint on my way back. It was then that I realized just what I had got myself into. A dangerous game that I was going to have to play out one act after the other, adlibbing if necessary, to avoid being ensnared by my lies. Luckily he waved me through. I grabbed my bicycle, taking care to conceal my immense relief.

This sense of relief was short-lived, however, as just afterwards I could make out the distinctive figure of our priest, Father Seignier, cycling towards me in the distance. I simply couldn't ride past without stopping to greet him. My involvement in the charitable activities of the local parish meant he was better acquainted with me than he was with most of his flock. I had no time to think of an excuse for my being here. During our recent conversations, I had guessed that he too sought to resist the enemy, if only for humanitarian reasons. But we had always kept our opinions on Vichy politics to ourselves. I decided I would give him the "official" version which, after all, wasn't far from the truth. I knew he would be surprised, but how could I lie to the person to whom I confessed my sins? He was no fool, and even though the Resistance justified a white lie, he would sooner or later get wind of my hypocrisy once tongues started wagging. I took solace in the fact that as a man of God he would not blab to anyone. Who knows, maybe he was on the same side as us and wanted the enemy out. I decided not to give him the chance to wonder what I was doing on the road to Polignac. Instead I would grab the bull by the horns and ask *him* what he was doing there! By now he was getting closer and I still hadn't assembled my ideas. Suddenly I found myself level with him. As expected, when he recognized me, he slowed down and stopped. His face was crimson, and I wondered if it was the physical exertion or the embarrassment at seeing me. Neither of us were supposed to be on this side of the border.

"Hello, Father."

"Good day, Noemie."

Then there was a heavy silence. Neither of us spoke another word. The explanation I had carefully rehearsed now stuck in my throat. Our eyes met and I sensed a mutual understanding, a tacit desire not to ask anything that could generate a lie, no matter how justified. At the same time, it would look very odd if I didn't express my surprise at his presence.

It would imply we both had something to hide. You could cut the atmosphere with a knife.

"So your duties bring you to the free zone, Father?" I asked light-heartedly to break the stalemate.

"Yes . . . the priest in Polignac is very ill and since Lignon is the nearest town, the diocese asked me to replace him. What about you, Noemie, where are you off to on that steed of yours?" he asked jocularly, pointing at my bicycle.

"I'm going to pick up a few bits and pieces for Armand at the pharmacy, Father. Usually, he has his supplies delivered but the delivery man couldn't get through this time."

The polite small talk over with, we could both be on our way. I prayed that he wouldn't check out the story of the delivery man I had just invented. Then I got back on my bicycle and went over our brief conversation in my head to check I hadn't said anything compromising. I felt surprisingly calm. Even though he had a valid reason for being in the free zone, the priest's awkwardness in my presence reassured me that he was counting on my discretion as much as I was on his.

I finally arrived at the village square. Given the peacefulness of the place, you would never have guessed that an active resistance movement was lurking behind closed doors, invisible and determined to give our country back its freedom. The mere thought of this galvanized me; I felt proud to be part of the process. My anxiety even disappeared entirely for a few moments. I parked my bicycle against a tree in front of the church and looked around the square. I could see a few passers-by, a couple of lovers on a bench, and a line of children walking in a crocodile, accompanied by an adult whom I guessed was their teacher. In the distance, I noticed two policemen knocking on someone's front door. I walked up the church steps and was amazed to discover that the beggar waiting at the exit was in fact a woman! Not that this changed anything. I went inside the church and lit a candle as Armand had instructed. I knelt down and crossed myself, before heading towards the exit, my heart pounding. Suddenly my mind went blank. I couldn't remember what I was supposed to say to the beggar. Seized by panic, I froze. The more I racked my brains trying to remember, the less it came to me. Something about putting money in the church collection box, but I couldn't remember Armand's exact words and my mind was in total disarray. I went and sat on a pew at the back of the church and took some deep breaths to calm down. I hoped I wasn't attracting attention with my strange behaviour. I observed an old lady, dressed in black, not far from me. She was praying on her knees. I could see her lips moving. Her devotion moved me. What was she asking the Lord for? The return of her son? Food for her grandchildren? The end of the war? What could we still expect from the Lord Almighty? Then I remembered why I was here. That tiny diversion had the effect of freeing the words that had been trapped in the inner recesses of my mind. When I reached the beggar woman, I heard her say the words I was expecting. The coast was now clear. Our verbal exchange had sounded so natural that I had to remind myself that this was all a ruse. Next, I set off in the direction of the town hall, pushing my bicycle. I scanned the square and was relieved to see that the policemen were no longer there. Had the beggar woman spotted them, like me? I located the greengrocer's and stole around the back looking for the stacked crates that Armand had told me about. Everything was as he had described. Between the tenth and eleventh rows, I quickly spotted the envelope that was awaiting me. I started trembling uncontrollably. Suddenly, I heard a noise. I pressed my back against the crates. Footsteps were approaching the back of the greengrocer's towards where I was standing. But there was nothing here except the crates. Two men appeared; it was the two policemen I had spotted earlier in the square. I smiled at them and put my finger to my lips. They stared at me in surprise.

"Please don't say anything," I whispered. "I'm hiding from someone I don't want to see near the church."

They stepped back to look in the direction I had just come from.

"Who is it?"

"I don't think they've come out of the church yet, but I'm not sure," I lied.

I carried on whispering to make my story sound genuine.

The policemen were smirking now but they were still somewhat suspicious and had a good look around. Luckily I hadn't moved and my body was concealing the gap in the crates where the letter was. My bicycle then caught their eye.

"Is this yours?"

"Yes," I whispered.

It then occurred to me that with all the unexpected happenings on the way, I had forgotten to take the envelope out of my bodice and put it in the briefcase in the saddlebag. It was still wedged in my skirt waistband. I congratulated myself on this oversight, as the policemen began opening my saddlebags. All they found was the empty briefcase. They winked at me as they left.

"Don't stay here too long, there are some unsavoury types around."

As soon as I couldn't hear their footsteps any longer, I quickly exchanged the documents. The envelope I retrieved was smaller than the one I slid in between the crates. I wedged it under my clothes and jumped back on my bicycle, first checking that the two policemen had indeed moved on. My next task was much easier; I picked up the pharmaceutical supplies and cycled back to Lignon. Fortunately there was no further incident—I had had enough excitement that day to last me a fortnight!

This experience taught me something rather incredible. Although I had been terrified, I had surpassed myself. I felt oddly euphoric. I had played my part so naturally and convincingly, all the while sweating profusely under my clothes.

The pride I felt at participating in such a meaningful cause for my country catapulted me into an indescribable state of exhilaration. I also understood how easy it was to let your guard down when you're driven by patriotism. The slightest error in judgment can be fatal. I shuddered in hindsight at the thought of the briefcase that could have so easily contained the precious envelope when the police searched it. It had been a near miss. I reminded myself that thousands of people in France go through this every day. Sometimes they are lucky, other times not.

For the past two days, I have been in a frenzy. All I think about is doing it again. But patience is a virtue, as they say. And then there's Gunther. I shudder at the thought of him finding out. The fact I detected clues in Armand's demeanour means Gunther could too. I will have to question him discreetly.

12

Angela, 15th June 1946

It feels like I've been in Bournelin forever. I arrived a month ago. I drift between that awful orphanage, the police station where they're working flat out trying to find out who I am and where I come from, and Justin's house, my haven of peace. I like the expression *haven of peace*. I remember reading it in a book. My memory has a mind of its own. Why does it let me remember that sort of thing but not who I am? Or what happened to me? If it wasn't so serious, it would be funny. For the past few days, I've been living at Justin's house. No more Sister Pigswill in the evening! At least for the moment. And I still see her at school. Justin and the superintendent think I'll be safer at Justin's house. "It's against the regulations, but we've got no choice, you can't be too careful," said the superintendent with his big moustache, huge belly and stinky wooden pipe. When he comes into a room, you first see his tummy then you hear him sucking on his pipe. He is nice, even though his moustache and his belly scare me a bit. I guessed he and Justin weren't telling me everything. They didn't want to frighten me. They looked like two children whispering behind their parents' backs. If the idea is to protect me, it means I must be in danger. I've lost my memory, but I still have my brain. I love the idea of living at Justin's house. But I know someone who won't be pleased!

From what I can gather, I may have escaped from the clutches of a very bad person. Justin and his chief are afraid that this man might come after me to stop me from talking to the police. He doesn't know that I've lost my memory. A policeman takes me to the orphanage in the morning and picks me up after lunch to take me to the police station, if Justin can't do it himself. I worry because when I'm in class at the orphanage, there is no one to protect me. It's not like at the police station or at Justin's house . . . If a stranger came to the orphanage to get me, the sisters wouldn't be able to stop him, especially if he had a gun. So, I'm on my guard all the time. And I tell myself that if someone I don't know comes to get me, I'll run and hide. I know every nook and cranny now. It's as easy as ABC for a child to hide here. Since I've had this plan, I feel better, even if I have to stay alert.

I still go to class every morning. A teacher comes to the orphanage to teach us. He is kind. It's a nice break from those old dragons. There are no separate classes—all of the children learn together. Since they don't know my exact age, they put me in with the nine-and ten-year-olds, but I do all the exercises of the class above. For some reason I can still remember what I learnt in my old school. I still know that one hectolitre is the equivalent of one hundred litres, and that the area of a triangle is equal to its base multiplied by its height, divided by two. The teacher is pleased with me and gives me good marks.

At twelve o'clock, we go to the canteen. The food is disgusting and is basically a few lentils swimming in water. The sisters say that because there is a war on, there is not much to eat and that we should be grateful for what God has put on our plates. Well, I wish God could taste what he puts on our plates! I'll leave him the weevils while I eat the lentils. But we always have something nice on Sundays. On that day the sisters serve us iced gingerbread or cinnamon cakes for dessert. I don't know where they get them, but I don't care as they are yummy. And the sisters love them too, we see them licking their fingers at their table. I can see why, as they eat the same food as us all week.

The day before yesterday, when I arrived at the police station in the early afternoon, Justin told me he had something important to show me. He was holding a picture in his hands. He looked embarrassed. We went and sat down in his office, as we do every day since I was found and brought here. It's horrible to have to say I was "found", like a piece of lost property. But that's what I am: a lost girl with no name. It's weird, because I know who I am in other ways and I am aware of my tastes, for example. I know that I love reading, listening to music, dancing, and I even write stories. I have opinions about everything. It makes Justin laugh. I talk about life at the police station, the orphanage, the news on the radio. I know a lot of things too. Justin says I'm "cultured" because when we're at home listening to music on his gramophone or on the radio, I often tell him about the musician we are listening to, other pieces he has composed and so on. The other day we were listening to Liszt's "Liebestraum No. 3". The notes literally dance all over the place. It makes you wonder how you can play it with only ten fingers! In my old life, I mean the one before I lost my memory, I used to play the piano. This was my favourite piece. I couldn't play it though, as it's really difficult for a small girl's hands, but I am determined to learn it one day. I also told Justin that Liszt's daughter, Cosima, married Richard Wagner, another famous musician, and that the two great artists worked together. Justin laughed and said that for someone who has lost their memory, I know an awful lot! Then he asked me how I knew all this. But I don't actually know . . . And I don't know where I come from, who my parents are, if I have brothers and sisters, or even where I live. These things are so important as they form the solid ground from which you grow. I realize now that I've lost that. I feel like I'm just bumping along, aimlessly. Even the girls at the orphanage know who they are; though most of them have suffered a lot because their parents have died or been deported. If my parents turn out to be dead, I'm not sure I want to get my memory back.

Speaking of which, when I told Justin about Cosima Liszt-Wagner, it set off a small spark in my brain, as if her name was linked to something other than just Liszt's daughter. I concentrated hard on the name "Cosima", trying to remember why it reminded me of something other than music. In my mind I could see a slightly chubby woman. Actually very chubby. And she was wearing a white apron over her big tummy. She was holding something like a ladle or a spoon in her hand and she was smiling. It was a nice vision. I must have liked her. But who is she? Justin noted it down (he likes to say "I'm taking note") in case it's a clue to help trace my family.

Anyway, back to the day before yesterday when Justin was acting very strangely.

"Angela," he said. "I'm going to show you a picture of a man and you're going to tell me if you recognize him, okay?"

The atmosphere in the office was suffocating, despite the window being open. Dr Bertin was with us too, as well as the superintendent. I couldn't understand why Justin was acting so bizarrely about showing me a picture of a man. When I asked, he simply replied, "We think that maybe he's the person who hurt you and caused your amnesia."

I didn't answer then. My heart was pounding. Now I could see why the atmosphere was so tense. They all looked really awkward. The superintendent took a long puff on his pipe, which hung out of the corner of his mouth, and beads of sweat ran down his forehead which he patted from time to time with his handkerchief. When I was ready, I told them to show me the picture.

Justin placed it on the table. The doctor stood next to me. I could feel them all watching me intently, which annoyed me. When I looked at the man in the photograph, my eyes grew as big as saucers. I looked at Justin and then at the doctor. Justin had sweat running down his brow too, but it wasn't because of the heat. He was frowning and looked worried.

"Do you recognize him, Angela?"

"Yes," I said, letting out my breath.

I saw Justin clench his fists on the table. He was clenching them so tightly, I thought they might break.

"Do you remember *where* you saw him?"

I tried to remember as it was rather blurry in my mind.

"In the square, I think."

"A square or a park?"

"I don't know, Justin. I think it was just before I was brought to the police station by those ladies."

He turned as white as a ghost.

"Were you alone?"

"I think so . . . No, actually I wasn't! There were some children nearby but they didn't seem bothered. They were watching from a distance."

Justin gulped. His face fell.

"What did he say to you?"

"I think he wanted to show me something I'd never seen before."

"What did you say?"

"I said no, I didn't want to, because I didn't trust him. He was dirty and he stank."

"And then what happened?"

"He said he would tell my parents if I didn't look at it."

Justin jumped out of his chair.

"Damn it! He did the same with the other children . . ." he exclaimed to his colleagues.

"Which children?" I asked.

"Keep going, Angela, keep going."

He was clearly finding it difficult to stay calm. Were we about to find out something important about me? I concentrated hard, trying to remember.

"He was so disgusting! I didn't want to look at him or touch him or anything!"

"Good God! And what did he say or do next?"

"He didn't say anything after that, because those two ladies, the ones who brought me here, came up to me and asked me what I was doing there on my own."

"And what about him?"

"He ran off, luckily!"

"So this happened in Bournelin square then?"

"Yes."

"He didn't touch you?"

"No."

"What about the other children who were nearby, did he touch them?"

"No, I don't think so."

"So, to recap, Angela, you recognize this man from the village square, but he didn't do anything to you."

"Yes, that's right."

I nodded my head to confirm what I'd said. Then I smiled when I saw how relieved Justin looked, as if I had just got top marks in a school test.

"The trauma obviously isn't related to this incident," Dr Bertin said then.

"I'm so relieved," said Justin again and again.

"Why?" I asked.

"Because that man does *very bad things* to children. Thank goodness those ladies were there, I can't imagine if on top of all the rest, you had to . . . Well, let's not talk about it anymore," he mumbled. Then he turned to the doctor.

"I'm still going to inform the Poinseuil station that the pervert dragged his sorry self all the way over here. Maybe they'll open up a proper investigation so that the poor children of Montjoly Park get justice. Who knows . . ."

"So it wasn't the bad man that hurt me then?" I asked.

"No, sweetheart, thank goodness!"

"But will it still help us?"

Justin nodded. "Yes, but we must keep going."

Meanwhile the doctor and the superintendent had gone, leaving me and Justin alone. I was so upset that it hadn't led to something that would help trace my parents. I understood now that Justin had been scared that the bad man had done something to me; that's why he was frowning at the beginning and smiling afterwards. When he pushed the door closed behind him after seeing the others out, he turned to me and opened his arms wide. I threw myself into them. It was so comforting to feel his warmth and strength after all the upset. I think we realized at that moment how fond we had become of each other.

"I was so scared, my angel, so scared!" he whispered into my hair.

The good news is that I'm slowly getting a few memories back. Or should I say nightmares. Recently I've been having a recurring dream of a woman screaming: "Go now, escape! Run fast, my darling! Run as fast as you can!" Justin asked me to describe her, but she doesn't have a face. I can't make out her features. She keeps telling me to escape and run. I have this dream a lot. Sometimes I can see small details which makes me think I have a brother or sister, because the lady with no face is holding another child against her. Sometimes she is blindfolded and sometimes she is tied up. She seems to be in a wooden cabin, not a house. It's small and there's not much light.

The police think there is a link between my nightmares and my fear of closed doors. They believe I was kidnapped and held prisoner, quite possibly with my parents. I was so dirty when I arrived at the station, like I hadn't washed for days, which could mean we were locked up for a long time.

Something bothers me even more than this nightmare. If I was being held hostage with my parents and I escaped, what will happen to them if I don't get my memory back? Or should I say, what might have already happened to them? I've been here a month now. But in all that time no one has come looking for me. No one at all!

13
Germain, June 1942

I've got lots to do at present. This spring has been gloriously sunny and the park has exploded into every shade of green imaginable. The vegetable garden is also in full swing so there's no shortage of jobs. But I prefer it like that. I work up quite a sweat. Sometimes I take my shirt off in the scorching heat if the lady of the house isn't around. I don't think she would appreciate seeing her gardener half-naked!

In fact, the other day, I was labouring in the park, not far from the house, when I sensed that I was being watched. I looked up and there were the bosses' two little 'uns standing there ogling me. They must have escaped Ernestine's eagle eye. They are sweet children, well-groomed and always polite—well, the little girl especially, because the boy can't talk properly yet. The girl, on the other hand, is a real chatterbox. She was staring at me intensely now, her eyes as round as saucers. I don't know if it was my outfit or what.

"Hello, Germain, could you make us a swing, please?" she asked finally.

"A swing, what's all this about? Did your parents tell you to ask me?"

"No, it's my idea," she said with a shrug as if she couldn't see why I was making a song and dance about it.

"Did you ask them first?"

"Yes, and Papa told me that with two ropes and a plank, you would do it while shaking a lamb's tail."

I chuckled.

"You mean 'in two shakes of a lamb's tail', I believe. But your father is right. I'll just have to ask him where he wants us to hang it. There's no shortage of trees, so he can take his pick."

The next day, the children had their swing. Quick and efficient that's me. I don't really like my bosses, particularly at the moment, but I'm not good at saying no. I love helping people out and being useful, and the kids were happy. They're thrilled with their new swing. Of course, Ernestine is moaning because she has to watch them outside now. But this could mean more opportunities for our little get togethers! Oh well, I suppose we all see things differently.

Despite being terribly busy, I don't neglect my other activities. By this I mean my efforts to kick out the evil forces that have been occupying our country for the last two years.

Now that the United States has entered the war, there is light at the end of the tunnel. But there's a lot of work to be done first. A year ago, me and my brother Etienne joined an intelligence network linked to de Gaulle's Free France movement. Etienne is group leader in our sector. He was trained as a radio operator by someone parachuted in from London. Since then, he's been coding and transmitting messages. But he won't be able to do this for very long as we must apply the 3/3 rule if we don't want to get caught. This means broadcasting for a duration of no more than three minutes, no more than three times from the same location, and the same person can broadcast for no longer than three months, to limit routine errors. Trouble is you then have to find new radio operators to do the job . . . His main concern is to broadcast as fast as possible, without being spotted. It's always a race against the clock because of the goniometers the Germans use to detect our radio waves. The other day, we had an extremely close shave. It sent shivers down my spine. We were at the property of one of our brothers-in-arms, and we were about to broadcast. There was Merlot, Etienne—alias Blaye—and me. We were broadcasting from the storage room at the bottom of Merlot's parents' garden—they had gone to live in the free zone as soon as the war broke out. It was a very useful hideout, and we could leave our equipment there, hidden inside old furniture. That junk is so heavy to carry around otherwise. Another good thing about the place is that it is out of sight, roomy and has an escape route through the alley at the back. We always strive to broadcast from a place with a double escape route so we can bolt if necessary. Except this time, Merlot hadn't checked the state of the locks which had rusted over and when the Krauts picked up our signal, we nearly got caught trying to flee. We had everything in place, the indoor antenna, the radio, it was all up and running. Etienne had plugged in the device and already punched in his call sign. We were in the heat of the action when we heard noises from the garden and we realized the Gestapo were coming towards the shed. That lot are hardly discreet. There were not one, not two, but three of them! I ran to lock the front door while Etienne switched everything off and hastily packed up the equipment. We scrambled towards the exit, but the door to the street at the back was jammed. The lock must have rusted over, as we couldn't turn the key. We could hear the Krauts trying to get into the outhouse. In their haste, they broke the glass. Merlot grabbed a hammer from the workbench and hit the lock with a force that none of us thought him capable of. Fear produces miracles sometimes. The whole thing shattered, and we were able to escape, but the Germans had us in their sights and opened fire. We owe our lives to the labyrinth of alleyways in this neighbourhood that got them off our trail. After that episode, we could never go back there again. The hideout was private but the fact that it was a detached building in the garden made it more easily detectable by the Germans' goniometer. Our signal is much harder to detect if we transmit from inside a building complex. There aren't many such places in Lignon.

For us, the hardest things to find are safe houses and reliable people. When someone wants to join our network, we have to go over their background check with a fine-tooth comb, to make sure they genuinely want to join the cause. Several of our agents have infiltrated the Vichy regime and it is these very agents who give us information to pass on to London. We know what infiltration means by now, so it would be the last straw to see our work sabotaged by a mole! Suspicion and caution are the watchwords of the day, along with bravery, courage, patriotism and other such values cherished by the rebellious French people.

We listen to Radio-Londres to check that our messages have arrived and to pick up others. We also receive instructions from our leaders, which we more or less follow, since not all the networks function in the same way. In fact, it's a bit messy. Everyone does their bit in their corner. On the one hand, it's safer this way because the more fragmented we are, the harder it is for the Krauts or even the French police to trace our actions back to us. But the disadvantage is that it's not very coordinated. Looking on the bright side, however, more and more patriots are joining us in one way or another. This is extremely important if our movement is to continue because a lot of groups disband. But we're holding on. If caught, our brothers-in-arms know the rules, i.e., you must try and hold out for forty-eight hours before speaking, or at the very least for twenty-four hours, if the pressure is unbearable. Time for us to erase all traces, take new code names and empty the hideouts. If I think about it, twenty-four hours is a hell of a long time, let alone forty-eight . . . We all wonder whether we would survive it. What the Krauts are capable of is unimaginable. They must be sick, crazy humans to have such barbaric ideas. And on top of physical torture, they put pressure on the "terrorists" as they call us, by threatening to attack our parents or children. Or they pretend that it was one of our own who denounced us, so that we have no scruples in ratting the group out. A lot of people crack at that point. Humans are certainly not equal in the courage and pain stakes. So we try not to think about it, otherwise our movement wouldn't exist. It's horrible to say it, but when one of our lot is freed, we can't trust them. We don't reintegrate them at first. We have to be extremely careful. No one knows what he or she might have revealed under torture . . . I say "he or she" as there are quite a few women in our ranks. They are skilled at passing on information and are as brave as the men.

My nickname is Petrus. I hate my real name so I'm pleased to have chosen a new one. In our group, we all have aliases that are linked to wine. We are in the Bordeaux region after all! The other day, a guy joined us that we were suspicious about. It wasn't just me, several of us had doubts about him. Finally, we accepted him, after painstakingly checking out his references which all turned out to be good. Nevertheless, we christened him "Plonk", as at first he left a strange taste in our mouths. Little things like that amuse us and it eases the tension.

Since I'm both a handyman and the doctor's gardener, people are used to seeing me coming and going in the village. This is great for our network as it facilitates the flow of information. The other day, however, I had the fright of my life. I mean another one! Being an active resistance member is by no means easy, and you can never let your guard down. The lady of the house had asked me to take some of our vegetables to Aurelia Blasco, the widow of a Spanish guerrilla who is raising her five children alone. That's the good thing about Mrs Lenoir. She is generous to those who are less fortunate than her. One way to earn your place in heaven, I suppose. Aurelia Blasco's eldest son, Pablo, is a member of our network. So, it's a fantastic way to get messages across. He is only eighteen years old, but since the Spanish Civil War, he knows better than anyone what the word "freedom" means. His father paid for it with his life. In vain too, as the Franco regime won. Despite all this, you have to keep fighting for your cause . . . One must always be brave and strive every day. Anyway, I had warned Pablo in advance that he would find a message in the lettuces.

I set off with my wheelbarrow laden with a crate of vegetables, well camouflaged beneath a blanket so as not to attract any covetous eyes. At the entrance to the village, I could see a checkpoint had been set up. I wondered why it had been put there. I had no choice but to pass through it. My heart was beating ten to the dozen as I arrived pushing my wheelbarrow, trying to appear calm and unruffled, while on the inside I was a nervous wreck. I presented my papers. The German guard lifted the blanket and looked at the contents of my wheelbarrow greedily.

"*Salat*?"

"Yes, salad: lettuce, radishes, cabbage, onions, chard . . ."

To distract his attention from the message hidden in the lettuces, like an idiot I started reeling off a list of the tasty vegetables in my barrow which he could have seized at any moment. He seemed very interested in my beautiful fresh produce and started pointing at it all as he turned to his fellow soldiers. He then barked two sentences at his colleague that made me jump, as I do every time I hear German spoken. I was just trying to imagine how I would get myself out of this mess should they decide to take my vegetables, when I heard his colleague bark back the answer, which was negative. He waved me through, a little annoyed at the missed opportunity. Once the danger was over, I couldn't resist mumbling under my breath: "No, you bastard, you're not getting your grubby hands on my *salat*, you filthy Kraut!"

Though the Germans put the fear of God into us at times, they are terrified of us too. Why do you think they call us "terrorists"? Our acts of sabotage and our booby traps are taking a toll on their morale, just as they're meant to. In some resistance networks, the motto is "kill the Krauts". It can happen any place, anytime, wherever and whenever they least expect it. The downside, however, is that our attacks are always followed by heavy reprisals. But we mustn't let ourselves be intimidated. We dream of organizing an attack on the Gestapo in Bordeaux in which Friedrich Dohse, their fiendish leader, is blown to smithereens. The icing on the cake would be if Poinsot was there with him. Poinsot is the head of the French police. Dohse couldn't hope for a more zealous and cruel collaborator than Poinsot. So, just one bomb, and wham! Two birds with one stone: gone! Well, until they're replaced, that is. But frankly, there wouldn't be many tears shed over those two. It's getting hard for people around here, especially in the city, by which I mean Bordeaux. The Germans seize everything they can, leaving only the crumbs for the inhabitants. To top it all, Poinsot and his henchmen have set up a vile denunciation system that has made the atmosphere even more oppressive. And as for the Jews, well, their situation is getting more and more alarming. They are treated like pariahs and now have to wear a special sign to differentiate them from the rest of the population. And then those convoys that go off to God knows where . . . It's all so sinister. Yesterday, I read in the local paper that the anti-Semitic exhibition organized by the deputy mayor, Marquet, has been a roaring success in Bordeaux. How sad. I don't actually know any Jews myself. At least, I don't think I do. And even if I did, what have these poor people done to be persecuted in this way? Etienne taught me that anti-Semitism is nothing new and that the Nazis didn't invent it. They just added another layer with all their nonsense about superior and inferior races, to justify their persecutions. They are absolutely filled with hatred.

In the meantime, Ernestine and I are still meeting in the potting shed. Even more so now than before, thanks to the swing. Imagine if the lady of the house found out! We don't do grand overtures; we get straight down to the nitty gritty. From time to time, I ask her to rummage through the Kraut's belongings when he's not there, to see if there's any information she can glean. I haven't told her that I'm in the Resistance as she blabs too much, but I did tell her that if she found any papers in his room, she should read them and tell me what they say. She doesn't even ask me why I want to know. I wonder if she does it on purpose . . . Sometimes she gives me tips like dates and places. We don't always know what's going to happen but we try to work it out. For example, when we find a note saying: "station, Tuesday 4:30 pm", we look at what trains are running that day, their destination and we try to ascertain if it's a departure, an arrival, or something else, by cross-checking our information. Then we pass it on. Sometimes it helps.

The problem is that she won't be able to snoop any more, as the Kraut cottoned on and complained to Mrs Lenoir. She summoned Ernestine and gave the girl quite a telling off right there in front of him. The fool didn't just root around for information, she also stole a square of chocolate here and a cigarette there, so of course he ended up noticing. Honestly, how stupid can you get! In any case, the humiliation stuck in her throat and she swore to me that her mistress wouldn't get to heaven by humiliating her in front of a Nazi. I'm just annoyed that I've lost my source.

Although it may not always appear so, we're passing on quite a bit of information to London. Our agents have even infiltrated the ports of Bordeaux and Bacalan. They monitor the arrivals and departures of the warships. I presume they are planning a sting operation to destroy enemy ships. Many positive things are happening now. On 1st May, we called on people to take to the streets. There was a lot of civilian resistance and big demonstrations took place in the cities in the south as well as in Paris. You should see the Krauts foaming at the mouth! So, to boost the morale of their war-weary troops, those in command—led by Goebbels—have rolled out another propaganda campaign. They have targeted cinemas, theatres, newspapers, wherever people meet and talk—no expense is spared when it comes to duping German soldiers and pretending all is rosy on all fronts.

And then there's that rumour about the "relief effort" being organized by the Vichy regime at the request of the Germans. They want French volunteers to go and work in Germany in exchange for prisoners of war. If I understand it correctly, the idea is to help Germany win the war and to thwart the rise of Bolshevism in Europe. In my opinion, all they'll succeed in doing is boosting our numbers, as there won't be many, if any, volunteers. We don't all have the same priorities when it comes to patriotism. When I heard Laval himself, the head of the French government, announce, "I am hoping for a German victory, because without it, Bolshevism will spread unchecked", I thought Etienne was going to throw the radio against the wall! People want to liberate France, they don't see Bolshevism as an immediate threat, or even a threat at all. Such a statement will just add fuel to the fire.

I nearly forgot to mention that I have discovered a fantastic new hiding place for weapons. The other day in the shed, while Ernestine and I were hard at it, rocking against the old sideboard in which I keep the small pots for seedlings, I suddenly heard a strange hollow noise. It intrigued me, so when Ernestine went back to the manor, I tried to found out where the sound was coming from. It was as if there was no wall behind the sideboard, even though I could clearly see it . . . So I tried to move the sideboard to one side slightly. Jesus Christ, it took every ounce of strength I had, as that thing is made of solid wood! It's what you call good quality tat. I could hear the pots wobbling around inside but I couldn't be bothered to take them all out. I eventually managed to shift the sideboard enough to squeeze behind it. I saw nothing at first, except a wooden panel on the floor, which looked like it had been placed there until someone found a use for it. It was safely out of the way behind the sideboard. But I still didn't have the answer to my question. Why was there a hollow sound? Then I removed the panel, and under it I could see an opening of about one metre by eighty centimetres: big enough for a man to slip through. Overcome with curiosity, and feeling very nervous, I slid down into the opening. I moved forward and was surprised to see that I could almost stand up straight inside. It was dark and scary down there, and the tunnel looked deep. It could well lead to the manor dungeons. I won't be going that far though, it's not that I've got the willies, but you just never know. I don't even know if there *are* any dungeons under the manor . . . But I immediately knew what this space would be useful for: hiding our weapons! It would be quite a job to get them down here and retrieve them again, but I don't think the boss comes to the shed very often. I doubt he even knows this hiding place exists. Even without venturing very far, you could get a lot inside. It's a good amount of storage space. I was already scheming how I could get the next deliveries of weapons down here, under cover of the blackout, of course. Our group had programmed weapons drop-offs by parachute over the next few days near Lignon, but we hadn't yet found anywhere safe to conceal them. I would waste no time telling Etienne about this new hideout. My "find" certainly perked me up. I put the panel and the sideboard back in place, carefully erasing any marks on the ground. You would have to be a talented sleuth to guess what lies beneath!

14
Solveig, September 2011

I love the end of summer in Toulouse. My flat on the Grande Rue Saint-Michel basks in a beautiful light and the air is cooler than in high season. I have got my energy back and have a thousand and one projects in mind: getting back to cooking after my laziness during these past hot months, making new covers for the living room cushions, learning that piano piece I came across and promised myself to play one day, plus making jam with the figs that the greengrocer set aside for me.

This morning I'm off to my yoga class. Yoga is like an old familiar friend. When my children grew up and gradually deserted the family home, I felt the need to keep myself busy and above all, take care of myself. While they were omnipresent in my life, I didn't have time to think or dwell on my dark thoughts. The children occupied my whole mind space and I was grateful to them for that. If ever I had a moment to myself, I would panic and rush to fill the void. When they flew the nest and were no longer tugging at my apron strings, I felt my old cage close around me again. This is when I knew I needed help. *If you don't take care of yourself, my girl, who will?* So I took the bull by the horns, as I loved to say when I was little, and set about finding an activity that would make me feel good about myself. That was in the 1980s. I quickly rejected aerobics and squash which were all the rage at the time. I wanted to do something zen, something that would relax and invigorate me, and nothing that involved jumping madly around. The idea was to nurture my body while keeping my mind in check so it wouldn't destroy me. *Mens sana in corpore sano.*

Then one day, Sylvette suggested I come to her yoga class with her. I was very reluctant, because hidden behind that word all I saw was an impossible array of postures, each one more uncomfortable than the last, not to mention the incomprehensible chanting. Instead, it was a revelation. I discovered a true life partner whose gentleness and benevolence fulfilled all my expectations. My husband used to tease me at first by calling it "your new lover". Later on, he called it simply "your lover" for short. It used to amaze me when he said this in front of friends who were inviting us to dinner or a party. He would ask me in all seriousness whether I would be seeing my lover that evening. I played along and answered equally seriously that I would move him to another night of the week. Wide-eyed looks came from all directions and I could tell the women were perplexed at the thought of our open marriage and that the men were shocked at my husband's permissiveness. I think I even read envy in some peoples' expressions as if to say, "what a couple! They must have fun together!" After pretending to be uber-progressive for a few moments, we would then reassure everyone, or disappoint them as the case may be, by admitting it was just a game and quite a silly one at that. But it still made us giggle like teenagers. It would be an untruth to say that yoga and meditation solved all my problems, but I think that without them, I would have slowly sunk into a depression or gone insane.

My job as a bookseller saved me too. Being surrounded by books was like having therapy. I loved meeting authors, organizing book-signing evenings, talking with readers about good titles, and seeing children absorbed in a book while lounging in the cosy little corner set up for them. All this helped me understand why I was on this earth and above all, why I had the right to stay here. My husband and children naturally imbued my life with great meaning. But my profession did too. Very much so in fact. And now I can say that at seventy-five years of age, I have finally attained a semblance of serenity, or something close. It has been a long and painful process, but I'm at peace now and when my time comes, I'll be able to say I did the best I could for myself and my loved ones. I'm not proud. It was merely my way of holding on, all this time, regardless of what life threw at me.

We all have our burdens, it's not just me. Take my best friend, Sylvette, for instance, who has been lugging very heavy emotional baggage around all her life too. We have known each other for almost forty years now. She's ten years younger than me. One day, she told me her story. In 1945, when the American troops came to liberate the towns and villages of France, her mother, Lucille, was just sixteen years old and living with her parents who produced cider and Calvados in Normandy. On a cold and grey January day, her parents had gone to a neighbouring village to negotiate the purchase of a wood adjacent to their property, as it was an ideal plot of land on which to plant additional orchards. Lucille stayed at home on the farm to work, as she had been doing for several years by then. This entailed preparing customer orders, sticking labels on bottles, milking the two dairy cows that her parents had bought at the start of the war, as well as fetching firewood for the house. These were tasks she had learned with her parents and did happily. As she made her way to the barn, a car drove into the farmyard at high speed and screeched to a halt. Four men got out. Lucille recognized them as the American soldiers who had been stationed in the village since the landings. They asked her if she had a keg of cider they could buy for a party that evening. As she was alone, she asked them to return later that day when her parents would be back. She wasn't allowed to sell the kegs herself as her father handled the wholesale business. She suggested they come around four o'clock that afternoon. The soldiers wanted to know if they had a cellar at the farm. Lucille felt a tad anxious and nodded, saying her father would be happy to show them around when they came to collect the keg. On that note, and much to Lucille's relief, they left. Fifteen minutes later, they returned. They were drinking directly from a bottle they had found somewhere and were passing it around to each other. From its colour, Lucille could tell it was Calvados. She was stood in the middle of the farmyard, holding a full can of milk which she was carrying to the kitchen to bottle up. They asked her again where the cellar was. She politely suggested they come back in the evening, as she had chores to do. The soldiers were drunk and were becoming increasingly rude and coarse. One of them started making inappropriate advances towards Lucille, who had to put the milk down to fight off the unwelcome hands. The other three soldiers seemed to find the game highly amusing and they joined in, all four of them touching the girl. "If you want us to leave, show us the cellar!" they shouted under the intoxicating effects of the alcohol. Lucille pointed to the cellar door which was visible from the farmyard. But instead of going inside, they continued to molest Lucille who eventually spilled the milk can. She tried to escape and ran towards the house, but the sheer number and strength of her assailants prevented her from getting far. They pushed her through the cellar door. While the other three were looking for something to drink, the fourth knocked Lucille to the ground and began to push up her long skirt. As the girl struggled, the others came over to pin her down and assist their friend. They then stripped her naked and raped her in turn. Then they left her there, curled up on the ground, shuddering with cold, shame and hatred. When her parents came home and saw the overturned milk can in the farmyard, they realized something was amiss. It took them a while to find the poor girl who was still lying on the cellar floor in a daze.

For her mother, Lucille was still a child, whereas for those brutes she was a woman, not that this changes anything of course. Her mother soothed her as best she could over the next few days, pleading with her to tell the police so that the bastards would pay for their crime. Lucille flatly refused, saying that she wouldn't be able to cope with the looks people would give her if she talked openly about the attack. The days went by and the image of Lucille curled up and moaning on the ground made her mother take matters into her own hands. After all, Lucille was a minor. She filed a complaint on her behalf, hoping to get retribution for her daughter and ease her wounds a little. Meanwhile, Lucille discovered she was pregnant. Another disgrace. After identifying her attackers to the police, and pending their trial, she went to the southwest of France to stay with her aunt and escape the watchful glances of the locals. Her mother learned afterwards from her sister that Lucille had tried to get rid of the baby. She had gone to see a doctor, but the doctor, a very devout man with a strong belief in the value of human life however small, untimely, or shameless it may be, refused her request. She returned several times begging him to help her. The doctor tried to reason with her, but at each visit, his refusal to intervene sent her into an uncontrollable rage. He argued that terminating the pregnancy would put her life in danger too. She said she didn't care, and that dying would release her from her misery. But the doctor did not wish to spend the rest of his days in jail and firmly dismissed her, suggesting that she should either accept the child as her own or give it to someone else to raise if she couldn't love and nurture the child herself. She left in anger never to return.

Lucille finally gave birth to a mixed-race child in September 1945. One of her assailants had been African-American and his seed had won the cynical race. This was yet another blow for Lucille, as despite feeling the same revulsion for all four GIs, people's stupidity and ambient racism were going to make things doubly hard for her. She also learned that out of the four GIs who had raped her, only the father of her child had been hanged. Baffled by this iniquitous judgment, her hatred for the three scumbags who had been spared merely intensified. Despite her parents' insistence that she return home to Normandy, she stayed with her aunt in Bordeaux and took her own life in May 1946. She left behind a simple note: "lenoir is scum". No one ever knew whether she was referring to her black attacker or the doctor who had refused to abort her baby.

What my friend Sylvette eventually found out was that the GI liberators—yes, the very same ones who strutted around on tanks chewing gum at the Liberation parade—didn't particularly like France or its inhabitants and hadn't exactly been happy at the prospect of cooperating in a rescue mission. So, to "sell" the Normandy operation to its soldiers, the American army had come up with the idea, which later proved catastrophic, of presenting France as a land of sexually liberated women, who were open to all kinds of experiences. So the GIs arrived, gleefully rubbing their hands at the prospect of what awaited them. Due to this toxic propaganda, a multitude of horny American soldiers had a hard time controlling themselves, and raped many women, including my friend's mother. While the Americans were on our soil, in the towns and cities where the garrisons were stationed, women couldn't go out alone at night, so afraid were they of being molested. To top it all, as happened in Lucille's case, it was the African-American GIs who were blamed for these rapes and paid for the crimes of their colleagues, often with their lives. The American military authorities preferred to make an example of these black GIs ("see how we punish the rapists") and in doing so preserved the fine reputation of the honourable white GI liberator. So, you can see that the image of the American soldier on his tank kissing a French girl was neither trivial nor pure chance. The GIs were praised for their heroic and selfless intervention in liberating us. On a more sinister note, however, France was on its knees, at the mercy of a superpower which, right from the start, had expected to have a share one way or another in this newly liberated nation. Sex was just one of many methods used to dominate the populace.

According to Sylvette, they blamed French civilians for not knowing how to behave, and used the latter's so-called "recklessness" as an excuse to control the population's movements as well as their access to healthcare. This was, in fact, a liberation that initially did more to constrain than liberate. Naturally this was hushed up on the world stage and not a word was printed in the international press, not even in the United States. *Omerta* was the order of the day. I was a little girl at the time and the Allied operations were staged in the north and east of France, but I remember how desperate my parents and so many others were for these landings. I think I can safely say that if my mother had encountered a GI on the streets of Lignon, she too would have kissed him joyfully. This doesn't make her a "loose woman" by any stretch of the imagination, just a happy, relieved wife and mother ecstatic at having her freedom back after five years of occupation. It's all a matter of context and interpretation.

My friend Sylvette was raised by her grandparents who spent their entire lives blaming themselves for making the sordid affair involving their daughter public. They loved their granddaughter as much as they could. The little girl asked them very early on why she was different from other children. They couldn't bring themselves to tell her the truth, so they pretended that her mother had fallen in love with a black GI who had to return home after the war. Poor Lucille must have been turning in her grave! To spare the child, they simply disguised one horror as another, as if it would make any difference. Except that little Sylvette was anything but stupid and sensed she was being lied to. When she was older, she made enquiries. She didn't have to go very far. The village gossips were only too eager to tell this dark-skinned little girl about the mystery surrounding her birth. What she discovered shocked her. Although she hadn't believed the romantic version of events related by her grandparents, she never would have expected to hear that she was the result of rape and that her childhood was shrouded in lies. She begged her grandparents to tell her the truth, the plain facts, not the sugar-coated version, after which she sank into a deep depression. Her grandparents tried to explain why they had lied to her, but the damage was done. These tragic events drove both her grandparents into an early grave, just two months apart.

Sylvette and I met in the psychiatric ward of Toulouse's main hospital. It was in this sad but auspicious setting that we both opened up about our respective experiences to another person for the very first time. From that moment on we were as thick as thieves. Some while later, when we were both back at home, she told me about the message her mother had scribbled down before she died.

"It's funny," she said. "'Lenoir', isn't that your maiden name?"

I nodded.

"So 'lenoir' could be your father," she went on. "He was a doctor in Bordeaux, wasn't he?"

I laughed and thanked her for insinuating that my father could have been the "scum" mentioned by her mother. I wasn't really paying much attention until she said, "I made some enquiries to find out exactly where my great-aunt lived."

"And?"

"Apparently, she lived in Lignon."

My heart missed a beat. I stared at her, stunned. By what irony of fate were our paths meant to cross?

"Sylvette, what *is* all this? It can't be sheer coincidence?"

"Yes and no."

"Tell me more," I said suspiciously.

"When I met you at the clinic, I quickly realized who you were, because as I told you, I had researched the village where my mother committed suicide, to try to understand exactly what happened. I also researched all the doctors in Lignon at that time and your father's name 'Lenoir' came up. When you told me you came from Lignon, I looked at your maiden name on your medical file at the end of your bed and couldn't believe my eyes. Can you imagine?"

"Why didn't you tell me?" I asked, astonished.

"Because our meeting was a coincidence, and you were in no fit state to take on my problems on top of your own at that time."

"Yes, but you could have told me afterwards?"

"Well, that's what I'm doing now, it's afterwards and I'm telling you."

"And you think that the 'lenoir' in her message was my father and not your biological father?"

"I'm not sure of anything. It's possible, but there were other doctors in Lignon besides your father . . . And then how do we know that she saw a doctor in Lignon itself? She could have gone to a neighbouring village. In that case, 'lenoir' would refer to my father. We'll never know."

"And if it *was* my father, would this change how you feel towards me?"

"Of course not, Solveig. If your father had carried out the abortion, I wouldn't be here now to tell the tale. So why would I be angry with him? Or even you for that matter?"

"You could blame him for not giving your mother more support when she needed it. He could have prevented her from taking her own life."

"No, there are too many question marks. And we must remember that this is the version of events told to my grandparents by the aunt who looked after my mother, so the truth probably got distorted somewhere along the line by the time it got to me. I really have no clear idea, absolutely no certainty at all, about my mother's mental state after what happened to her. Just look at her suicide note. Not a single word for me, or even her parents . . ."

I decided not to tell Sylvette that I had kept all my father's appointment books. After all, she hadn't told me everything either at first. I wanted to be the one to investigate. I knew that Sylvette was born in September 1945. That was more than enough to go on for now.

15

Noemie, August 1942

This war is spiralling further and further into horror and chaos every day. Thousands of Jews were rounded up last month to be transported to who knows where. What did the Nazis have in mind when they decided to do this? It's very disturbing. These poor people must leave everything behind, their homes, furniture, money . . . They are only allowed to take a few personal effects with them. I heard that some of their houses have already been appropriated by new tenants, which implies they won't be coming back. One evening last week we had a few guests over for a dinner party. We had invited the lawyer, Mr Boivin, and his obnoxious stuck-up wife, Father Seignier, the local priest whom I had met on the road to Polignac, and the Montorgueils, a prominent family of wine-makers who owned a vineyard on the outskirts of Lignon. I increasingly loathe these social gatherings, but it would be frowned upon, even suspicious, if we didn't return their invitations. What's more, Armand thinks it's an excellent way of testing the water, to find out the general frame of mind of the population. The lawyer and the priest are good sources of information for us. It goes without saying that the done thing at these dinners is to support the collaboration and minimize its terrible consequences. And it goes without saying that Armand and I play the role of the devoted Pétain loyalists perfectly.

On such occasions, I ask Ernestine to stay on and serve the dinner. Cosima had prepared a chicken from our own henhouse—the poor thing sacrificed for such a thoroughly tedious purpose—a gratin of vegetables from the garden and baked apples for dessert. Armand was an attentive host, looking very dapper and at ease in his dark grey impeccably ironed suit, which he only brings out for such soirées. I glanced at my husband, thinking how attractive he was. He has lost some weight over the last few months and his serious expression behind his small round spectacles all of a sudden made him irresistible to me. Why was I risking everything with Gunther when I had the most seductive man in the world by my side? Apparently, Mrs Montorgueil seemed to agree with me, going by the way she was devouring my husband with her beady eyes. It's true that her companion with his flabby chin and big stomach isn't a patch on Armand; there's no comparison. Suddenly the conversation, which until then had only touched on light-hearted subjects, took on a more serious tone when Janine Boivin, the lawyer's wife, mentioned the roundups.

"I don't know what to make of those raids that took place last month," she said in her loud, high-pitched voice.

"It's very violent," replied Calixte Montorgueil, her chin trembling. "Apparently it was the French police who carried them out, so we have to trust the Marshal knows what he's doing. He is obviously carrying out German orders. But I imagine those people will be returned to their homes soon, I don't see any alternative."

"I do hope you are right," said Father Seignier, a middle-aged man whom I generally enjoyed listening to. "But if you look closely at what's been happening in France, it's exactly the same as what's been going on in Germany since the mid-1930s. Jews are being subjected to increasingly violent persecution of all kinds. I have a vague feeling that these roundups constitute the final stage of the Reich's racial policy. Why else would they take the trouble to deport thousands of Jews, deploying an incredible amount of resources such as trains, personnel, reception facilities, not to mention the camps, and to rob them of all their possessions, if they intend to release them again at the end of the war?"

"Okay, so assuming they imprison the Jews, they'll surely have to free them at some point?" squealed Janine Boivin.

"Or not," cut in Father Seignier provocatively.

"What exactly do you mean, Father?" she asked then.

"I mean that it is hardly logical for a state as organized as the Reich, which is itself at war and needs able-bodied men for the battlefield, to waste time, money, energy and resources simply to deport people it deems undesirable."

"I agree with you, Father," chipped in Armand. "I even . . ."

"Maybe they just want them to go and live elsewhere!" interrupted Mrs Boivin.

"Then why lock them up?" replied the priest.

"And what would stop them from coming back after the war?" added Armand.

"Yes, what would stop them?" asked Mrs Montorgueil in turn, clearly wishing to ingratiate herself with Armand, whom she had been flirting with all evening.

"Since they have nothing left here, they'll have no reason to come back," replied Mrs Boivin with her implacable logic.

"They are being sent to Poland," said Father Seignier, looking at her steadily. "You know as well as I do that Poland has been under German occupation since 1939. You've heard about the Warsaw ghetto, no doubt? The fate of the Jews in Poland is even worse than in France. Well, until now that is."

"But they're not planning to make mincemeat out of them, are they?!" shrieked Janine Boivin forgetting that she was talking about actual human lives.

"I don't have the answer to that question, but I do wonder. And the answer emerging in my mind horrifies me. It seems they are being sent to what they call 'labour camps'. But I must admit I have my doubts. I ask myself again and again, but the same answer keeps rearing its ugly head a little more persistently each time," said the priest gravely.

"Well, personally, I don't care if they don't come back. They give me the jitters . . ." sighed Mrs Boivin. "Besides, they always take the lion's share of everything . . . they had to have it coming to them one day, didn't they? But I can't see the Marshal condoning such a thing. You must be mistaken, Father," she concluded arrogantly, as if she knew something the others didn't.

"With all due respect, Mrs Boivin, do you not think that the Marshal, for whom I have the utmost respect of course, in his position has the same elements as I do at his disposal to pass judgment on this 'thing', as you call it? I have heard the most dreadful rumours," he added in a hushed tone.

Father Seignier's last words were met with a leaden silence, as if this final sentence were indisputable proof that his suspicions were correct.

"That's a bit over the top, Father," said Mr Boivin boldly. "We all know the Marshal isn't a big fan of Jews, even though he doesn't air his views on the subject in public, but to imagine a scenario as radical as the one you're suggesting seems rather exaggerated to me."

Once again, a thick silence engulfed the room. No one sought to find out more by quizzing the priest about the famous rumours. I was eager to ask him where he had heard such things, but I had to feign indifference so I could keep in character as the obedient bourgeois French housewife who had faith in her country's politics and leaders. The poor man looked down at his plate, visibly stricken.

"Well, it'll mean fewer mouths to feed in France! And in this day and age that's quite something!" added Mrs Montorgueil, whose forced laughter broke the silence. All eyes focused on her. No one seemed to know if she was serious or joking.

Everyone knew her to be very close to the Marshal and an active collaborator. I had an inkling she had denounced the son of a family from Lignon, who had escaped from a stalag. The poor lad's arrest had caused the family immense distress and suffering.

"Well, if we're not even allowed a sense of humour any more . . ." she went on, seeing that the other guests were bemused by her comment, and glancing at Armand to seek his support.

"A sense of humour . . ." repeated the priest, visibly dismayed.

"What about you, Noemie, what do you think of all this?" asked Mrs Boivin.

"Oh, you know me, I'm the perfect Aryan wife. I don't think. My husband does that for me! We each have our role to play."

The guests felt obliged to laugh. Armand glared at me, telling me with his eyes not to overdo it. I had drunk a little wine and was getting tipsy.

"I don't believe a word of it! Anyway, my dear Noemie, at least we can't accuse you of supporting the black market!" shrieked Mrs Montorgueil cheerfully to change the subject. "We have just had a most delicious dinner cooked using 'reputable' produce."

"I don't see why we should pay five times more for food when we can produce it ourselves!" I said gaily, trying to lighten the atmosphere. "I don't know what we would do without our gardener Germain!"

"But at the same time, let's not delude ourselves, we all use it at some time or other!" said Mrs Montorgueil, looking around conspiratorially at the other guests. "Haven't we all had enough of drinking that disgusting coffee that isn't real coffee and sweetening it with sugar that isn't real sugar! We all have our tricks!"

"How would we survive otherwise?" I agreed, trying not to let my irony show. "Everything is sent to Germany! But it's for a good cause, isn't it?"

The conversation then came round to the German soldier living under our roof. Was it an advantage or a disadvantage? Wasn't his intrusion into our family life dreadfully bothersome? These plus many other similar questions which the assembled company delighted in asking us, and to which we reeled off the same ready-made answers, being as evasive as possible, while satisfying a multitude of opinions on the subject.

On evenings like these, when Ernestine is present, I know she is eagerly listening to all of these snippets of conversation. And since she is no good at disguising how she feels, I can see that she disapproves. Sometimes I almost have to restrain myself from telling her that Armand and I are merely play-acting. She may not be the cleverest girl, but she must have cottoned on that for the last two years, everyone has been lying to each other. Sometimes you say black to one person and white to someone else. Often, we throw out a red herring to confuse the issue, as people's opinion is so divided. You can't always tell which side someone is on either. In fact, many don't even have an opinion at all and are content to just get through each day. Sometimes I wonder what will come out of all this. Supposing the Germans win the war, what are they going to do with France and the French people? Will they really force us to speak German, and erase our culture? And if France and the Allies win, how will the Resistance get its revenge on the collaborating Vichy government? Will there be a civil war? For the moment, everything is underground for fear of denunciation and reprisals. But if we win the battle—I like to fantasize even if it seems a remote possibility at present—how will today's resistance fighters deal with those who collaborated with the enemy? They can't just accept what the Vichy government did! I tremble in anticipation, however much I pray for this victory.

These dinners are such an ordeal for me. The worst thing is that through these selfish, narrow-minded people, I can now see what sort of couple Armand and I formed before the war. We were well-meaning bourgeois folk, intent on preserving our social status and comforts. However, the war was a big wake up call, forcing us to accept that we no longer share the same outlook on life as our old friends and acquaintances. We are not fighting the same war. They are battling the spectre of communism, while we are battling against the Germans by any means possible.

Fortunately, the children keep us entertained. Their spontaneity gives us respite from the everyday horrors of war. We laugh and play with them. Their innocence is refreshing and sometimes gives us a whole new perspective on absurd situations. The other day, Solveig asked why Cosima and I don't bake cakes any more. Valentin then joined in asking, "What's a cake?" It's true that we haven't baked a cake at home in a long while. The shortage of flour and butter makes it almost impossible. And when we do happen to have these ingredients, we use them for more important things. The fact that Valentin, who is only three years old, didn't know what a cake was, made me think. He worries me too because he is very skinny. He needs more protein. He has been weak since he was born and I watch over him constantly. This exasperates his father who says I'm like a mother hen and that my fussing is making him even weaker. But I don't see how a mother's love can harm a three-year-old.

Our daughter is a different kettle of fish altogether. Solveig is a gifted child. She is six years old, bright as a button, inquisitive and an avid reader. She has an insatiable appetite for intellectual stimulation. The problem is that she reads material she shouldn't. And when she doesn't understand, she persists in asking questions until she gets the answer that satisfies her. A few days ago, she came looking for me in the garden towards the end of the afternoon. I was tidying up the garden pavilion, sweeping up the wisteria leaves and enjoying the early dusk in the park. I noticed she was looking pensive, so I wasn't surprised when she finally piped up with a question.

"Mother, are Jews really people?

"Yes, my darling. Why do you ask?"

"Because in Mrs Truchot's shop window there is a sign that says: 'No dogs or Jews'. It's weird, don't you think? It's a bit like saying 'No Jews or potatoes'."

I realized at that point that Solveig had grasped that it made no more sense to refer to Jews and animals on the same sign than it did to equate Jews with inanimate objects. And I liked her choice of comparison which was intentionally trivial. But was I supposed to explain to her what the sign meant and why it was there? This was tantamount to revealing the horrors and nonsense of this war and shattering her childhood innocence and dreams. I stopped sweeping and asked her to come and sit down. We had already explained the war to her, but we hadn't gone into the racial policies. Now she gave me no choice, as she rattled off another question in her reedy little voice.

"Why doesn't Mrs Truchot want Jews in her shop? I can understand about the dogs because sometimes they go to the toilet everywhere and they smell. But why stop people entering?"

She raised her palms in the air as she asked this last question, to show her confusion. The disbelief and incredulity in her face, her wide eyes and stern frown, reassured me that Armand and I had raised her correctly and instilled the right values in her. At only six years old, our daughter was already touched by the misfortunes of others, whoever they were and wherever they came from. Although I was pleased to see such compassion in her, I felt sad knowing that my revelations would inevitably bruise her young conscience.

"It's complicated, Solveig. It is the Germans who force us to hate the Jews. It is not just Mrs Truchot."

"Germans like the UG you mean?"

I was startled. She had obviously figured out from my conversations with Armand that the UG was Gunther.

"Yes, like Mr Kohler."

"And he doesn't like Jews either?"

Often, when Gunther came home in the evening, Solveig would stand behind a door and spy on him. He intrigued her.

"Why don't you ask him?" I answered, immediately regretting my impulsive response. I didn't want my daughter to bond with Gunther. The atmosphere in our house was already charged enough as it was.

"Really? Can I ask him?"

"Why not, if he doesn't scare you . . ." I said, wishing I could take back my words.

"I thought we weren't meant to speak to him. But you talk to him a lot."

My heart started racing.

"You think I talk to him a lot?"

"Yes. All the time! And Ernestine told Germain that you sometimes go up to the second floor."

"It was to take care of him when he was wounded, remember?" I said hastily.

"Ernestine says that you've been going up even after he got better."

"What is this? So I no longer have the right to come and go as I please in my own house? You shouldn't listen to everything Ernestine says. Besides, I'm going to remind her to keep her nose out of our business from now on. When did you hear her say this?"

"The other day, when we were playing on the swing."

Damn, the staff are talking about me behind my back and suspect something.

"Well I still think you like the UG," she went on.

I raised my voice, attempting to show her just how wrong she was.

"Don't talk nonsense, Solveig!"

"Here he is!" she replied.

I turned around and saw Gunther coming towards us. I must have been bright red with embarrassment. He immediately caught on that he had arrived at a tricky moment. He must have heard the end of our conversation.

"Am I disturbing you ladies?" he asked.

"No, not at all, Mr Kohler, my daughter has a question she wishes to ask you."

I had hoped that by saying this the little madam would keep her mouth shut, but she didn't. Quite the contrary in fact.

"Do you want to ask me something, Solveig?"

"Yes. I asked Mother why Germans don't like Jews and she told me to ask you as you're German."

Gunther gave me a meaningful look and said what a funny idea of mine it was. He then sat down next to Solveig on the pavilion bench.

"I don't know if I can answer your question, Solveig."

"Why not?"

"Because not all Germans think the same way about Jews."

"But do *you* like Jews?"

Gunther seemed disconcerted by Solveig's blunt questioning.

"How am I supposed to answer her?" he asked, looking at me.

"Only you know that," I replied.

And then for some reason, all my disgust, loathing and hatred for the Nazi regime surged forth and I couldn't contain the rage which spilled out of me any longer. Poor Gunther didn't see a thing coming.

"Tell her about your Führer and his evil ideas, about his underlings and his minions who lick his boots and obey him to the letter, even if it means causing humiliation and suffering. Tell her that your people think they are superior to everyone else and that they are eaten up with jealousy towards the Jewish community. I don't know! Figure out a way to tell the truth that a six-year-old can understand!"

"Okay then, should I also tell her about your precious Marshal, who doesn't have any scruples either?" he retorted.

"In reality, you can't accept the whole reason why you're here occupying our country. You're happy enough to fight for your Nazi Reich, aren't you? 'Fight' being rather an exaggeration because the war has been rather cushy for you so far hasn't it? But you don't take any responsibility for what this war actually represents!" I roared.

Solveig, surprised by this venomous exchange, was looking at us each in turn as if she were watching a tennis match.

"Concerning the Jewish question, no, admittedly, I don't take responsibility," said Gunther, standing up. "And to answer your question, Solveig, yes, I do like Jews."

He then walked off leaving Solveig and I sat there, lost for words in the wake of this unexpected answer. I suddenly remembered that Gunther's German fiancée, the pretty girl in the picture, had a Jewish name. A wave of remorse swept over me. I had ridiculed him and taken things too far. I lost myself in my thoughts and guilt until I heard my daughter's little voice pipe up once more.

"So why don't Germans like Jews then, Mother?"

16

Gunther, August 1942

I have spent the last few months travelling back and forth between Lignon and other garrisons. I'm happy to return. I've been watching helplessly at what is happening around us. Jews of foreign descent are being deported to camps in the east. I fear the noose will soon tighten around me too and I can't tell a soul. The Wehrmacht is full of *Mischlinge* like me. There must even be some of us among the senior officers. Why do they blindly obey the Führer's orders? Is it a mug's game? Hitler knows exactly who is useful to him. I read a quote in the newspaper the other day attributed to Goering. "I decide who is a Jew and who isn't." That says it all. As long as a half or quarter Jew serves their purpose or can be used as cannon fodder, the Reich turns a blind eye, or even "aryanizes" those whom it deems particularly valuable. In other words, it cleanses them of their stigma by giving them Aryan status.

But there comes a point when you simply can't condemn your own people. I am willing to fight for my country, but I cannot help the Nazis persecute my own. I may not be practising the faith, as my family are atheists, but I have the same ethnicity as these people who have committed no crime and do not deserve the terrible fate the Reich has inflicted on them. I'm facing a big dilemma because serving my country essentially means condoning its racial policy. This makes me uncomfortable. Maybe I'm imagining it but I sometimes feel that the soldiers in my regiment look at me in a strange way.

About twenty new soldiers have recently joined the garrison. They have just come back from the front in Russia and are very affected by what they went through. They are itching for a fight, it's obvious. You can see how traumatized they are by the violence of their words and deeds. I realize now how war can be experienced in many different ways. They brag about the number of men they killed, some in cold blood just to "finish them off" at the end of the operation. The only thing I have ever shot at was a hare on a field trip!

I am very worried as I have had no news from my family since October 1941. Cologne, my hometown, was bombed by the Royal Air Force at the end of May. There were no less than a thousand bombers in the sky that night. Their aim was to strike hard and fast to undermine our confidence and intimidate us. I found this out thanks to my French sources as the official Nazi propaganda made no mention of it. Indeed, hardly any information of this nature reaches us at all because the military authorities go to extreme lengths to maintain morale among the troops. But we hear it from elsewhere which is worse, as it makes it harder to know what is true or false. Anyway, for almost a year now, I have no idea if my loved ones are still alive.

The other day, while I was walking in the manor gardens during the late afternoon to clear my head, I came across a man I had never seen before. He was pushing a wheelbarrow of potatoes towards the gate at the bottom of the park. When he saw me, he stopped short and let go of the barrow. My uniform always seems to have that effect.

"You startled me!" he said.

"Why? You've got nothing illegal in there, have you?!" I joked.

"No, not at all. It's just potatoes! By the way I'm Germain's—the gardener's—brother. Etienne."

"Hello, I'm Gunther Kohler. I'm staying at the manor."

"Yes, I know, my brother told me. I'd better be on my way; I have to deliver these potatoes in town."

"I'll escort you then, they could fall into the wrong hands!"

"Oh, don't trouble yourself, Herr Kohler, it's not far. And I'll hide them under some foliage that my brother cut for me," he explained.

"It's no bother at all, don't worry," I said.

"Thank you, that's awfully nice of you! You know, I think that if everyone made an effort, we could easily get on and live in harmony together. It's true, all that matters is that everyone can eat their fill, work, live as a family. The rest isn't important."

For once I was conversing with someone who wasn't openly hostile. I wanted to enjoy the company of this young man who seemed very pleasant. We headed to the bottom of the park and, just before leaving, camouflaged the potatoes with some foliage left there for the purpose by Germain. We went out through the gate and chatted the whole way as we walked along the winding streets of Lignon. Our convoy caused astonishment. Etienne was ill at ease walking along with a German by his side, I could tell. He was nervous, but it would have been unwise to transport such a precious cargo alone during this period of extreme food shortages. My presence protected his load from either being confiscated by my colleagues or stolen by an opportunistic thief. No crook would dare to rob him with me standing there. It was a pleasure to be able to do him this service. Though the sun was low in the sky, it was still very hot and I was dripping with sweat under my uniform, but I felt good about myself.

I love French summers. The long, drawn-out evenings are delightful. The intense bright light of the afternoon fades away, lending itself to silky contrasts of colour reflected by the stone walls of the houses, the tiles, the trees, and the greenery of the parks and small gardens. In villages like Lignon, you can smell the scent of the stubble fields nearby. Nature seems to come back to life once the mid-afternoon heatwave has passed. Even the chiming of the church clock seems lighter and less aggressive as it announces the cool evening hours interspersed with the chirping of crickets. For a moment, you could almost forget there was a war on . . . When I return to my country, I think this unique atmosphere will be one of my most precious happy memories of this place. And Noemie of course. Noemie, who is pulling away from me and alas I cannot stop her. This isn't the Noemie I knew. Another woman seems to have stepped into her shoes, someone cold and distant. During the two years we have been together, my love for her hasn't waned. I would do anything to be walking by her side right now, even pushing a wheelbarrow of potatoes. Something so simple yet so out of reach.

"What do you do in life, Etienne, when you're not delivering potatoes?"

I sensed he was embarrassed by my question. I quickly understood why.

"I am a teacher."

"There is no shame in helping your brother deliver potatoes!" I said to put him at ease. "A teacher of what?"

"Natural history."

"Do you mind if I ask where?"

"In Bordeaux."

"And it's the school holidays now of course?"

"Exactly! During the holidays I make the most of my time off and return to Lignon to help my family. And yourself, Herr Kohler? What do you do when you're not being a soldier?"

"I am a cellist in Cologne, where my parents and my fiancée live. I have had no news of them for almost a year now.

I am very worried because there were terrible bombings in the spring. They must have left the city."

"I am very sorry. Maybe it is just a problem with the post?"

"I doubt it . . . But I'm clinging to the fact that the letter got lost and they will send me another one very soon. When I write to them, the mail gets returned to me. Probably because the address no longer exists . . . It's just so hard not knowing . . ."

Etienne and I finally arrived at a house where a lady opened the front door. You should have seen her face when she saw me. I thought she was going to pass out. It must have been my uniform. Etienne reassured her and told her why I was there. When she finally regained her composure and spoke, I noticed she had an Italian or Spanish accent, I don't know which as I can't distinguish between the two. We left the wheelbarrow in the courtyard and Etienne waved goodbye.

"You don't want your wheelbarrow back?" I asked, surprised.

"Oh no, Aurelia has to store the potatoes in her shed, it'll take her a while. Germain will come and get it tomorrow."

"But I've got the time if you want to do it now?" I suggested. "We can unload them and put them away for you."

"I need to make room for them first," replied Aurelia curtly, although I struggled to understand her accent. "And right now I have to make the soup. Thank you, Etienne. And thank Mrs Lenoir for me. Excuse me, but I've got to go, I've got things to do."

And with that she disappeared into the house without saying another word. Etienne and I then said our goodbyes. I told him not to hesitate to contact me should he ever need an escort. I like being useful.

Meeting him did me a world of good, as I feel like I'm losing my footing. I don't trust anyone. I am very lonely.

I can't confide in Noemie any more. For a while now, she has been very evasive. On the rare occasion we manage to see each other alone, she relaxes a little and there is just enough time for a quick kiss before she comes back to reality again. She thinks that the gardener knows about us. I try to reassure her and tell her that it's not the end of the world. What would he gain from telling Mr Lenoir? Then she talks about her daughter and the worry it's causing her, as Solveig is very inquisitive and asks her mother a lot of questions. Noemie is not herself at the moment, and this is reflected in our relationship. Even though she assures me that everything is fine, apart from a few legitimate concerns I can tell she is lying. She's not the same person any more. She's hiding something from me, but I can't figure out what. Yesterday, I tried to find out more from Solveig. While she was playing alone under the pavilion with a doll, enjoying the end of the summer afternoon, I went up to her. She seemed very absorbed in her game.

"Hello, Solveig! Are you alone? Ernestine isn't with you?"

"She's gone to the potager to fetch some vegetables. Well, that's what she said . . . You know, I haven't forgotten," she added.

"Forgotten what, Solveig?"

"That you didn't answer my question about the Germans and the Jews."

"I think I told you I didn't hate Jews, didn't I?"

"Yes, but what about other Germans?"

"It's difficult to answer that, you know. Even I can't understand it . . . You have a pretty doll, don't you? What's her name?"

"Sophie. But shush!"

"Why shush?"

"Because Sophie is doing residence. You mustn't tell anyone!"

"She's doing what?"

"Residence. Don't you know what that is?"

"I do. At least I think I do. But how do *you* know about that?"

I was very afraid of the answer. She pouted and shrugged as if to say that she couldn't remember where she had got the idea.

"Residence is a secret war!" she explained with disconcerting relevance. "To make you and your people lose the war!"

"You mean the Resistance?"

"What's the difference?"

"Just a few letters, but you're right."

I was dying to ask her some questions, while at the same time dreading what she might tell me.

"Do you know any people who are in the Resistance?" I finally plucked up the courage to ask.

"Maybe," she announced, more to arouse my curiosity than anything else, in my opinion. "But I'm not stupid enough to tell you who! Because I want you to leave our house and leave my mother alone."

Here was yet another person whose aggression towards me felt like a slap in the face. I liked this little girl and for reasons I couldn't explain I felt bruised by her hurtful words. Her lucidity was astounding.

I got up and walked off. I could feel her gazing at my receding back and I was willing to bet that despite being only six years old, she was well aware of her small victory.

17
Mid-June 1946

I returned to the cabin. Jojo and I had a serious car accident on the way back from our expedition and I spent six weeks in hospital recovering from my injuries. I mustn't complain though as he is still fighting for his life. He is in a severe coma and suffered multiple fractures. If he pulls through, I've no idea what state he will be in. My throat tightens just thinking about it. Jojo's car, a Luc Court "Torpedo", was getting rather old and careered off the road, sending us both flying. The steering just gave up and I lost control. I was driving even though I don't have a license. The Torpedo span off the road and flung us out. Someone in a cattle truck spotted us when they saw smoke rising from the bonnet.

Because of the accident, I couldn't go back to the cabin until today. It was idiotic of us to leave them locked up there . . . But how could I have known I wouldn't be able to return straight away? It's not like I could tell the police either. In the beginning, I just wanted to teach those bourgeois nobs a good lesson. And I knew I had the means to prevent them talking after I released them.

I had been pondering over my revenge for a long time . . . It's a dish that's best served cold. I often wondered what that expression meant and now I know. I thought long and hard before making this decision. Especially for the little 'uns. They are sweet and it's not their fault, the poor mites. But if I really wanted to hurt their parents, I would have to take them too. When you get their children involved, parents go ballistic. So how did we convince them to come with us? Well, at first it was almost too easy, child's play, if you will. I offered them a picnic and a day out in Jojo's car, and they jumped at the idea. Times are still hard, despite the war being over. Life is struggling to get back to the way it used to be and any distractions are welcome. Besides, who could say no to a ride along quiet country roads in a cabriolet in springtime?

It was a little tight, squeezing us all into the car. The idea was to picnic in a wood that we know well, as our grand-parents used to own this land. There's even a primitive cabin, literally four walls and a roof. During the war, the place was used as a hideout for one of our groups. It lent itself well to the purpose as it was isolated and well-hidden, tucked away in the forest. You could even practise shooting as there were no neighbours around to hear you.

We had to walk some way to get to the cabin though. They didn't understand why we wanted to picnic so deep inside the forest. We pretended there was a stream there where the children could swim, that kind of thing. We tied them up and locked them in the cabin, intending to come back two or three days later to release them. But unfortunately, things didn't go to plan.

What's done is done. But the problem is that the girl escaped through a gap in the door. It was too small for an adult, but there was just enough space for a child to crawl through. I don't know how long ago she escaped, nor in what state she's in. I did search for her thinking that she might not have got very far. I found bits of material caught on brambles near the cabin, but no other traces of her. I couldn't tell which direction she had gone in either. If she has been found, she will have told her rescuers everything already. But it's odd they didn't come for me at the hospital. Maybe she got lost in the forest. Things are not looking good for me though.

I cleaned up the cabin so there was no evidence left. But now I must find the girl, dead or alive, otherwise it'll be my neck on the line.

18

Angela, end of June 1946

I'm scared. I've been staying at Justin's house for five weeks now. The police are worried that my family's kidnappers might find me. They think I escaped and that my family may still be held prisoner somewhere. And if those bad men discover I'm missing, they'll come looking for me. The investigators have widened their search, but police stations in towns and cities within a thirty-mile radius and as far as Bordeaux have turned up nothing so far. No families or young girls appear to have been reported missing. Justin looks after me at night and for part of the day. I really like living at his house. It's a shame Eliette is there all the time. She sticks to him like glue. Plus, she doesn't like me. They argued about me the other night. They were trying to talk quietly but I could still hear them through my bedroom wall. Their words were muffled, but they still made me cry.

"Be careful, Justin, you're getting too attached to that child!"

"What do you want me to do, eh? Her parents are probably dead by now! She'll most likely have to go back to the orphanage until she comes of age. I'm trying to give her some affection and a semblance of family life while we sort out this whole mess. After that, it'll be too late, because she'll be in the hands of the sisters, and we both know what that means!"

"Exactly! So why make her think that life is a piece of cake? It'll just be all the harder for her when she goes back there."

"She's no fool. She knows the future is bleak so she's making the most of it before she finds out what fate has in store for her. Between us, I think she's terrified. She's strong and hides how she's really feeling. Her inner strength stops her from going under. Yet, every morning when I drop her off at the orphanage, I can sense how scared she is. It's like she's afraid what each new day will bring. Will it reveal the truth and shatter all her hopes? Try and put yourself in her shoes, Eliette."

"I'm trying, Justin, I promise. But she seems to love you so much, it's unhealthy."

"So what if she does? Are you jealous? Of a child? Now you're being ridiculous. Besides you and I are only friends. We haven't made any commitments to each other as far as I know?"

Eliette seemed dumbstruck by his bluntness and took a while to react.

"That's not a very nice thing to say. I think I'd better go, it's for the best."

"Yes, you should."

"You're not the person I knew, Justin. This whole thing has gone to your head and you're changing. It's like you're stalling the investigation to delay the moment you have to bid her farewell."

"Now you're the one who's not being very nice. I have no leads; do you hear? Not a single one! This is the worst investigation I've ever had to deal with. It's not surprising that it has had such an impact on my personal and professional life."

I heard the front door slam as she left. I stuffed my handkerchief in my mouth and the tears rolled down my cheeks. Since this whole thing began I haven't cried that much. People cry when they are upset, or when they are being told off, or because they've lost something they liked. But I don't actually remember what I've lost, so the tears never come. I just feel numb. Except if Justin is angry with me of course, which doesn't happen very often, or if I've hurt myself, or if I feel really terrible. That night, I made up for it though. I cried for a long time. Justin came to check on me before he went to bed, to see if I was asleep. He stroked my hair in the dark before he realized I was still awake.

"Are you crying?"

". . ."

"You need to get some sleep now, Angela."

"I heard you two arguing," I sobbed finally.

"You mustn't worry. She'll be back."

"It's not Eliette I'm worried about. I don't care about her, it's because you said my parents are dead."

"But we don't know that, Angela. Maybe they're out there looking for you. We'll find them eventually. I said that to justify all the attention I give you. While I'm taking care of you, she feels neglected and gets upset."

I pulled myself up onto my elbow.

"But she's not your girlfriend!"

"No . . . not really, but we're very close, as we've always spent a lot of time together. Look, it doesn't matter. You must get some sleep now."

"Justin?"

"Yes?"

"If my parents are dead, can I live with you?"

"You're getting ahead of yourself, Angela. We're going to do everything we can to find out what's happened and get you back home."

"Will we still see each other when I'm back home again?"

"Of course we will. How could I do without you now that I've found you, you cheeky little monkey!"

"I'm not a cheeky little monkey!"

"No, you're an *ADORABLE* little monkey!"

I could feel my eyes closing. They were stinging from crying so much. Then I fell fast asleep.

The next day, when I got up, Justin had lit a candle and placed it in front of his mother's portrait. She died a few years ago.

"What are you doing?" I asked.

"Today, it's exactly three years since my mother passed away. This is her candle. It's my way of letting her know I'm thinking about her."

Suddenly I had a flash. A woman placing a candle on a small table against the wall with pictures and portraits on. The "console of the dead". That's what came back to me. My mother, who still has no face in my mind, used to do exactly the same thing as Justin. On the anniversary of someone's death, she would place a candle in front of the dead person's picture on her bureau. I never understood why she called it the "console of the dead". Dead people don't need consoling, it's living people who get sad. I must have spoken out loud because Justin looked over at me.

"What did you say, Angela? Did you say 'console'? What's that?"

"The 'console of the dead'. It was a table in my house where there were pictures of my dead grandparents, aunts and uncles. My mother used to do the same as you. She used to say to me, 'Look, today, it's been ten years since grandfather passed away. Come, you're going to help me put a candle on the console of the dead'. I don't know why she called it that. I mean, it's not like you can console dead people!"

Justin smiled. He dragged a chair up and sat me on his lap.

"It's great that you can remember all this!"

He waited a little to see if I had anything else to say before going on.

"That piece of furniture is called a 'console', Angela. A console is a kind of small slim table. It has nothing to do with the verb 'to console'."

"But Mother used to talk to our dead relatives, or to her parents at least. She used to thank them for looking after us and making sure we didn't want for anything. But I don't really see how they could do that if they were dead."

"Didn't she tell you that dead people go to heaven?"

"Yes. But when you're dead, you're dead! One day I asked the priest why the dead can see us from up above but we can't see them from down here. He gave me some ridiculous answer, so I guessed that if he didn't have a better explanation than that, then it must all be nonsense. They probably tell us that to make it less sad when someone dies."

"Maybe you're right . . . Can you remember anything else, Angela?"

I then realized that for a whole five minutes I had been talking about my old life. But when I tried to remember more, the only image that surfaced was of a tall dark-haired man and the word 'Jew'.

"'Jew' did you say?" Justin said, when I described this memory.

I nodded.

"That's strange. Do you think it was long ago? Can you see a forest, for example, or a locked house?"

"No. It's in a garden, with my mother and a tall dark-haired man who talks weirdly."

"Do you see your mother? Can you describe her?"

"No, I can only see a shadow. You know, like when you dream about someone, you see the shape of their body, but not always their face."

"Was it during the war? Or after?"

I shrugged.

"The gentleman who was talking strangely, do you think he was Jewish?"

Justin looked me in the eye. It was as if he wanted to get inside my head to find more clues, as if tugging on this thread could unravel all my memories.

"What was his name?" he asked.

"Something that sounded like a chocolate bar."

"A Jew with a chocolate bar name? Good heavens, it's been ages since I've seen any chocolate! Okay, let's think of a few brands . . . Menier? Suchard?"

". . ."

"Can you remember what your father's job was? Or your grandfather? Anything at all could help us. Or the name of the priest? What about your schoolteacher?"

As always, my mind goes blank when I try too hard to remember. And what does come back to me little by little is of no use to Justin. Justin made enquiries about a person called Cosima after my vision the other day, because Cosima is an unusual name. He thought it might be a lead, but after checking with police stations and town halls in the area, he came away with nothing.

As we were talking, I took off my jacket because I was hot and Justin noticed the red marks on my arms which showed up clearly against my fair skin.

"What are those? Did you hurt yourself?"

"Yes . . . I scraped myself against the hedge at the police station."

"Let me see. That doesn't look like bramble scratches . . ."

I looked down, ashamed I had lied to him.

"Did you do this to yourself, Angela?"

I nodded.

"But why are you harming yourself?" he asked me looking concerned.

". . ."

"Are you punishing yourself?"

"Yes," I said, feeling more ashamed than ever.

"But why?"

"Because I'm hurting my parents by not remembering anything."

"But it's not your fault, my angel!"

"Yes, it *is* my fault. I shouldn't have fallen in the forest."

"Don't you remember what the doctor said? You may have lost your memory because you were terrified. You're a victim, Angela, a victim of what happened to you, a victim of your amnesia! None of what happened is your fault! And we still don't know what has happened to your parents. Maybe they are simply waiting for you somewhere, a bit further away; don't worry, we'll find out where they are!"

He hugged me tightly.

"I'm the one to blame here, not you, Angela. It's me, because I'm not getting anywhere with this investigation. Every lead turns out to be yet another dead end. I don't know what to do any more. The truth is I'm inept, I'm useless."

"No, Justin! You're doing everything you can. I can see how hard you're trying to find out what happened to me."

"But you must stop hurting yourself, do you hear? Besides, what did you do it with?"

"Your razor."

"My what? Jesus Christ, you could have injured yourself very badly. You could have severed a vein or something and bled to death! It's very dangerous!"

"I know."

"And you didn't think of that?"

"No, because you're here. Also I didn't want to bother you."

He hugged me even harder than the first time, and I thought I heard a sob. When he pulled away from me, his eyes looked wet.

"We're going to find them, Angela. I promise you, I'll move heaven and earth to find them. But please, for pity's sake, stop hurting yourself. Promise me."

"I promise."

I didn't tell him about the cockroaches, because he wouldn't understand. It's just something I do and it's not dangerous.

When I'm in that small box room I sleep in, I see bugs on the floor at night by the light of the streetlamp that comes in through the skylight. I think they are cockroaches. They run amazingly fast and have really long antennae. Sometimes during the night I find one of them in my bed and I challenge myself to let it crawl over my skin. I tell myself that if I am brave enough not to move, then the police will find my parents. One evening, I could even feel the antennae of one of them tickling my neck. I didn't move. It was disgusting but I was happy because I managed to stay still, so I'm sure now that we'll find them.

We got ready and left the house to go to the orphanage. As we walked down a small street, I saw an advertisement painted on a house gable. I had already seen it many times before and it made me smile because it showed Little Red Riding Hood and the wolf, who had his eye on something tempting inside the little girl's basket. But this time, I stopped dead in front of it, which forced Justin to stop too. He looked at me curiously.

"It was 'Kohler'!" I said, pointing at the picture.

"What's 'Kohler'?" asked Justin, looking up.

"Kohler chocolate. The man I remembered who spoke strangely was called Kohler."

But that wasn't even the half of it. Something even more amazing happened later that day at the police station.

19

Armand, September 1942

Time passes quickly, so the saying goes, but this doesn't appear to apply in wartime. The months go by laboriously slowly as the country grows increasingly weary. Laval has appointed René Bousquet as head of the Vichy police force. There is much political zeal in the air . . . The collaboration is firing on all cylinders, while on the other side of the barricades the Resistance is growing, consolidating and mobilizing its troops. Noemie and I work for the Civil and Military Organization. The OCM is an active network whose membership is growing by the day. Being a doctor makes things easier for me because how does one distinguish between the genuine patients coming to my house and those who are members of the Resistance bringing me information and documents? Noemie, alias Grieg, is in charge of passing on what we receive. To justify her outings, she registered as a volunteer with the Red Cross and goes there every day as well as wherever the network sends her.

The French people are hungry, not like us. We're the lucky ones, thanks to our vegetable garden and the hens. He's very resourceful is our Germain! Thank goodness, because since the end of June we have been hiding a Jewish family: our friends Gabriel and Mélanie Bach, Gabriel's mother Éthel and Salomon, their fifteen-year-old son. Their eldest son, Jonathan, preferred to go into hiding elsewhere, as he has his own connections. They moved into our cellar. Or rather the underground passage which leads off the main cellar. It's an extremely useful hollowed-out underground space. The story goes that a previous owner was married to a cantankerous woman and sought to console himself in the arms of more welcoming members of the opposite sex. While his wife was away, he had this underground tunnel dug, which leads all the way to the potting shed, meaning he could leave the house and the park without being seen. Some village gossips even say that he received his mistresses in the shed itself. But we never discovered if there was any truth to the rumours.

Legend or not, this passageway is a godsend in times like these. The entrance and exit are invisible, both on the house and garden sides. You'd have to have your wits about you to detect the openings. It was also dug a long time ago so there are no living inhabitants in Lignon who would remember the antics of the previous owner and thus the existence of the tunnel. In fact, it makes a perfect hiding place. The Bachs are of German descent but have lived in France for about fifteen years. They anticipated their imminent fate and escaped before the roundup that took place in Bordeaux in July. Gabriel believes that sooner or later, foreign and French Jews will all be lumped together. The current distinction was negotiated between the Vichy police chief and the SS generals. But for how long will French Jews be spared? If the Vichy police don't arrest them, then the Gestapo will, and the latter is less "picky" as it were. Better to make the first move and disappear.

All summer long, the atmosphere in our country has been stifling. What's more, work on the submarine base in Bordeaux will soon be completed which means the enemy will have a fortress in which to protect its fleet of U-boats against the Allied bombardments. The huge reinforced concrete bunker will be almost impossible to destroy.

It goes without saying that between our underground activities and the family we are hiding, Noemie and I have to be particularly careful. The comings and goings of our staff, the children, and Kohler's presence on the second floor don't make things any easier. Fortunately, Kohler's schedule is like clockwork, which has helped us narrowly avert disaster on many an occasion.

Our friends have now got settled in beneath the manor. It's not the most comfortable of lodgings to say the least, but they are well fed and out of harm's way. I'm not sure their Jewish acquaintances can say the same right now. Gabriel reminds me of this regularly, despite his family being fraught with worry and on edge all day long. Confinement for any length of time can sharpen tempers and exacerbate simmering tensions. They surface once a day for twenty minutes or so to get some air and daylight, either before my patients and staff arrive or after they've gone home, and it's not uncommon to hear them arguing. Noemie begs them to lower their voices, while seeking to reassure them. *Don't worry, it's only temporary. It feels like things are moving. It's just a matter of time* ... It grieves me to say it, but they're living like rats in a sewer. Impatience and uncertainty clearly don't mix. How long will the situation go on for? And what's more, they feel beholden to me. I reassure my friend that he would do the same for us, but it's not easy, especially as there is no good justification for them to be treated as outcasts in this way. We can't even put them in the main cellar, which is certainly more spacious, as it would be far too risky. The bulk of their belongings are in the passageway that leads out of the main cellar and whose entrance is concealed. I doubt the Casanova who had this tunnel dug had any idea what purpose it would serve a few decades later. Not in my wildest dreams would I have imagined that one portion of our population would have to be protected from the other ...

The other day, Gabriel claimed to have heard noises in the tunnel. He was unable to describe exactly what he had heard.

I thought it was probably merely the sounds of our everyday lives—footsteps on the stairs, children playing and so on—in the house above coming down through the floorboards. After all, I have never stayed long enough in that tunnel to know what you can hear from down there. To reassure Gabriel, I took a flashlight and walked all the way along the tunnel, something I haven't done for several years. In some places, earth had fallen from the walls and accumulated on the ground, but I was still able to push my way through. I couldn't have been too far from the potting shed when I noticed some shadowy objects on the ground. I shone my flashlight onto them. Suitcases. I was intrigued now because I certainly didn't remember leaving anything in that part of the tunnel. I opened one and couldn't believe my eyes when I discovered the weapons inside. My mind started racing. I quickly deduced that only Germain could have put weapons here; he must have discovered the access shaft in the potting shed. And there I was thinking this passageway was tamper proof! My next thought was that Germain might have detected the Bachs' presence at the other end of the tunnel. If he was involved in clandestine operations like us, however, he was unlikely to denounce us. To be on the safe side, I decided not to tell Gabriel about my discovery to avoid alarming him. I didn't think it would make any sense to tell Germain either, as he needed to continue believing that his hiding place was secure. If I tell him what I discovered, he will worry unnecessarily. Secrecy is of the highest importance in the Resistance. If Germain is working at this end of the tunnel, that explains the sounds resonating in the cellar where the Bachs are. So I went back and confirmed to Gabriel that it was indeed ambient household noise that he could hear. I felt guilty about lying to him, but my silence was the only way I could ensure both he and Germain would have peace of mind. The war has taught me the art of dissimulation and words are no exception.

I had to go to Bordeaux recently to attend an important meeting organized by our network. I took advantage of the trip to check on something that had been bothering me. I had heard that the housing of former Jewish tenants was being looted and reassigned. So I went to the Bachs' home to see what had become of it after they fled. I rang the bell, assuming the place was empty, but then a lady opened the door. She seemed very much at ease in their flat. When I glanced furtively inside, I could see that she had replaced my friends' furniture with her own. I didn't go in, of course. I pretended to have got the wrong address and left, my stomach in knots. So the rumours were true then. I didn't tell Gabriel. He doesn't need this type of news right now and it won't change anything. The world has gone mad.

The atmosphere is very tense these days, because the Gestapo has just ordered the execution of seventy more hostages from the Souge camp, in retaliation for attacks against German officers in Paris. Apparently, these killings are also aimed at the prefecture as an intimidation tactic because it is deemed to be dragging its heels when it comes to deporting Jews. Friedrich Dohse and his henchmen call this "obstruction" and label the Souge prisoners as "dangerous terrorists" to justify these arbitrary executions. Sometimes, at the end of the day, I pretend I have work to do in my office, and break down, alone and in silence. It's the only way I can relieve the unbearable pressure and mental anguish of witnessing such an appalling state of affairs.

20

Justin, end of June 1946

I'm really worried about Angela. She has started cutting herself as a punishment for not getting her memory back. I'll have to talk to Dr Bertin about it. Yesterday, when I saw the little girl's arms, I was horrified. Eliette is right, I *am* very fond of her. How could I not be? At the station we have all fallen for this sweet, witty little girl, who never fails to entertain us, despite her amnesia. I was so shocked by her mutilated arms that I stormed into my boss's office and insisted that we widen our search efforts around Bournelin or even launch a national missing person appeal. Damn it! We need to extend our investigation and think beyond the boundaries! If Angela's family lived within thirty miles of here we would surely have found something by now. Logically speaking, if her family isn't out there looking for her, then something is preventing them from doing so. Kohler's name is a new lead, however. We're going to check it out. It's given me fresh hope.

And then at the end of the afternoon, as I was looking in the offices for Angela to go home, something incredible happened. Angela was in the courtyard playing hopscotch that she had drawn on the ground with chalk that Eliette had given her. Trying to keep busy in the afternoons, she has transformed the area outside the station into a playground. There are all sorts of games: hopscotch, her own version of snakes and ladders, and a grid with numbered squares and circles spaced apart to form a path she jumps along, step by step, trying not to fall. As I approached, I saw that she was engrossed in her game and hadn't heard me coming. Then she rushed towards me and took a pebble out of her pocket. It was flat and smooth, about the size of her palm. She had drawn a face on it with chalk; a little girl's face with plaits, just like she had been wearing on the day we found her.

"This is Solveig!" she declared out of the blue, showing me the face on the pebble.

"Solveig? That's a pretty name. Why Solveig?"

"Because I like that name."

"Where have you heard it?"

She put her finger to her lips as if to hush me and then with her other index finger, pointed up into the air, as if she wanted me to listen. From the window of a neighbouring house a familiar tune could be heard. A light soprano voice with the occasional dramatic note floated on the breeze.

"Do you recognize it?" she whispered.

"It rings a bell . . . one second, let me listen carefully . . ."

I concentrated on the music, but she immediately answered her own question.

"'Solveig's Song'!"

"Ah! yes, that's it . . . " I said, curious to know why Angela associated her drawing with this song. "It's a pretty drawing . . . But how do you know this song?"

"I think we listened to it at home. My mother used to sing it. She loved this song. Mother used to sing really well."

I saw her close her eyes to focus on the mental images that were coming back to her.

"And I even think . . . "

I didn't want to disturb her train of thought. To rush her would have distracted her from what she was trying to extract from the depths of her memory. She opened her eyes again, as if in a trance.

"I even think she named me after this song."

I saw her little face change right there in front of me. Her concentration transformed into visible relief and then a big smile lit up her pretty face.

"I think my name is Solveig!"

"I understand, Ang . . . Solveig! That's fantastic! Well done my angel!"

"My name is Solveig!" she shouted, jumping into my arms.

I lifted her up and spun round on the spot with her, both of us beside ourselves with joy. The chief put his head through the door that opened onto the courtyard and asked me what all the rejoicing was about. I put Solveig down and told him. He congratulated her too and appeared relieved by this new recollection, which constituted important evidence for the investigation. Maybe her surname will come back to her soon too, I thought.

This morning I had experienced a glimmer of hope, thanks to the man with the chocolate name, but now I was ecstatic. In a short amount of time, Angela-Solveig had managed to remember some key snippets of information from her past, and given us various new leads to pursue. She was delighted at having rediscovered her real name; the first step to getting her identity back. Maybe the floodgates were finally going to open and the memories which surfaced would provide the missing pieces of the jigsaw that would enable us to find her family. There was at last a light at the end of the tunnel.

21
Germain, March 1943

We had a near miss. Two in fact.

One was last August when the Fritz decided to accompany Etienne on his potato delivery to Aurelia Blasco. Why on earth he chose to poke his nose in, I don't know. My poor brother had to put up with him the whole way. So he served him up lashings of Pétain-style patriotism to keep him happy. He was so disgusted he washed his mouth out with soap and water afterwards. The stupid German even helped him hide the potatoes under some foliage to avoid attracting any greedy glances on the way. Etienne was terrified the whole time that the jolting of the wheelbarrow would betray the presence of the weapons under the vegetables. You should have seen the wheelbarrow that day. There were so many layers of weapons concealed inside it resembled a Neapolitan ice cream! My brother is very well spoken on the whole but that night he told me: "I was shitting bricks the whole way!" Aurelia Blasco apparently told him in her heavy Spanish accent never to pull a stunt like that on her again. But as he pointed out to her, he didn't have a choice. He would never have willingly asked that Kraut to walk him to her house, knowing what he had in the wheelbarrow! Of course, if he had refused, it would have looked suspicious . . . But the whole incident turned out to be a blessing in disguise because last month Etienne got himself arrested. All because of a stupid misunderstanding.

This was our second near miss: a raid carried out by the Milice at the Café de la Poste. That lot are worse than the

Gestapo. It was Laval who had the bright idea of creating the French Militia, an organization of crazy fascist lunatics headed up by Darnand, on the grounds that the police needed back up. They are worse than rabid dogs! Witnesses have seen them shooting old people and the sick in cold blood, and even threatening children to force the resistance fighters to talk. These militia scumbags are a depraved, corrupt bunch. They spy on people, monitoring everything down to the slightest detail, including their comings and goings, or any behaviour they think is strange. So we have to be even more vigilant. Problem is, they are also extremely vigilant. So, at the Café de la Poste, they had cornered a few resistance fighters from I don't know which network who just happened to be in there. Etienne was in the café at the time, having a coffee at the counter. They were immediately suspicious—that lot are so stupid, it doesn't take a lot. I mean a guy having a coffee in a bar? He obviously must be up to something! So they arrested him along with the others. At first he was very frightened and regretted not having his cyanide capsule with him. Nevertheless, it was a good thing he didn't have it with him that day, because it turns out that the Milice had no idea just what a big fish they had caught. But we only found this out later. At the time, Etienne wondered why they had taken him in and whether the thugs knew about his level of involvement in the Resistance. First they took him to the headquarters and then to the *Kommandantur*. From there, they transported him to the Château du Hâ in Bordeaux where resistance members were imprisoned.

He told me that when the prisoners saw a patriot leave for interrogation or come back beaten to a pulp they would all start singing the French national anthem, "La Marseillaise". Apparently, it drove the Krauts crazy. When it was his turn, he prepared himself for torture and promised himself to hold on as long as he could. He didn't want the others to go down because of him. They tied him to a chair and started to intimidate him verbally. He wouldn't tell me exactly what they did to him; we avoid telling each other things like that as it could put others off joining or scare off existing members. But he was already covered in blood by the time he spotted Kohler enter the room with some new prisoners. It took Kohler a while to place him, but Etienne could tell by the look on his face that he had recognized him.

"What's *he* doing here?" Kohler eventually asked the thugs who were beating up my brother.

"He's from Lignon. Arrested with some buddies of his at the Café de la Poste by the Milice."

"Well, the Milice have got it wrong. I know this man; he has nothing to do with the Resistance."

"How can you be so sure? "

"I work out of the Lignon *Kommandantur* and my job is to escort prisoners caught in the area. I am telling you that this man is not a terrorist. On the contrary, he's a true patriot. You're making a big mistake!"

"What if *you're* the one making a mistake?"

"Then I'll assume responsibility for it," replied Kohler firmly.

"I'll mention in the report that you ordered me to release him then."

"As you wish."

Etienne, who had learned a little German at school, could roughly make out what the two men were saying. They ended up releasing him and he took the first train back to Lignon. When he told me I couldn't believe my ears.

"You lucky bastard!" I said.

We laugh about it now, but the incident really shook him up. He came very close to being tortured like so many of our comrades who were caught. After that episode, we didn't put him back in the field right away, in strict compliance with the rules. When a comrade is released quickly like that, it arouses suspicion. It usually means he talked. Etienne on the other hand hadn't even really been tortured. Personally, I believe what he says, but the others had their doubts. They think that it could be a ploy by the Fritz to trap Etienne, which is quite possible. Looking back, it was a remarkably close shave. The Lenoirs' German certainly gave our nerves a good jangle.

In other news, we have had plenty of fresh recruits since they set up the Compulsory Work Service or STO last month, conscripting young French men for forced labour in Germany. Not me though. I'm too old. You have to have been born between 1920 and 1922 to be conscripted, but many young men don't want to go and work for the Krauts, so instead they join our ranks. It's not easy, as resistance groups are springing up all over the place in a scattered, disconnected and indiscriminate fashion and it all needs to be coordinated and organized. Fortunately, Etienne has been reintegrated in the meantime.

Life is tough for the Resistance fighters in their rural hideouts. They're exposed to the cold and the rain, and food is scarce, repetitive and not very nutritious. Getting hold of provisions is complicated. As a result, the guys hunt and gather whatever they can. We try to find farmers who are on our side and agree to give us provisions, but it's not easy. They're risking their lives by helping us. Sometimes the guys steal. We don't really approve of this, but because food is thin on the ground they are tired and tempers are frayed. They are champing at the bit to see some action. My goodness they're young and full of spirit! But first they have to be trained in the art of handling weapons, camouflage strategies, and clandestine warfare. And, most importantly, how to exercise the utmost caution.

Not long ago I heard some noise coming from the cellar. Like voices echoing. It gives me the jitters . . . Maybe there are things living down there. What if I come face to face with a ghost one day, what do I do then? If I was man enough, I'd go inside and find out for myself, but I'm too damn scared.

As for life at the manor, things are not going too smoothly between Mrs Lenoir and her Kraut. I hardly ever see them in the garden now. Ernestine told me they went on a romantic little jaunt to Bordeaux last winter. How the hell does she manage to find out such things? She told me that her mistress hasn't been up to the second floor for a while now. I wonder what could have happened. Ernestine tells me all about the fancy dinners they host up at the house. It's enough to make you vomit. We clearly don't live in the same world!

22

Noemie, May 1943

Things are going from bad to worse. For the past few weeks I've been completely overwhelmed by events, and feel like I've got no control over anything. Since the Germans lost the battle of Stalingrad last February, public opinion is unanimous that the war has taken a heavy toll on the Germans. The power struggle has been reversed and the morale of French troops has soared. This is a huge relief, in an otherwise catastrophic situation. The Germans have plundered our country, leaving behind only anger and bitterness. But this could also be seen as a good thing, as it incites people to get involved and join us in the Resistance.

Since Armand gave me my first mission, I haven't looked back. I am a regular messenger, going from postbox to postbox. I pick up and pass on orders destined for our Resistance fighters. Sometimes, I also distribute leaflets. Obviously we can't live totally hidden away like they do. I have already taken a lot of risks. Luckily for us, when you are deemed a pillar of the community, you're the last ones to be suspected. The lawyer's wife, who of course knows nothing about our clandestine efforts, was extolling the virtues of our respective social positions just yesterday at a society dinner. She pointed out that we were not obliged to take sides: "We're not like the butter, cheese and egg traders profiting from the black market or the shopkeepers, or even the civil servants." That woman never knows when to keep her big mouth shut. She thinks you can judge a book by its cover. I'm willing to bet that in the French police force, there are plenty of officers who are reluctant to execute Vichy orders and choose instead to engage in underground combat, like us. But a policeman will always be a loyal collaborator in this poor woman's eyes. People do seem to love classifying others, putting them into convenient boxes according to their social status and occupation, and oblivious to their true nature. Though to be honest, her shallow reasoning and sweeping statements quite suit us for the time being. They help disguise what we're really up to. Armand understands the game well, since as a doctor he has to treat anyone and everyone. We are chameleons. We change colour depending on who is watching us. It is rather disturbing, as we must be extremely vigilant at all times so as not to get our roles mixed up. For some people I'm the doctor's wife, for others, I'm the lady of the house, and for another group altogether, I'm a Resistance fighter. Yet I am also a mother who has had to answer many awkward questions from her children during this difficult period.

And to top it all off, I'm also somebody's mistress. And that somebody is German no less. Or at least I was, because I recently ended my relationship with Gunther. I just couldn't carry on leading a double life any longer. My feelings gradually faded; I think fear was at the heart of it. I could never figure out if I could trust him or if it were better to keep quiet. I partly didn't reveal my feelings so that I wouldn't cause him a moral dilemma in terms of what he told his commanders. But what's the point of being with someone if you can't share your troubles or show them your true emotions and fears? I tremble at the thought of him discovering what Armand and I are up to. And terrified that he'll spot the Bachs in our cellar. I had an extremely near miss last week when Mélanie Bach emerged from the cellar in the middle of the day. This happens sometimes when our staff have gone home and there is no one left in the house except me and Armand. We can't leave them like rats in the dark with just candlelight. We agreed that at certain times of the day the risk of them being seen was almost zero. So they come out in pairs and stand by the windows behind the curtains, to savour the light they are deprived of in the cellar, or take a shower. That morning, Mélanie and I had just prepared ourselves a cup of National, that horrible coffee substitute that tastes nothing like coffee, when I heard the front door open. Armand's patients usually ring the bell first, and someone comes to open it. So it wasn't a patient. Paralyzed with fear and holding my cup of National, I signalled to Mélanie to hide in the storeroom adjoining the kitchen. But it was too late, Gunther was already walking past the kitchen door on his way upstairs. The door was half open and he stuck his head through the crack.

"Sorry, Mrs Lenoir, I didn't know you had a visitor, there's no car outside. Here, I brought you two packs of cigarettes. They were distributed to us this morning."

"Do come in, Mr Kohler! And thank you for the tobacco."

I opened the pack as calmly as possible and lit one for myself, after offering them to Gunther and Mélanie.

"This is my friend, Véronique. She is just passing through. She came to consult Armand, as she's not been feeling well. See how poorly she looks!" I said, exhaling the smoke.

"Indeed," he said politely, staring at the M-shaped pendant on a gold chain around her neck. "No doubt due to the food shortages . . . If I can drop you somewhere, madam, let me know. I have a car. I'm leaving in fifteen minutes. I just came to pick some things up I'd forgotten."

I didn't give Mélanie the chance to reply.

"No need to trouble yourself, Mr Kohler. I'll take Véronique home when Armand has seen her. She's waiting for him to finish with his current patient. She lives nearby."

I drew a chair up for Mélanie, partly to encourage Gunther to leave us, and thanked him again for the tobacco.

Once he had left, we didn't know what to do. If Mélanie returned to the cellar, her sudden disappearance would be suspicious. I went to Armand's surgery to ask him to stage a doctor's appointment with Mélanie immediately, until Gunther was out of our hair, in case it should occur to him to check the matter out.

Ever since this episode, I have been hoping to find another solution for the Bach family. We are sailing dangerously close to the wind. If we didn't have a German staying with us, I could have handled the pressure. But it's tricky when the fox is guarding the chicken coop. I can't sleep at night. I break out in a cold sweat whenever I sense danger. I often wonder how understanding my ex-lover would be if he found out what was going on under our roof, literally metres away from him. Would he turn a blind eye? Would he give me an official warning? Would he denounce us without a second thought? I realized how difficult it is to really know someone, deep down. Even Armand, my husband of almost eight years, sometimes seems like a stranger to me. Hidden facets of his personality, his vulnerability and sensitivity, and snippets of his life before we met never fail to surprise me. The other evening, as I passed in front of his office, I heard sobbing. All his patients had long since left. He had locked himself in there to cry. I think he breaks down at times but prefers to be alone, most likely to avoid adding to my torment. Or perhaps out of pride; men are loath to show their weaknesses. Love is only half of the story; both husband and wife have their demons, and their secrets, with varying degrees of intention and awareness. In this case, though, I wasn't willing to take that risk with Gunther. Ever since we first got together, his role as a Wehrmacht soldier cast a shadow over our relationship. Sometimes I wonder what drove me into his arms. I must admit that as soon as I clapped eyes on him, I found him surprisingly handsome. He didn't have those classic

German features, which normally repel me. I was spellbound by him. Then we were slowly drawn to each other by our intellectual affinity, but the bitterness of our differences often marred the sweetness of our exchanges. I don't think it was merely the attraction of forbidden fruit that made me do it. My marriage was stuck in a rut and the routine was oppressive for an energetic young woman like me. And the thought of seducing someone other than my husband had crossed my mind from time to time, though I never went through with it. The very idea seemed insane to me because I was so mired in my own self-righteousness. I must have wanted to escape from myself. Not just from my outer shell, but also from whom I really was, and push myself to my limits, discover my real identity, beyond the burning sexual desire I had for him which soon eclipsed our meeting of minds. And I learned a great deal in fact. My outlook on life, events, and even my marriage has changed. Adversity has brought me and my husband closer together. We have rekindled our love through our mutual desire to resist oppression. So, quite naturally, there was gradually no longer any room for Gunther in my life.

The Bachs will have to go. I have become obsessed by the idea. But when I brought it up, Armand just stared at me, puzzled.

"Do you realize what you are asking me to do, Noemie? Do you really want me to tell Gabriel that we're throwing them out on the street?"

"No, of course not, we will have to find a solution first!"

"What solution? Do you have any? Where do we send them? And how? Do we take them out of the cellar when it gets dark, when the blackout starts? Or in the middle of the day, in full view of everyone?"

"We just have to find somewhere else for them. We can smuggle them outside one by one, as if they were your patients. Among the properties your father left you, isn't there . . . I don't know, a tiny cottage somewhere hidden away or a cabin in the woods? At this time of year they wouldn't suffer from the cold . . ."

"Even if there were, it'll already have been taken over by the Resistance."

"Armand, I'm really scared . . ."

We were in our bedroom at the time, sitting on one side of the bed. The children were asleep and the house was silent, as it is every night at the moment. We were whispering so as not to be heard. Armand took my hands in his.

"Listen, I understand. I know what you mean. Not a day goes by, not even a single moment, that I don't live in fear of the Gestapo knocking on our door, whether to take us in for our Resistance activities or for hiding the Bachs. But no matter how many times I mull it over, I reach the same conclusion: we simply have no choice. We must fight to liberate our country, just as we must protect our friends. You know as well as I do what happens to those who aren't lucky enough to go into hiding. Why do you think Gabriel and Mélanie are willing to live underground in our cellar? Because they know what will happen if they fall into the hands of the Nazis. Gabriel knows. He is convinced. Many don't come back. We don't know exactly what goes on at the camps in Germany and Poland, but what's certain is that when the trains arrive a certain horror awaits them. We can't do that to them, Noemie. We were both raised as good Christians, so now is the time to be Christian. Beyond going to mass, baptizing our children, getting married before God and giving vegetables to Aurelia Blasco, all of which are not exceptional acts in any way, now is the time to look fear in the face for the sake of our friends and put real meaning into the word 'Christian'. Imagine if the situation were the other way round and we were Jews needing help . . ."

"I think I would understand the immense danger I was putting my friends in," I replied.

"It's easy to say that when you're not the one risking being deported."

"Armand, what will happen to our children if we get caught? Have you thought about that?"

"Of course I've thought about it. When they are old enough to understand, they'll be proud of their parents . . ."

"They'll also be orphans!" I pointed out.

"If we continue to be vigilant, we won't get caught!"

We weren't aware of it, but we had raised our voices by now.

"The UG may already know that we are hiding a family. Just the other day when he ran into Mélanie in the kitchen I noticed that the tone of his voice was rather strange, as if he'd guessed!" I said.

"So you know his tone so well that you can tell when it's 'unusual'? I honestly think you're imagining things, Noemie."

"But Armand, I know he noticed the M-shaped pendant around her neck just after I had told him that her name was Véronique! I felt like such an idiot!"

"Her pendant could refer to a relative or someone close to her. What does he know?"

"I can see I'm wasting my time, you obviously don't realize the extent of the danger."

"Of course I do, Noemie! Listen, the war will probably be over very soon, we must hold on a while longer. And continue to take risks. If we win, just think how proud we will be of ourselves! We'll have done our duty right until the end, without slipping up!"

I swallowed. Maybe Armand can claim not to have made any mistakes, but I certainly can't. If we do win the war, I dread to think what will happen to all the French women who succumbed to the enemy's charms. Thank God I broke up with Gunther when I did.

"I'm sorry, but I'm not at that stage yet. What if we lose the war?"

"The Germans themselves no longer believe they're going to win! But they are not allowed to admit it in public, or they risk being labelled defeatist and sentenced to death. But trust me, they already know they've lost!"

After a pause, he went on. "Look, if you want out, then leave the network. That way, nothing will happen to you, and if I am caught, at least the children will still have their mother."

We didn't find any common ground that night. There is no way I'm giving up the fight after coming this far. Armand is right, the tide is turning and I don't believe it would be fair for me to wash my hands of it now. I think back to the beginning of the war, when the mere sight of a German made me tremble. I've come a long way since then. I've done a lot of work on myself too, in order to join the Resistance with my husband and the other militants. I have learned to be more courageous and now I'm able to play the part. I'm good at it too. My relationship with Gunther served me well somehow. Though I don't know exactly who I am any more, because I'm so used to lying to everyone.

Gunther took our separation badly, proclaiming his undying love for me and begging me not to leave him. I thought about it long and hard before taking the decision. I weighed up the pros and cons of continuing our relationship and my arguments turned out to be less focused on pleasure than self-interest, given the context. Should I keep him as an ally, in case we get into trouble, or should I get rid of him to limit all contact and the risk of him discovering our secrets? When I finally told him, I assumed he was half expecting it, since we haven't seen each other much over the last few months—privately, I mean. I often pretended I couldn't see him because my daughter was getting suspicious or because Ernestine was prone to gossip. As he had received no news from his parents for over two years, he leaned on me and drew the sort of comfort from me that one normally gets from their family. He was merely content to know that we loved each other and were there for one other. My feelings had been cooling for a while, but he clearly hadn't gauged the extent of my detachment. I thought he would agree that it was the wise thing to do, so I was taken aback by the violence of his reaction even though I had been careful to tread gently.

"Gunther, I think it would be wise if we stopped seeing each other, at least for a while."

"What do you mean? Has your husband found out?"

I grabbed at the lifeline he was throwing me.

"I don't know. Sometimes I wonder . . ." I said unconvincingly.

"There's something else . . . Isn't there, Noemie?"

"Yes, there is."

"Tell me. Tell me what's going on."

"I'm sick and tired of seeing you on the sly . . ."

"You're a terrible liar . . ."

He clenched his jaw. He was sitting on the bed with his eyes on the floor. I had been standing and now sat down next to him.

"Gunther, you must be reasonable. I've been taking huge risks for us for over two years now. I'm tired of having to sneak around, lie and pretend. Not to mention that Solveig is getting suspicious. One of these days she's going to catch us, and I couldn't cope with that."

"You can't do that to me, Noemie, not now."

"Why 'not now'?"

"I can't tell you, because I'm running a big risk myself by revealing certain things to you."

"Don't you trust me?"

"Of course I do . . ."

In hindsight, I didn't want to be taken into Gunther's confidence. I was burdened with enough secrets of my own. I had taken advantage of Ernestine's absence to hurry up to the second floor and couldn't stay for long.

"I must go. Ernestine will be coming up to her room soon."

"You're not leaving me, are you? You still love me, don't you?"

"No, Gunther, no!" I answered, annoyed now. My answer was intentionally blunt; I wanted to give him a shock.

"No, please, Noemie. You can't do this to me!"

"And why not? If I don't have feelings for you any more?!"

At that point, he exploded with fury. I feared he would be heard downstairs and gave him a black look while putting my finger to my lips to warn him to lower his voice.

"I don't care if they hear me. I've got nothing to lose any more!"

"What do you mean, you've got nothing to lose? What about me?"

I was suddenly gripped with fear. If this was his attitude, what would he be capable of?

"If Armand finds out about us, your life won't be worth living!" I answered, opting for intimidation.

"Nor will yours!"

"Gunther, don't be like this! Please accept that this is how things are going to be. We can still be good friends."

He looked furious and clenched his jaw again. Suddenly I found him quite ugly. I didn't know what I had ever seen in him. My tall, dark and handsome German had disappeared leaving a hard-faced stranger in his place.

I heard a noise on the stairs. Ernestine. I signalled to Gunther to be quiet. When we heard her bedroom door close, I slipped out without so much as a glance at the man I had once loved so dearly.

On my way downstairs, I ran into Solveig. I had thought she was in bed asleep, but she explained that she had needed the toilet. She was clutching a book. Solveig spends a lot of her time reading when she's not in class. I don't know where she gets her reading material. When I asked her, she said she got it from school. The teacher called us in recently to tell us that she was distracted during her lessons. The other day, she refused to sing "Maréchal, nous voilà", the patriotic song dedicated to Marshal Pétain. When the teacher asked her why, she claimed that the lyrics implied it was a song for boys:

Marshal, here we are!
Before you, the saviour of France.
We swear this, we, your boys,
To serve you and follow in your footsteps.

He explained that all children had to sing it, but she wouldn't listen. She asked him out of the blue why they didn't sing, "General, here we are" instead, referring to General de Gaulle. I don't know where she got that name from! We try not to talk about the war in front of the children, and try not to ever mention General de Gaulle, as we know that children are wont to innocently repeat anything. She must have heard it from someone else. After all, it's a name that crops up often enough in conversation or in the press and she reads everything in sight. In any case, she has understood somehow that General de Gaulle is Pétain's rival, a fact which cannot be denied. To cut a long story short, I felt awkward in front of the teacher but at the same time I wanted to laugh. I felt rather proud of my daughter, even though she had caused us embarrassment. The teacher warned us to be more discreet in future and I swore to him that she hadn't heard that name at home. Then he told us that she regularly finishes her work before everyone else and as she's bored, she gets into mischief, and distracts the others. She plays with her pen and covers her desk in ink. So, to keep her busy, he had given her a notebook and asked her to write some poetry. But Solveig didn't do as he suggested and decided instead to turn it into a journal and write about her life. Since then, she hasn't put it down. She wrote on the cover "My blue notebook". It's her secret diary. None of us are allowed to read it. To be honest, we're just happy she has found something to keep herself busy. Though I could do without these extra worries.

And as if life wasn't complicated enough, the other day I caught Cosima red-handed stealing vegetables from us. As much as I tell myself that people are fighting for survival in these difficult times, I cannot accept that my staff are stealing from me under my very nose. In wartime, vegetables are like gold dust and now that we have the Bachs to feed as well, we have to be extremely careful. Besides, it's hard to feed another four mouths without it being noticed. It would have been simpler to tell Cosima, but in hindsight I can see I was right not to. I also have the provisions that Gunther gives us. This covers our tracks, by concealing the real quantities of vegetables produced in our potager. Plus we have our ration cards of course. Now that I've parted ways with Gunther, I'm not sure we'll get any more food from him . . . We'll see. Anyway, the long and short of it is Cosima has been stealing from us. I don't know how long it's been going on. I caught her at it last Thursday. Germain had placed a crate full of vegetables on the kitchen table earlier in the day. Cosima then prepared a soup and in the evening, the crate was empty and so was the pantry. Normally there would have been a few vegetables left over. As I was hunting around, I spied Cosima through the window, cycling down the driveway towards the gate. There was a canvas bag hanging from the handlebars of her bicycle, which was swinging her off balance and preventing her from riding straight. I called out to her from the window, pretending I had something urgent to discuss for the next day, and went out to meet her. She did everything she could to keep me away from the bicycle, but I pretended I wanted to walk her to the gate.

"Give me that bag, Cosima, I'll carry it," I offered innocently.

Despite her pleas, I unhooked the bag from the handlebars. I hoped I was wrong, but the vegetables from Germain's harvest that morning were indeed inside. She asked me to forgive her, told me that it was the first and last time, that her family was hungry, the youngest was sick, and so on. Don't get me wrong, I'm not insensitive to my employees' difficulties, but I won't tolerate deceit. I would have preferred her to ask me outright. We could have worked something out. I told her not to come back the next day or any day after that, except to pick up her wages. She left dragging her feet, muttering something in Italian that clearly wasn't very polite. Out of sympathy for her family's woes, I let her keep the vegetables. She came back the next day, with her tail between her legs, hoping I'd changed my mind in the meantime. She obviously doesn't know me; I have toughened up since the start of the war. I paid her what I owed her and said goodbye. She said I wasn't being very Christian and then she threatened me with God's wrath and told me I would repent. So be it. Though I do wonder where God has got to amidst all of this bloody chaos . . .

23
Justin, end of June 1946

This morning, after dropping Solveig off at the orphanage for school, I arrived at the police station feeling more upbeat than usual. I felt like we were finally making headway and the pace was accelerating. Maybe we were finally going to turn a corner in this damn investigation. I had to see the chief to tell him about the new arrangements for continuing the search. I hadn't slept a wink all night and had hatched various plans, which I wanted to present to him.

As I walked through the lobby to his office, I caught sight of that day's copy of the local newspaper, which had been delivered to the station and left at the reception desk with the letters. The headline on the front page read: "Family disappears in disturbing circumstances". I grabbed the paper, my heart racing, and began to read, swearing under my breath at my colleague who had neglected his post. My eyes skimmed the article, eager to get to the next paragraph, dying to find out what it said. The family lived in Lignon, just beyond the thirty-mile perimeter that we had set up at the beginning of the investigation. Apparently, concerned friends of theirs had raised the alarm. The father, Armand Lenoir, was a doctor and hadn't opened up his surgery for more than six weeks, which had never happened before. The house hadn't been locked up, which you would expect if the inhabitants had planned to be away for a long time. On the contrary, the shutters had been left open. The family had two children aged seven and ten: a boy and a girl. I could feel my heart pounding in my head now.

The Lenoirs' friends had seen the maid who showed them a message left in the entrance hall, which read simply: "We are going away for a few days. N and A." So the staff hadn't been worried at first, merely surprised that their employers hadn't had the presence of mind to inform them in advance or lock up their house, simply leaving them a hastily scribbled note. Anxious that the family had never returned, their friends then went to the police about ten days ago, who opened an investigation into their disappearance.

I immediately grabbed the telephone to call the Lignon station. My hand was shaking, and all I could focus on was the newspaper in front of me and the article with a picture of a beautiful manor house. I was finally going to find out. After the usual niceties, I hastily got down to business.

"Do you have any news on the family that disappeared?"

"We asked around the neighbourhood and interviewed their staff. But nobody knows anything," my colleague replied.

"What is the little girl's name?"

"Um . . . wait, I'm just looking. The parents are . . . Armand and Noemie Lenoir and—"

"Yes, but the girl, what's the girl's name?!"

"I'm getting there, I'm getting there . . . err . . . Valentin and Solveig are the children. Why?"

I closed my eyes in both fear and relief.

"Because we took in a little girl here, just over a month ago. Her name is Solveig."

"Really? But where did she come from?"

"We don't know, because she arrived here with amnesia, which was the result of a fall or some sort of trauma she suffered. We suspect she may have been kidnapped. She has only just remembered her first name."

"Damn! But Bournelin is more than thirty miles away, I doubt this has any connection . . ."

"I think it does," I retorted quickly. "Solveig is an unusual name. What did the Lenoirs' staff have to say?"

"That they haven't seen their employers for a month and a half. The maid hasn't worked since and the gardener has been away."

"The dates coincide. Where has the gardener been?"

"He was allegedly visiting his family in the north, I don't know where exactly . . ."

"On holiday? For a month? And nobody noticed anything before? Didn't the children go to school?" I asked.

"Yes, but the school was closed for a few days in mid-May due to a storm that tore off part of the roof, and when it reopened, the teachers didn't react straight away."

"What does that mean? Two children from the same family no longer turn up for class and their teachers don't even wonder why?" I said, puzzled.

"Apparently, they received a note saying the children would be absent for a while."

"Did they keep the letter?" I asked then.

"Look, Mayol, we're still investigating, just give us some time. We're going to find out what happened to that family. They could have just up and left and are living the good life somewhere else."

I felt like I was reliving the exchange I had had with the imbecile from the Poinseuil station. I started shouted without realizing it.

"You don't seem to get it! I'm telling you that this family has been kidnapped and held prisoner somewhere! And their ten-year-old daughter managed to escape!"

24
Gunther, August 1943

Things are going downhill fast. Somebody must have denounced me to the authorities. I was summoned to base immediately. My commanders were sitting around an empty table and told me to enter. They didn't ask me to take a seat, so I deduced that this was going to be short and unpleasant. And I wasn't mistaken.

"You are Sergeant Kohler, are you not?"

"Yes, Major."

"Do you recognize this document?" he asked then, showing me the form I had signed when I joined the Wehrmacht, confirming my Aryan ancestry. I immediately knew where he was going with this line of questioning.

"Yes, Major."

"Is this your signature?"

"Yes, Major."

"Are you absolutely sure you are of Aryan descent, Sergeant Kohler?"

"My grandparents are Jewish, but my father is Aryan and my parents are atheists."

"That does not make you Aryan, Sergeant Kohler."

"With all due respect, Major, it doesn't make me Jewish either."

"But it does make you a *Mischling*, and a liar and manipulator as well."

Despair crept over me. I tried not to show it or let it get the better of me. I stood my ground. I have been living on edge for the last three years, in fear of being found out. Over time, anger at having to hide who I am has built up in me and simply reinforced my pride in my origins. What exactly was I supposed to apologize for? I looked steadily at my superior.

"I wanted to serve my country, Major."

"You have to be *worthy* of your country to serve it."

"I think I have been worthy so far, Major. I've done my job to the best of my ability and I don't think my superiors have had any complaints about me."

"What do you do again?" he asked, shuffling his papers around in his search for the answer. "Oh, yes, you were the one visiting local chicken farms, scratching around for a few supplies."

"My work kept the units stationed in the area fed for over two years, Major."

"Let's not exaggerate, shall we? I think you're being a tad presumptuous! In any case, *Feldwebel* Kohler, you will go to Bordeaux train station tomorrow to await the next departure to an Organization Todt camp. I suppose you've heard of them?"

I had indeed heard of them. As a *Mischling*, I knew only too well what would happen to me if they found out I was Jewish. Throughout the war, the Reich's position on the status of *Mischlinge* had changed several times, taking one step forward and two steps back. *Mischlinge* had been allowed to join the military initially, but then in 1940 the rules had changed and they were discharged from the army and became civilians. They had been left to fend for themselves with all the risks that being a Jew in Germany at that time entailed. Some while later, the Reich's urgent need for manpower meant they were redrafted. The German war machine had no choice but to be less discriminating. So, naturally I knew all about where I was being sent. The OT was a forced labour camp. All the so-called "undesirables" were sent there, including prisoners of war, *Mischlinge* and other defectors. They were tasked with building or rebuilding the infrastructure that the Reich desperately needed to be able to pursue the war and ultimately fight its way to victory. My only hope now was that I wouldn't be assigned to the V-2 factories. Rumour had it that every fifth rocket exploded on the assembly line.

I felt like a vice was gripping my skull. I fixed my gaze on a spot on the wall somewhere above the Major's head. Suddenly, I remembered my mother's warnings before I enlisted, and then I understood just how right she had been. Fate had spared me so far, but the tide was turning, and my future looked bleak. The Major repeated his question.

"I suppose you've heard of them?"

"Yes, Major," I whispered.

"Unless . . ." he said suddenly.

Astonished, I plucked up the courage to look my superior officer in the eye. I felt a spark of hope.

"Unless, Major?" I echoed suspiciously.

"There are rumours about . . . the family that you're living with."

"What sort of rumours, Major?"

"In your opinion, is there anything . . . how shall I put it . . . *unusual* going on?"

"I don't know what you're talking about, Major," I said, summoning up what energy I had left to hide my discomfort.

I felt cold sweat run down my back. What on earth was going on at the manor? At that moment I would have preferred to have been dismissed on the spot rather than be offered this dubious way out.

"Come on, you're the one living there! You must have noticed?"

"Noticed what, Major? If you could tell me more . . ."

My pulse slowed. His last sentence cast me as an observer of a situation, not as a protagonist. So he couldn't be alluding to my affair with Noemie, though I would have been surprised if he was.

"Strange comings and goings, for example."

"No, I haven't noticed anything."

I had no trouble answering, as I genuinely didn't know what he was referring to.

"Look, I'm not going to beat about the bush. It seems that this family is hiding another family, Jews to be specific."

I was stunned to learn this. Had I not wanted to see it, or was I really so blind as to not be aware of what was doing on right under my own nose? How could another family be living under the same roof without me realizing? I went over the last few months in my mind and then it clicked that the Major was right. Something *was* going on at the manor. Even Noemie's behaviour towards me probably had something to do with it. I suddenly remembered the scene in the kitchen with her friend, whom I had never seen before. The friend whom she had introduced as Véronique, even though the woman had been wearing an M-shaped pendant and had appeared from out of nowhere in the kitchen. She must be one of them. And her deathly pallor was that pasty colour you go when you're locked up inside with no fresh air or daylight, not the effects of an illness as Noemie had claimed.

"Let me be clear, *Feldwebel* Kohler. If you can confirm this information, we can arrest this family and you can retain your position in Lignon. If not, in three days' time, you will be sent to one of the OT units, to join the other *Mischlinge*."

I clicked my heels together as I saluted him before heading for the door.

"One more thing, *Feldwebel* Kohler!"

I turned around, anxious to hear what else he had to tell me.

"It goes without saying that we cannot let the Lenoir couple go unpunished for ridiculing the German authorities in this way . . . Remember, three days, and not a minute more!"

I had the impression that he was testing me. As if he knew all about my relationship with Noemie, including the fact that she had left me. His expression seemed to be saying, "I'm offering you your revenge on a platter". My paranoia was clearly getting the better of me and causing my imagination to run riot.

This unpleasant and unexpected interview meant I got home an hour later than usual. I was in a state of turmoil and couldn't think straight. I had no idea what to do. I was in a lose-lose situation. Either I gave him the proof he wanted and retained my position in Lignon—finding somewhere else to live in the process—which effectively meant I would be signing the Lenoirs' death warrant as well as that of the Jewish family they were protecting. Or I could keep my mouth shut, save the Lenoirs' skin and be carted off to the OT to get myself blown to pieces. Neither option was very palatable. The dilemma gnawed away at me and played on my conscience. How could I betray my mother's origins by denouncing my own? Her warnings flashed through my mind for the umpteenth time. Here I am, up to my neck in it. I'm in the worst possible situation a man can face, choosing between his own life and that of the woman he loves, with the gassing of an entire Jewish family as collateral damage. I say "gassing", because we've recently learned what happens to Jews in the camps. They are gassed to death. Only the Nazis could dream up something so outrageous. They are all about "output". Yet another example of their implacable discipline: fast, clean and efficient. What am I going to do?

Am I really so angry with Noemie that I would hand her over to the Gestapo? If I'm seeking revenge, is there not a simpler and more dignified way? My thoughts swirled around in my head as I pushed open the front door of the manor that evening. I was contemplating telling Noemie that I was probably going to leave. Even though it's over between us, I still love her. I'm still very much in love. Madly so. But my curiosity was also getting the better of me and I wanted to find out more about what the Major had said. After all, I only had three days in which to make my decision.

There was something else on my mind too. I hadn't had any news from my family for two years. I hadn't dared inquire at the *Kommandantur*, lest they discover my secret while looking into my family's whereabouts. It was as if everyone I knew and cared about had turned their back on me. I was alone in the world with a monstrous decision to make.

The Lenoirs' staff had already gone home. Just as I entered the hallway, I heard unfamiliar voices coming from the kitchen. Who could that be? I hadn't seen any vehicles parked out front. Suddenly they went silent. I had entered the house as was my custom and had not made any particular effort to be quiet. They must have all been on edge. Armand Lenoir came out of the kitchen to see who it was. When he noticed me, I sensed that he was surprised and embarrassed, but he quickly adopted a casual tone.

"Herr Kohler! Just the person I wanted to see. I have a document for you that must be returned to army headquarters. Could you come into my surgery for a moment, please?"

I had the curious impression that he hadn't wanted to see me at all, and simply needed to put some distance between me and the kitchen. When we came out of his office, he offered me a glass of brandy. By then, the kitchen was deserted. Even Noemie had disappeared. Then I noticed the pile of cups in the sink. I didn't see who could have used them as nobody had entered or left the manor since my return.

25

Solveig, September 2011

I do have some fond memories of my youth too. I remember, for example, the day I tried to seduce Justin. It's strange, because at the time I thought it was one of the worst days of my life, but it turned out to be the opposite. I had grown up with him and he had become a father figure and a big brother all rolled into one. Although we were not related by blood, our bond was as strong as any traditional family's. Day in, day out, I admired and adored him, pinning all my hopes of a better, more enjoyable, fairer life on him. He was my pillar of strength, the railing I clung to, the anchor that stopped me drifting away. I lived in constant fear of losing him. As the years went by, my childhood affection for him gradually turned into a teenage crush, and then into a young woman's love. At least that's what I believed. But what could I possibly know about love? I dreamed of the day we would get married, me in a beautiful white dress, with a train as long as the church aisle, and him in a dark suit looking as handsome as ever. His looks had captivated me ever since I first saw him, on that famous day when I arrived at the police station, just ten years old with straggly hair. During my adolescence, I tried hard to show him my best side, so that he would finally recognize me as the young woman I was becoming. It was a waste of time though, as he only ever thought of me as a child. He believed it was his duty to protect me and so any boy who got too close, whatever his intentions, had to contend with Justin's wrath. I remember one time, at a fun fair, when I must have been about thirteen years old, and a young man from a neighbouring village had bought me a toffee apple. Justin and Eliette had become separated from me in the crowd. When they saw me walking towards them accompanied by this boy and with a toffee apple in my hand, Justin gave me a good grilling.

"Where have you been, Solveig? We were looking for you!"

"I was with Charles. He wanted to buy me a toffee apple."

"I told you to warn us if you want to go off on your own."

Then, he turned his attention to Charles, and started interrogating him.

"And who are you?"

"Charles Fournier-Meynard, sir."

"How old are you?"

"Seventeen, sir."

"You're much too young to be walking around on a young man's arm, Solveig. Besides, we're going home now," Justin said sternly.

The lecture over, the poor lad sheepishly took his leave, politely saying goodbye to us all.

"Why can't I stay with him? He's sweet and considerate!" I whined, as soon as Charles' back was turned.

"Because you're too young."

"But you don't want me to see children of my own age either!"

"That's not true. You can see your girlfriends if you want."

"Girlfriends! But not boyfriends!"

"Boys can have bad intentions towards girls."

"Good heavens! Do you want me to become a nun or what?"

"Not at all, I'm just trying to protect you. And put you on your guard."

While I was angry at losing my young knight in shining armour, I secretly revelled in the way Justin wanted to keep me all for himself. He claimed to be protecting me, but I used to tell myself that his obsession with keeping boys away was because he was jealous.

As time went by, I got more and more worried that he would fall in love with someone else. Therefore, one day I decided to take action. It was one Sunday in June 1953; I had just turned seventeen. That day, I woke up feeling bright and cheerful. I put on a pretty red dress that Monica, a local dressmaker, had made for me. Monica was German. She was fond of me because she saw me as rootless like herself, even though our backgrounds had nothing in common. She had recklessly fallen in love with a Frenchman during the Liberation, when she was a nurse with the Red Cross, and hadn't dared return home when she fell pregnant. The two lovers had fled, got married and came to settle here in this remote village where no one knew them. I was impressed by her curvy figure, as at seventeen, I was almost as flat-chested and narrow-hipped as I had been at twelve years old. But this was my natural build and I quite liked having a lithe agile body, noting in passing that men seemed to like it too. By which I mean all men except Justin, who only ever saw me as the little girl he had taken in at Bournelin police station seven years earlier. I had been planning my modus operandi for ages and I was finally ready. I had no idea how Justin would react and this made me jittery. By this time, I was a boarder at the local secondary school and only came home on Saturdays. The holidays were approaching, and on weekends, when I had finished my schoolwork, I would take advantage of the long summer days to walk in the countryside, sit in the shade reading, or swim in the stream a few miles away. My bicycle would take me wherever I wanted to go. I felt as light as a feather. Even my deepest wounds seemed to have faded, giving me some welcome respite, at least till summer was over. I knew, however, that autumn would then return, bringing with it the usual demons.

When I came out of my room that morning, I was upset to see that Eliette was inevitably already there. I was fed up with that woman clinging to Justin. Over the years, she has put on weight and her skin has turned all grey and pasty. Their relationship turned a corner last month though, as Justin, tired of resisting—at least that's how I interpreted it—had agreed to get engaged to her, rather than spend the rest of his days as a bachelor. They were both thirty-one years old and neither of them wanted to end up alone. But I could see that Justin had no enthusiasm for her marriage plans. He seemed to be resigned to the fact that despite not being madly in love with her, he would at least have a life-long companion in his childhood friend. Anyone could see that Eliette didn't send his pulse racing. And meanwhile I lusted after him in secret.

I had tried to show him how I felt a few times, but he could never see beyond my childish playfulness. So the news of their engagement forced me to take action, otherwise I risked losing him altogether. I tensed up at the mere sight of Eliette's engagement ring. This wasn't going to put me off though. That's her hard luck. What worried me more was that Justin liked having her around. So I was going to have to tread carefully.

Justin was eating breakfast when I appeared. He was holding his coffee cup in his hand, elbows on the table and was just raising his cup to his lips when he saw me and froze. As he looked at me, open-mouthed, I felt reassured that I had picked the right outfit. I was wearing my curly blonde hair loose. Normally I wear it up, especially in the summer, but I had decided to let it go a bit wild that day. Justin opened the old *laguiole* knife that he had inherited from his father, cut me a slice of bread and handed me the jam.

"Wow, you look really pretty this morning, Solveig," he said suddenly, after we'd exchanged the usual morning pleasantries. "Do you have any plans?"

He gave me a knowing wink.

"Yes, I do actually!" I fired back.

I was sitting across from him, holding my coffee cup with my elbows planted on the table, mirroring his posture. I stared into his eyes. He was wearing a white shirt, slightly open at the neck, and his sleeves were rolled up to reveal his tanned forearms. He looked even more handsome in casual clothes than he did in his police uniform.

"Is it a secret?" he asked.

"I don't know," I replied, smiling mysteriously.

He turned to Eliette who was watching us impassively and didn't seem to suspect what I had in mind. He looked at her questioningly and she just shrugged. Then she went to the door to greet the milkman, who called every Sunday morning.

At this point, I told myself to go for it. Meanwhile, Justin had got up from the table to wash his bowl. I quickly finished my coffee and went up to him. He had his back to the sink and was wiping his hands when I told myself that it was now or never.

I wrapped my arms around him. This was nothing out of the ordinary, as we often used to hug each other playfully. But this time, the way I pressed my body against his was quite different from our usual innocent larking about. I lifted my face up and brought my mouth closer to his. He gaped at me in astonishment. His hands pressing into my back felt hot against my dress. Emboldened by the passion stirring inside me, I gently placed my lips on his. He pulled back and slowly extricated himself from my arms. Then he stared at me as if to say, "What on earth are you doing, Solveig?!" He held my hands in his. He furrowed his brow and looked confused.

We could hear Eliette and the milkman chatting away on the doorstep. He brought my hands to his lips and gave them a quick kiss.

"I have to go . . ."

"Where are you going?"

"I don't know, but I'm off now."

"Justin, you're not making sense. You must know where you're going!"

He walked towards the door, looking awkward, and mumbling to himself. Then he left the room. The next thing I heard was the rattle of his bicycle and I watched through the window as he pedalled away. Eliette came back into the kitchen looking concerned. She had just run into Justin and couldn't understand why he was behaving so oddly all of a sudden.

"What's wrong with him?" she asked me.

"I don't know," I replied, offhandedly.

"You must know, you were with him here in the kitchen!"

Seeing that stupid look on her face, I wanted to hit her, and tell her to get out of our lives for good because he didn't love her anyway. But I was scared I would lose Justin if I upset her, so I went instead to my room to brood over what had gone wrong.

He didn't come back until that evening. Eliette spent the day at her parents' house preparing for the wedding with her sisters. I spent my Sunday alone, not knowing where Justin was or where he had eaten lunch. Eventually I took off my beautiful red dress and put my ordinary everyday clothes back on. I sat down at the kitchen table to write my essay based on a quote by Julien Green: "The avenues of daydreams are the devil's favourite promenade." The subject inspired me and there were plenty of examples to draw from in literature. I felt like a real-life Emma Bovary, in the throes of passion, waiting for the man she secretly loved. Then Justin walked into the kitchen and sat down opposite me. I pretended to be doing my schoolwork and ignored him, just as he had ignored me for the whole day. His hair looked wet, even though it hadn't rained. He smiled as if amused by my indifference. Then he broke the silence.

"Solveig, we need to talk, don't we?"

"Hmm," I answered and carried on writing with my eyes glued to the page.

"Can you stop that and look at me, please?"

"This essay is due in tomorrow, what do you want to talk about?" I snapped.

He laughed outright, amused by my exaggerated nonchalance. Despite the circumstances, I was secretly glad. It had been torture having to wait all day, but the truth was I was sure of myself. I see now just how immature I was.

"Solveig, look at me, please."

Looking bored, I dropped my dip pen on the table and looked at him as if to say, "Hurry up and get on with it, I'm a very busy person". His damp, slightly dishevelled hair made him look like a big child. I chuckled as I looked at him and couldn't resist asking him why his hair was wet. He said he had gone for a swim in the river to clear his head.

"How was the water?"

"Nice. Thank you." Then he paused a few seconds before asking, "Solveig, why did you kiss me this morning?"

"Because I've been wanting to, for ages now. And you do too," I said, picking up my pen and starting to write.

"You're very sure of yourself . . ."

"Honestly, Justin, you can't look me in the eye and tell me you love Eliette. What you two have isn't love."

"Of course it is! Why do you say that?"

"Have you two seen each other? You can't marry her! You're really handsome . . . and she's . . . she's . . ."

"Don't insult her, please!"

"You have to tell her you don't love her and cancel the wedding!"

"Why would I do that? I'm single, and so is she. We're good together, so we may as well be together. Why should I listen to you?"

"Is that how you plan to live the rest of your life? Spending it with a girl who's mad about you, whom you're not even attracted to, just to avoid being alone?"

"What would you know about it?"

"I have eyes."

"You don't know anything at all! Really, Solveig, what's your problem, why are you meddling in our affairs?"

I felt wounded by the sincerity of his anger.

"And look at all my other failed relationships,' he went on. "Remember Bernadette?"

"Bernadette? Was that the sweet brunette with the short hair?"

"That's right. We really liked each other . . . Then one day, she just vanished from the face of the earth with no warning . . . I never understood what got into her. I must have done something wrong to make her flee like that!"

I couldn't stop myself from smiling. How could I forget Bernadette! I couldn't tell Justin that I had got rid of the woman by telling her he was cheating on her with Eliette. My story had been all the more convincing because they were always together . . . When Bernadette heard that, she packed her bags and scarpered. I was so happy. I'm not proud of myself, but it meant that Justin was free again, for me. That was the plan anyway, but then another one appeared on the scene not long after. Georgette, known as Jo. I had to come up with a new idea to get rid of her. I played the homosexuality card which worked wonders. After hearing Justin was gay, which was considered extremely shameful in those days, she couldn't be seen for dust! I admitted all this to Justin much later on, when I was an adult, and he had laughed, calling me a calculating and manipulative brat.

"You're wrong, Solveig, I'm very fond of Eliette. It may not be heady passion and fireworks, as we've known each other for so long, but we do love each other, whatever you may think. What exactly do you want from me, anyway?"

"I want *you*. I love you."

"Like one loves a father."

"Like one loves a *man*!" I retorted. "I may be young, but I know the difference."

"And just how do you know the difference?" he asked.

He must have realized at that moment that I was no longer a child, but a woman.

"Do you want me to draw you a picture or show you?" I replied, infuriated. Then I got up, annoyed at the way the discussion was going. Justin followed suit and came over to me. He took my hands in his.

"Angel, you know I love you very much," he said gently. "You're as much a part of my life as Eliette. If not more so. But what I feel for you is fatherly affection. And even though I'm not yours or anyone else's biological father, I know just how powerful, how unconditional, how absolute, a father's love for his daughter can be."

I could hardly hold back the tears. He had called me "Angel", the nickname he had given me all those years ago at the police station. Since then, he only ever used it if the situation was particularly grave or painful.

"Admittedly, you are seventeen years old now, sweetheart, but you're still very young."

I was about to protest, but he stopped me, indicating that I should let him finish.

"And even though I'm not your real father, or even your adoptive father, I consider myself your father in every sense of the word and have always taken that role extremely seriously. You know that I will always do anything for you, to make you happy. I understand how you must feel. Over the years, your circumstances have caused you to idolize me, out of gratitude, recognition and admiration, which I guess explains how you feel today. But please don't mix things up, my Angel. My feelings are genuine, sincere, and solid, unlike the fleeting romantic feelings you claim to have for me. I could only ever love you as my daughter. I love and respect you too much for anything else. What kind of a father would I be if I took advantage of you now that you've grown into a beautiful young woman?"

He came up to me and gave me a huge fatherly hug. I started to cry uncontrollably on his shoulder. His words had shattered my original intentions and I could see now how childish I had been. Just five minutes ago I had been acting the fool and provoking him, with the self-assurance of a teenager who didn't know what she was doing, knew nothing about love and who was lost in the maze of her emotions. Justin had always been like a father. So of course he couldn't be anything else to me.

"Do you understand, Angel?" he whispered in my ear.

And there, snuggled in his arms, all choked up, I finally grasped the extent of his love for me.

26

Armand, August 1943

The other evening, Kohler took us by surprise. Usually, by that time, he is safely locked away in his room on the second floor. The Bachs had come out of their tunnel to get some air. The cellar door is located in the scullery, which makes it easier to retreat if there is a threat. We were just enjoying a pleasant moment in the kitchen together when we heard the front door open. We all looked at each other aghast and wondered who on earth it could be at this hour. After the initial shock, Noemie took charge and signalled to them to head to the scullery and go back into hiding, while she cleared the table of our refreshments and I composed myself. When Kohler walked past the kitchen door, I intercepted him as if I had something important to say. He looked displeased. Had he heard us? I invented an excuse to lure him away from the kitchen and into my office. When we returned a few moments later, he still looked annoyed. His jaw was clenched and his eyes were watery.

I couldn't bring myself to let him go up to the second floor without first gauging his state of mind and whether he had picked up on the Bachs' presence in the kitchen. I offered him a drink, praying to God that Noemie had finished clearing the table. I saw with relief that the cups were in the sink. I could see his eyes scanning the room, looking for anything which would confirm that he had indeed heard voices.

"Would you like a brandy? I've got a nice Fine Bordeaux," I suggested, trying to distract him.

"If there's any left, Mr Lenoir!" he said. His irony was not lost on me.

"Well, we still have a few treasures hidden away luckily!"

"I can see that . . . What exactly are you planning to do, Mr Lenoir?" he whispered. "Toast our great Franco-German friendship?"

"Listen, Gunther—do you mind if I call you Gunther? Here we are, two patriots, but, most importantly, two *men*, with our inherent strengths and weaknesses. I thought you were going to pass out in my surgery just now. You look rather off colour. Take a minute, forget about the war and talk to me, as you would to your own doctor, and tell me what's happening. The brandy will help."

Contrary to what he thought, I had no intention of becoming his friend. I was just trying to find out if he had guessed what was going on, to better assess the danger we were in. The Bachs' fate was entirely in the hands of Gunther, Noemie and I. In front of me was a visibly weakened individual, in a fragile state. I intended to take advantage of this to worm some information out of him. I'm good at that. The nature of my profession means that my patients often tell me their innermost secrets. I filled two glasses, offered him one and invited him to sit down.

"You'll see, it's very good," I told him.

We sipped our brandy in silence. The burning sensation of the alcohol in my throat soothed me. After a first taste, Gunther nodded, agreeing with me. Then he downed the rest in one gulp.

"It's helping . . . I really needed that."

"Are you in trouble, Gunther?" I asked.

"Up to my eyes, Mr Lenoir."

"Call me Armand, please."

"We shouldn't be fraternizing like this," he said with a smile.

"Okay, then let's pretend it's a medical appointment."

"What about you, is everything okay, Armand?"

"We're making do, you know. We just want the war to end, like everyone else."

"And for Germany to lose . . ." Gunther added gravely, looking down at his empty glass. He didn't finish his sentence.

I poured him another drink which he eagerly accepted, gulping it down too. I could tell he was in a quandary and couldn't decide whether to stay alert, thus fulfilling his role as the enemy, or to let go of his inhibitions and savour the liquor I was offering. We both knew that the latter would prevail. I waited patiently for him to tell me what was torturing him. He seemed to be searching for his words in the bottom of his glass.

"I'm in a big dilemma . . ."

"What kind of dilemma?"

"Either I report you to the Gestapo for hiding a Jewish family in your house and retain my position in Lignon as a respectable soldier worthy of serving his country . . ."

Again, he trailed off before finishing his sentence. His words seemed to have frozen the very air around us. I even thought for a moment that the kitchen clock had stopped ticking. I feigned surprise, while I processed my shock. Whereas he avoided looking me in the eye, I stared at him intently, hoping to see beyond his words and into the inner workings of his mind.

"Or . . . ? You didn't finish, Gunther," I said calmly, as if the first part of his sentence didn't concern me or even merit my attention.

"Or they'll send me to the Organization Todt . . . Have you heard of it?"

"Yes, I've heard of the OT. But why you? I thought it was reserved for prisoners or people unworthy of the Reich?"

"Well, I guess I am what you'd call 'unworthy'. And they're offering to give me back my self-worth by turning you in," he replied cynically.

"But what are they accusing you of?"

"I'm Jewish, Armand. Would you pour me some more of that liquid magic, please?" he asked, looking at the brandy bottle. He had said those two sentences without pausing, as if he hoped that the first would be drowned out by the second. I handed him the bottle wondering whether I had heard correctly. He filled his glass and knocked it back in one go.

"What do you mean, Jewish? I thought the Wehrmacht had long since expelled any Jews from its ranks?"

"They did. But I hid my Jewishness from them. Well, my half-Jewishness. I am a *Mischling*. Do you know what that is? We're a filthy lot, us *Mischlinge* . . ." He laughed and his laughter turned into hiccups. "And they've found out. I don't know how . . . The deal they're offering me is this: either I hand you over or they send me to an OT camp . . ."

"And who says that we are hiding Jews? The very idea of it!"

Gunther looked pointedly at the cups in the sink and handed me his empty glass while indicating the bottle. I burst out laughing.

"We had tea with the children and Ernestine earlier on," I said, refilling his glass.

He was the one who chuckled then, as if to imply that I couldn't pull the wool over his eyes this time.

"In any case, the Gestapo are already convinced of it. So I'm not the only one around here who's been betrayed."

"And if it were true, would you really go so far as to denounce your own people, just to avoid being sent to the OT? You know as well as I do, the outcome won't be the same for you as it will be for them."

"I didn't say that, Armand, *I didn't say that.*" He hiccupped as his drunkenness caught up with him. "Anyway, I don't care. I'll get myself blown up assembling V-2s, but at least I'll have a clear conscience."

"Isn't there another way out?"

"Yes, desertion," he said simply. "For desertion, it's execution by firing squad. At least with the V-2s, I have a slight chance of staying alive . . . Or . . . I could denounce you . . . I don't know what to do yet."

He swayed in his chair and almost fell over backwards. My brain was racing. Suspicion was tantamount to certainty that the Bachs were in our house, so there was no point lying. Luckily, I had only had one glass of brandy and still had my wits about me.

"Even if you don't report us, the Gestapo won't give up and will come and search the place anyway. Suppose we tell the family to flee, and you help us by getting your colleagues off the scent. Then when they come and search, they'll find nothing, which means they can't send you to an OT unit, can they?"

"Yes, but they'll be embarrassed! The fact I'm a *Mischling* is a big problem for the Wehrmacht. They will only spare me if I give them something in return. An entire Jewish family and two unpatriotic French rebels, you can't get better than that."

"So what do you intend to do, Gunther?" I asked.

"Right now? Go to bed."

"Do I have anything to fear from you?"

"No, nothing from me. Because there's Noemie . . ." He polished off his drink and poured himself his fifth brandy.

"What's my wife got to do with anything?" I didn't understand why he had mentioned her. From his dejected look, it was as if he had just buried his parents. He shook his head and tears streamed down his face.

"What's wrong, Gunther?" I asked, touching his arm.

"Nothing's wrong. It's just that you shouldn't separate a mother from her children. And that's what'll happen if I turn you in," he sobbed.

I quickly took control of the situation. "Look Gunther, you're not in your right mind. Get a good night's rest, and tomorrow we'll work something out. We'll find a solution that works for everyone and causes minimal damage."

I helped him up the stairs to the second floor. Luckily Ernestine was away for the night, staying with her family, so we didn't need to worry about any indiscretions on her behalf.

"So the gardener's whore isn't home, then?" blurted out Gunther drunkenly as we walked past her room.

"Listen to yourself, Gunther! Alcohol doesn't excuse everything, you know. You can't go around insulting people like that!"

"Oh, so you haven't heard?"

"Heard what?" I snapped, feeling weary now.

"That your gardener has been having it away with your maid in the potting shed, right there between the pruning shears and the spades!"

"Look, get some sleep now, Gunther, it'll do you more good than spouting nonsense. Good night!"

He collapsed onto the bed, fully dressed and still wearing his shoes. He gave a long slobbering moan, but I couldn't make out the words. It was a far cry from the legendary German meticulousness. As I left the room, I tried to make sense of what had just happened. The surreal scene from which I had just emerged made me doubt my sobriety. My nerves were so frazzled that I went back downstairs again and locked myself in my office. Behind closed doors I let out a loud uncontrollable groan that came from deep within. Nervous spasms shook my chest, and my stomach was tied up in knots. I let my body free itself from the tensions that had been accumulating for months. Once my nerves had calmed down, I felt a huge sense of relief. Gunther's last words then came back to me, and in my mind's eye I could see Germain hard at it with Ernestine in the potting shed. The maid's blonde curls were bouncing around her head in time with the gardener's frantic back and forth movements, both of them crying out with pleasure. The vision was so real that I started to laugh uncontrollably. My guffaws got louder and louder until I had tears in my eyes from laughing so much, and from the absurdity of the situation I now found myself in. When I had recovered, I took a deep breath and told myself that tomorrow was another day. Then I left the surgery and went back upstairs. Noemie had been out of her mind with worry, waiting for me to come to bed.

27

Justin, end of June 1946

As soon as I finished my conversation with the Lignon police, I hung up and ran to the chief's office to show him the newspaper and ask him to send me over there to help with the investigation. Our little Angela was the Lenoirs' child. Our units would have to join forces on the investigation. Ideally, we should have gone to Lignon to obtain a photograph of the family to make sure it really was her. But maybe there was a faster way to find out. I called Dr Bertin beforehand to tell him what I had planned and ask for his advice. He approved of my idea.

I went to the orphanage to fetch Solveig. The sisters were disgruntled at my disrupting the class to pick up a pupil, but I had no time to lose and the stakes were high. I gave them a big smile and their stern faces relaxed. I think I'm back in their good books now. On our way to the police station, I asked Solveig if the name "Lignon" meant anything to her.

"No. What's Lignon?"

"It's a village about thirty-five miles from here."

The name obviously didn't mean anything to her, but she understood that it was important somehow.

"Why are you talking about Lignon? Do you think I'm from there?"

"Yes, I think you are . . ."

I expected more questions to follow such as how I'd found out she was from Lignon in the first place, but she said nothing. I think she guessed I knew more, but the expected interrogation never came. It stood to reason that if her family had been found safe and sound, I would have told her so immediately. The absence of such news did not bode well. I was sure Solveig had figured this out and preferred not to know. Ignorance is bliss. Although for weeks all she could think about was retrieving her memory, she now seemed to be seeking refuge in her amnesia.

I was going to have to talk to her about the headway we were making in the investigation. I was torn between excitement at finally discovering the truth and my concern at the outcome. Were her family still alive? I had my doubts as no one was out there looking for a lost little girl, which would surely have been the case if they had merely been "living the good life" somewhere, as my colleague from Lignon had put it. When I arrived at the station, I phoned Dr Bertin again and asked him to get here quickly, because things were not going as planned. Solveig's behaviour was worrying me. It wasn't like her to bury her head in the sand. Up to now, she had faced each step of the investigation with great courage. Then I went out into the station yard to search for a pebble similar to the one she had used to introduce me to "Solveig". I had just had another idea.

When the doctor arrived, I told him how concerned I was and asked Solveig to join us. I then took out the stone on which I had drawn a face identical to the girl Solveig had drawn on her pebble, but with short hair and no plaits.

"Solveig, this is Valentin Lenoir."

She looked at the picture intently, as if she was processing the information.

"It doesn't look like Valentin, Valentin has glasses," she said after a few moments, in a quivery voice. It struck her at precisely that moment that she was talking about a boy she had known before she lost her memory.

"Do you know Valentin?" I pressed.

Stunned, she swallowed then stammered, "He's my little brother." She jumped off her chair and threw herself into my arms. She began to cry loudly and between her sobs, she uttered the magical words: "My name is Solveig Lenoir! My name is Solveig Lenoir! My name is Solveig Lenoir!"

I must confess I couldn't hold back my tears as I heard her pronounce her whole name. This was a milestone and boy, what a milestone! But the hardest part was probably still to come. One thing at a time. I let her vent her high spirits at having got her full name back. Suddenly, she looked up at me.

"How do you know my little brother's name?" she asked determinedly.

Relieved that she was asking, I set the rest of my plan in motion. With Dr Bertin's permission, I planned to show her the photograph of the manor house in the newspaper. We needed to buy time, but we didn't know if her amnesia had gone completely or if there were still grey areas in her memory. I explained to Solveig that a family had indeed disappeared in Lignon on 7th or 8th May. Her family. She looked me straight in the eye, trying to guess at the truth by the look on my face more than from what I was going to tell her. She knew me well. She nodded to let me know that she was listening attentively.

"My parents? And my little brother? Where are they?" she asked, before I could go any further.

"We don't know that yet, Solveig. But we have new leads now, so our colleagues from Lignon will help us try to find them. Can I show you the photograph from the newspaper so you can tell me if it's your house?"

I had the newspaper face down on the table in front of me, with my hand resting on it. She grabbed it and turned it over to look at the front page. What was going on in her little head at that moment was anyone's guess. She turned to me and I could see by her frown that she was confused. Snippets of memory seemed to be coming back little by little, but the black and white photograph of a house had clearly triggered nothing in her mind. To be honest, the fact that Solveig had remembered her real names was sufficient for us to connect her to this family's disappearance, although I had hoped that this photograph would unleash other memories.

A colleague pushed open my office door that we always left ajar when Solveig was in the room, and announced that Lignon station had left a message. My eyes prompted him to continue. Seeing that Solveig was in my arms and had her back to him, he whispered, "They asked the housekeeper if the family's little girl had any distinguishing features. She said she had a brown spot on her neck, that resembled a flattened heart."

He pointed to the base of his own neck to indicate the exact spot.

I had often thought that this little birthmark would be crucial to us in identifying Angela. But it was almost superfluous now, given all of the missing pieces of the jigsaw we had found today.

The chief arrived at that moment, inhaling deeply on his pipe. We all looked at each other, relieved but mindful of the task ahead. I asked Solveig to return to the courtyard to play for a while. She left the room reluctantly.

We now knew where the child had come from so we could move forward with the investigation. What Solveig had remembered while she was here, and what we had learned about her from spending time with her, would provide the basis for the investigation. The chief then told me he had spoken to Sergeant Rousseau from Lignon, who had agreed I should go there to assist them.

"Shall I take Solveig with me?" I asked.

"No, not for the moment. They are interviewing the witnesses, namely employees, acquaintances, and all those in the

Lenoirs' inner circle. Our number one priority is to find this family. We mustn't add to the child's trauma, nor make her think that she is responsible for finding her parents. She has been through enough already."

"But maybe if she recognizes people her memory will come back? We must take advantage of any detail she can give us. I could also take Bertin with me. He'll know better than me how and to what extent we can draw on her memories."

The chief took the pipe out of his mouth and looked inside the bowl, as if the answer lay in the burnt tobacco. "Okay, Justin, it's a go for Bertin. But be careful with the child. We must be sensitive to her needs."

28

Gunther, August 1943

The morning after my alcohol-fuelled evening with Armand, I had to make a decision. He was hovering in the kitchen and pounced on me before I could leave. He said he had pushed back his first appointments to go over things with me. He asked me to sit down, then poured me a cup of National, that disgusting French coffee substitute. The family was still asleep. We heard the church clock chiming seven. It was so calm and peaceful at this time in the morning. The only disturbance to the peace was the echo of our inner turmoil which manifested itself in our haggard faces and sweat-drenched shirts, despite the chilly morning air.

"Have you made your decision, Gunther? Could you tell me what you have decided and whether I need to fear for the people I am protecting and my family?" he asked.

I hadn't slept all night, weighing up both sides. I had come to the conclusion that whatever I chose, my life would be utterly destroyed. I would suffer psychological torture if I turned in both families, and physical torture if I joined the OT. I opted for what seemed like the lesser of two evils, namely physical suffering, knowing it would be over once the hostilities ceased. Helping Jews slip through the Reich's net, and saving a couple from the firing squad and two children from becoming orphans, would surely redeem me.

"You have nothing to fear from me, Armand. I will tell the Wehrmacht I haven't noticed any abnormal goings-on in your house."

"Why would you do that?" he asked.

"I'd rather save my conscience helping you, than buy back my so-called dignity from them. Morally speaking, the burden will be easier to bear. Nevertheless, as you rightly said last night, they won't give up until they've checked for themselves. We need to organize your friends' escape. I can help you with this."

"What do you have in mind?"

"Where are the family hiding?"

He hesitated before responding, which is understandable, as until a few hours ago, I had been the UG, someone they loathed and despised. Trust isn't built overnight. So it was only natural that he should question my sincerity. I looked him straight in the eye to reassure him.

"In the cellar," he confessed after a pause. "The manor has an underground passageway leading out from the cellar."

"That's why I didn't notice anything. How many of them are there?"

"Four. A couple, their teenage son and their grandmother."

"Since our troops now occupy the southern zone, the only solution would be to get them to Spain where they could try to take a boat to the United States or elsewhere."

Armand Lenoir looked down at his clasped hands on the table. He seemed to be mobilizing all his intellectual resources to find a viable solution. The way he blinked his eyes and twisted his mouth betrayed his mental agitation.

"I may have a solution . . ." he said finally. "I have . . . contacts. I may be able to get them to the Spanish border. We'll have to find a smuggler for the Pyrenees. I know they have money to pay someone. It's risky, but we have no choice."

"Are your contacts reliable?"

"As reliable as you can get."

The speed with which Lenoir responded surprised me. These days, it's very difficult to know exactly whom you can trust, be it your friend or your neighbour. I guessed that his "contacts" were of a different order, but at this stage I didn't care to find out. If he is involved in terrorist actions, we'll deal with it later. I had a fleeting vision of Noemie all alone at the manor, while her husband was being arrested. I quickly banished it from my mind and focused on the matter at hand.

"Can your contacts be reached during the day?" I asked then.

"Yes, I'll make sure of it."

"Okay, so I now have to see on my side how to get your friends out of the house without them being spotted. The easiest way would be to do it under cover of the blackout. I'll try to find out if there is a patrol scheduled for tonight and, if so, what route they'll take."

"I'll see you back here tonight when you get home," Lenoir replied. "In the meantime, I'll tell the Bachs to prepare to leave. I hope their grandmother will hold up. She hasn't had much stamina lately . . ."

"Yes, it's not going to be easy with an elderly person. Ah, their name is Bach? With a name like that they deserve better," I said, trying to make light of the situation for a moment.

"I must tell Noemie about our plan. She'll be a little surprised."

"Please don't tell her about the Gestapo blackmailing me," I said nervously. "Just tell her that I'm helping you get your Jewish friends out."

"Okay, but why? You know, my wife is very . . ."

"Please . . ."

For some reason, I didn't want Noemie to know about my Jewish origins. Probably because I had hidden them from her the whole time we were together.

Lenoir and I left to go about our respective business and carry out the tasks we had agreed upon. It was going to be a long day. That evening, when I got back to the manor with the information I had gathered, the Gestapo's trademark black Mercedes was already parked in front of the house.

29

Justin, end of June 1946

When we got to Lignon, the police station was buzzing. A team with dogs had just left to comb the surrounding countryside. While I went to join my colleagues in the interview room, Dr Bertin and Solveig were stretching their legs after the car journey. Six years of war meant the road had been in a terrible state and we had had to drive slowly. On top of that, we nearly had a head-on collision with a wild boar. I hate to imagine what state the vehicle would be in after hitting something as colossal as that. We took our time though, and thankfully arrived in one piece.

Sergeant Rousseau knew I was coming, so he had summoned all the Lenoir employees for further questioning. Meanwhile, Bertin took care of Solveig and showed her pictures of her family.

"Did you find out who wrote the note informing the school of the children's absence?" I asked Rousseau before the interrogation began.

"Yes, it was Ernestine, the maid."

"Did she know anything?"

"No, I don't think so, but we'll try and get the facts straight at least."

We went back to the beginning, starting with the maid, Ernestine Delfieux. She told us she had learned that her employers had gone away after finding a small note on the console table in the hallway.

"Did you recognize the handwriting on the note? I asked.

"Yes, Mr Lenoir wrote it."

"Didn't that surprise you? Did they often go off on a whim like that?"

"Well, no . . . They never went on holiday. Especially with the war on. They haven't gone anywhere much in the last few years. That's why I thought they had every right to go off and enjoy themselves."

"And you didn't think it was odd they didn't warn you they were going?"

"Yes, I did, a little . . . But I thought that it must have been a last-minute decision to get away for a while. And I knew where they hid a spare key, so I was able to work the first few days. There is always so much to be done in a house like that: tidying up, sweeping the floors, cleaning the windows, not to mention polishing the silverware and airing the carpets, because carpets do tend to hold the dust, you know, and—"

"Yet, during all that time, you didn't once think of notifying the police?" I interrupted.

"What? So I could get yelled at by Mrs Lenoir? No thank you!"

"Did she often yell at you?"

"No, but when she did, she could be really mean!"

"You didn't like her?"

"I didn't like or dislike her. She was the lady of the house, that's all. But she did have a good side. She looked after her staff. I'll give the lady her dues; she wasn't penny pinching."

"All right, so I'll ask you again: why didn't you alert the police earlier? After one or two weeks had passed, surely your employers would have understood your concern for their safety?"

"I don't know . . . I didn't want to interfere. They'd gone away together as a family, so it didn't ring any warning bells."

"But don't you agree that dropping everything to go off like that isn't exactly normal behaviour?" I insisted. "They hastily scribbled a note, didn't breathe a word to their staff or the school, and didn't even lock up their house! Do you have any idea where they could have gone?"

"Err, no . . . I don't know. They didn't have much of a family, not in this area, nor elsewhere for that matter. Neither Mr or Mrs Lenoir had any brothers or sisters."

"Did you at any time believe they may have been kidnapped?"

"Good God, no! Kidnapped? People are only kidnapped for money, aren't they? There wasn't a ransom demand was there?"

"No, not that we know of . . . But people are abducted for other reasons too, such as to hurt them, or get revenge . . ."

"But who would want to hurt them?"

"That's what we're trying to establish, Miss Delfieux . . . Does the name Kohler ring a bell?"

"Yes, he was the UG. I mean, the German who lived at the manor. He was based in Lignon and stayed with us almost three years . . . I mean with them."

So the strange voice Solveig had remembered was a German accent.

"Did the Lenoirs receive a requisition order to take him in?"

"Yes."

"How did the Lenoirs cope with the new living arrangement?"

"It depends on who you're talking about . . ."

"What do you mean?" I asked, puzzled.

"Nothing . . . I'm not supposed to gossip."

"You lived with them after all, you must have seen or heard things?"

"Oh yes, I certainly heard things!" she laughed.

"What are you referring to? Be more specific, Miss Delfieux," I said sternly. "Their lives are at stake!"

"I don't think it's got anything to do with their disappearance," she retorted.

"We'll be the judge of that, if you don't mind. We can't rule anything out at this stage."

"Do you have any idea what they'll do to me for telling you this?"

"What are you getting at, Miss Delfieux? You should know that right now, if they didn't disappear of their own free will, which seems to be the most plausible assumption, your employers are most likely dead. But we need to find them. And the more we dig into their lives, the more likely we are to find a lead."

She sighed. "The Fritz and the lady of the house . . ."

"What about them?"

"They liked each other."

"Did they? And Armand Lenoir, did he know?"

"I don't think so!"

"If you knew about it, why didn't he?"

"Because I slept on the second floor in the room next to the UG."

"The UG?"

"The Uninvited Guest, you know, the German!"

"Did their affair last right through the war?"

"No, I don't think so. From what I gathered, Mrs Lenoir wanted to end things."

"And how did Kohler take it?"

"Badly. When I used to pass him in the corridor, he looked sad and dejected, like a beaten dog."

"And you, how did you get on with him?"

She raised her head sharply, as if she had received an electric shock. "Well, I didn't like him, did I? He was a Kraut after all!"

"Were your employers collaborators?"

"I don't know. I'd say so . . . but I'm not completely sure."

"Why aren't you sure?"

"Mrs Lenoir didn't like Krauts on the whole. But at the same time, Mr Lenoir was friendly with the local police commissioner. And they socialized with Lignon's big wigs, who all supported Vichy. So I would say yes . . . But Mrs Lenoir was more discreet about her political opinions than she was about . . ."

"About what?"

"Her secret rendezvous with the UG."

"I still find it hard to believe that Mr Lenoir was that blind to it all!" I said.

"He spent all day in his surgery with his patients, and she was a good actress, she knew how to pull the wool over his eyes when she wanted."

"I've noticed you're talking about her in the past tense?" I said suspiciously.

"I beg your pardon?" she said, in surprise.

"You said: 'she knew' and 'when she wanted', as if you are sure you aren't going to see her again."

"If I was sure I wouldn't see her again, I wouldn't have made all that fuss earlier, begging you not to repeat what I said about her and the Fritz, now would I?!"

"Well, it could also have been a ploy . . . You know, I've seen and heard everything in this job. It usually happens when people get comfortable and start talking away and that's when they corner themselves, by using the imperfect tense for example. Let's rewind. You knew that Mrs Lenoir was having an affair with this German, and you said nothing?"

"Are you mad? I wanted to keep my job! But it really annoyed me seeing her fooling around with a Fritz. It annoyed Germain too, for that matter!"

"Germain?"

"The gardener."

"And how did Germain get on with his employers?"

"Ask him yourself. You're the one doing the interrogating!"

"What about you and Germain, did you get on?"

"Well, yes. We got on," she said, blushing a little.

"But did you get on well?"

"We got on all right, like normal staff who work for the same house, that's all," she said, going scarlet with embarrassment, which didn't escape either me or Sergeant Rousseau.

"If that were all, as you say, you wouldn't be so red in the face, Miss!" I retorted.

"Okay, well, sometimes we'd meet in the shed to . . ."

"To what?"

If it weren't for the grave circumstances in which we were questioning this young woman, we would have found her quite amusing.

"I don't have to spell it out, do I?! But don't go telling the bosses, my job will be on the line and so will his!"

"Ho, ho! Germain, you scallywag!" said Rousseau.

"Do you know him?" I said, turning to my colleague.

"Yes, a little. We went to school together."

"Tell us, Miss Delfieux, what do you think of little Solveig?" I asked, resuming the interview.

"She's a lovely child, and very bright. Sometimes a bit of a rascal, but never mean. If something bad has happened to them, it hurts me most of all for her, and her little brother, of course. A sweet little fellow."

"Did you know that she has been found?" I said, deciding now was the time to share this bombshell.

She flinched. "Solveig? And she's . . . alive?"

"Very much so."

"But . . . I don't understand . . . Why doesn't she tell you where her parents are, if they all left together?"

"Because she has amnesia."

"Am . . . what?"

"Amnesia. She lost her memory due to either an emotional or physical shock, it's hard to say which. That's what makes us think that her parents didn't disappear of their own accord."

"Jesus!"

"Do you want to see her?"

She hesitated. "Well . . . yes," she said finally, shrugging as if it were obvious.

We let Bertin and Solveig in. Solveig clung to me. She was frowning and you could see how distressed she was. Ernestine Delfieux looked at her in amazement and reached out her hand. The little girl was told who Ernestine was, but she just shook her head. She clearly had no memory of the maid whatsoever. She held on to me tightly.

"And Cosima, do you remember Cosima?" asked the maid.

"You remember, Solveig, you talked about a certain Cosima the other day," I said, deciding to intervene. "Do you remember? A stout lady with an apron?"

"Yes, that's right," Ernestine continued, "she was the cook. She was fired because she stole some vegetables to feed her family."

"How long ago was that?" I asked.

"Two years ago . . . maybe three?"

The sergeant and I looked at each other, both thinking the same thing: a new lead. Personally I found Ernestine not so much eager to awaken Solveig's memory than to point us towards someone else who had a motive for attacking the family.

"Miss Delfieux, everything leads us to believe that they were held prisoner in the woods. Do you have any idea where that could be? A favourite picnic spot, or a wood belonging to friends of theirs?" I asked.

"I don't see . . ."

"We found Solveig in Bournelin, just over thirty-five miles from here. She didn't go there alone and she didn't walk. They must have gone by car or bus . . ."

The maid merely pouted in response. She clearly had no idea.

"Who in their circle has a car?" I asked.

"He's a doctor, so they have quite a few friends with cars . . . Off the top of my head I'd say the lawyer, Boivin, or the Montorgueils, the Fourniers, and, well, quite a few others to be honest."

"Do you know what cars they drive? I mean, cars which could fit five people inside? Room enough for the Lenoirs plus the driver?"

She paused to think. "Maybe the Boivins' could. The Montorgueils' is pretty big, too. And the Fourniers'. They live in Bordeaux. But they drive up here from time to time. I don't know much about cars to tell you the truth . . ."

"In your opinion, who could bear them a grudge?" I asked bluntly.

"All I know is . . ." She paused for a moment before going on. "You know as well as I do, that the war has only just ended, and that it has caused many arguments and much jealousy, anger and unpleasantness, for everyone . . ."

"One last thing, Miss Ernestine. Why did you warn the school that the children wouldn't be coming?"

"I thought I was doing the right thing. We assumed they had chosen to leave . . ."

When the interview was over, we left Ernestine with Bertin to talk to Solveig. Who knew, something valuable could emerge from their conversation. I asked Sergeant Rousseau if we could bring Mr Kohler in for questioning. Solveig had mentioned his name a few days ago, but I had got sidetracked when I came across the newspaper article and hadn't had a chance to follow up on this potential lead.

"We'd have to track him down first . . . It won't be easy. We could ask the Wehrmacht, I suppose . . . Do you think he could be involved?" asked the sergeant.

"If Noemie Lenoir left him, he may have taken it badly . . . To tell the truth, I don't know what to think, I'm just scratching around trying to find clues . . . But it could be a lead worth exploring. What was your impression of Ernestine?"

"You want the truth? Nothing much. She doesn't seem to harbour any particular grudge against her employers, and she doesn't seem to like them much either. But no real motive for doing away with them though . . . She's a bit slippery, that one, like an eel. What's your take on her?"

"Same," I replied. "She pulled a face when I told her that Solveig had been found, but that's understandable if she thought the whole family had disappeared. Though she did use the past tense when she talked about them . . . Her attitude towards Solveig is slightly strange too. I sense that she doesn't really want Solveig to get her memory back. I'll ask Bertin how their interview went and how she behaved towards the girl."

As it was getting close to lunch time, we decided to quickly drop by the manor before eating. Dr Bertin and Solveig came with us. We had high hopes that this visit would trigger some kind of flashback for Solveig. I asked Bertin what had come out of the discussion between Ernestine and the child. He told me that each time Solveig had replied "no" to a question, all the maid had found to say in response was "holy mackerel". Then he recounted the rest of their exchange.

"And your brother? Do you remember Valentin?"

"Only what he looked like. He had brown hair and glasses," answered Solveig, who seemed intimidated by this chatterbox of a woman who seemed to know her very well.

"Holy mackerel! Don't you remember anything else?"

". . ."

"And your cat? Don't you remember your cat? He's grey. Such a beautiful grey colour."

"Yes! Err, I think so . . ."

"That's the spirit! Oh, don't worry, I've been feeding him every day since you . . . I mean you and your parents . . . you . . . you've . . . well, you'll find him. He's probably in the garden at this time of day . . . Do you remember what his name is?"

". . ."

"Holy mackerel! Figaro, his name is Figaro . . . And your doll, do you remember your doll, Sophie?"

". . ."

"Holy mackerel!"

And so it went on. The doctor soon realized that this woman wasn't going to be of much help to Solveig. She obviously hadn't grasped just how serious the situation was. She seemed rather more curious about Solveig's amnesia than concerned for the family's welfare.

30

Armand, August 1943

The day after our infamous conversation, the German and I agreed upon a course of action to get us out of this mess. I was in my surgery attending to a patient when I heard tires crunching on the gravel. From the slamming of the doors and the determination of the footsteps marching up to the porch, I guessed who it was. That lot are not exactly discreet. On the contrary, they like to make their presence known. Then there was the inevitable violent knocking on the front door. It's not something I will ever get used to. A wave of anxiety swept over me. My heart was racing and I felt myself break into a cold sweat.

Noemie was out on a mission and Ernestine must have been outside with the children. So I asked my patient to wait while I went to the door. Although it was already late in the afternoon, my waiting room was packed. Through the frosted glass of the front door I glimpsed the dreaded uniforms. There were three of them. I summoned up all the strength I had to appear calm and unconcerned. I had barely opened the door when they pushed past me into the hallway.

"Do you know why we are here, Herr Lenoir?" the oldest one yelled at me.

"No, but I presume you're going to tell me?"

"*Feldwebel* Kohler isn't here?"

"Not that I know of. I'm currently seeing patients. He normally comes home a bit later."

"But today is not a normal day, Mr Lenoir."

I began to panic. Had I done the right thing in trusting the UG? He could have done anything with the information I had given him. It hit me then just how foolish I had been.

"What can I do for you?" I asked.

"I have been told that you are hiding Jews here?"

"You have been misinformed, sir."

"All right, I'll put it another way, because you don't seem to quite understand. I *know* that you are hiding Jews here."

"I think you meant to say 'assume'. I don't see how you could 'know' something imaginary. And my reply to you would be that you are mistaken. My wife and I are loyal to the Vichy regime and I assure you that there are about as many Jews here as there are in the ranks of the Gestapo, if you'll permit me a small joke," I smiled.

"This is no time for humour, Herr Lenoir," he snarled.

He signalled to his henchmen to begin searching the house. I was pretty sure that the hiding place was sound. I just hoped that the Bachs hadn't left anything in the cellar that could betray their presence. I needed to give them the signal we had agreed on which would warn them that they needed to evacuate the cellar and retreat into the hidden passageway. I had to make two rather loud knocks on the wooden floor. I pretended to move back to let the Gestapo through and in the process knocked over a small oak table with a vase on it. While trying to pick it up and clear away the debris, it slipped out of my hands, falling on the floor a second time. I hoped that the signal would be loud enough to reach them. Meanwhile the house was inspected from top to bottom. But they found nothing.

"There must be a cellar in this manor?" barked the man I assumed was the leader of the troop.

"Of course there is. You have to go through the scullery to access it," I explained.

I went with them to the kitchen. They all trooped down into the cellar. They stayed there for a few minutes, as if they were convinced there was something to be found down there. I could hear them talking. Then none the wiser, they came back up. I then realized that it couldn't have been the UG who had betrayed me.

As they searched the ground floor, I wondered what pretext I could use to divert attention away from our house for a while and buy us precious time to get the Bachs out of the cellar. I had heard that the Langlois Resistance group had changed location recently as their hideout was no longer safe. This *maquis* was an offshoot of the Notre-Dame troop, the other large and well-known Resistance organization in the area in addition to the one that Noemie and I had joined. Whereas the group had occupied the forest of La Trappe for a time, I had heard they had moved to the other side of the hill, to an area known as the Crêtes. A patient had carelessly let the cat out of the bag, knowing that I was involved in a similar organization. So I decided to tell the Gestapo about their old hideout, knowing that they would find nothing there. Meanwhile, I would deal with the Bachs. When they found the forest empty, they would immediately summon me to their headquarters, and I would explain that the Resistance fighters must have been tipped off, and so on and so forth and that would be the end of the matter. They would no doubt give me a hard time, but my arguments would be well prepared.

"I'm not convinced by this visit, Herr Lenoir . . . I think you'll be seeing us again soon."

"As you wish," I replied. "But instead of wasting your time here, you should really be looking at the forest of La Trappe. You'll no doubt find something more interesting there than here."

"What do you mean? What lurks in the woods apart from deer and foxes?" he asked, looking incredulous. He stared me right in the eye, trying to figure out if I was serious or not. I nodded to confirm my statement and dispel his doubts. Suddenly, the three of them turned around and stormed out as quickly as they had burst in. I sat down for a moment to gather my thoughts and slow down my racing heart. Meanwhile, Kohler had arrived and was waiting for me discreetly. He joined me in the hallway.

"Mr Lenoir, please don't think that I . . ."

"I don't think anything, Kohler. We just need to act quickly now to get the family out of here. I've given those rabid dogs something to chew on in the meantime, but they'll be back."

"What exactly do you mean by 'something to chew on'?"

"Something to distract them and buy us time. I've tipped them off about a Resistance group camped in the area; but they won't find anything there."

"They'll come back and demand an explanation," he warned.

"Don't worry, I'll take care of it. Did you find out about the patrols?"

"Yes, if we get them out around eleven o'clock tonight, they shouldn't run into anyone from here to the bridge. After that they'll have to keep their heads down."

"Great. I'll make sure my contact arrives a little earlier. The Bachs should be ready to leave by now. The plan is to get them to Spain. It's a fairly established route. They'll work out the rest once they're there, depending on the grandmother's state of health."

"I'll come down and help you later," said Gunther, taking the stairs.

"I don't think that's a good idea," I said, heading for my surgery. I wasn't sure if he had heard me from where he was standing.

That very evening, shortly before the designated hour, Gabriel and his family gathered in the hallway ready to depart. The grandmother didn't seem to be in the best of health but she insisted that she was ready to leave. Their faces were grim. Noemie had given Ernestine the night off. When they saw Kohler coming downstairs in his uniform, they froze. Both Gabriel and Noemie, whom I hadn't warned in advance, looked at me uncomprehendingly.

"Sergeant Kohler knows," I reassured them hastily. "Don't be afraid. He's on our side. He has verified that the patrol units are at the other end of the village at this time of night."

Kohler confirmed this with a nod, but Salomon looked daggers at me. I spared them the reasons for involving Kohler in their departure, as we had no time to lose. I heard the whistle outside signalling that the coast was clear. As planned, Gunther went to check that it was safe. He walked through the manor gates, stepped a little way into the street, and waved to the family to come out. Then my contact escorted the Bachs away. I watched them leave, my heart pounding, hoping to God they would make it. The grandmother was hobbling along after them. Then the little group disappeared into the night. I would receive word from them in a few days' time when they arrived at the border.

Noemie and I went to bed that night breathing a huge sigh of relief. We believed we had done the right thing. It would be better for them and for us. We hoped with all our hearts that they would make it to a place where they would finally be able to live freely and without fear. It was as if a lead weight had been lifted from our shoulders. For a year now, the fear of them being discovered in our house has terrorized us. Noemie asked me why I had confided in Gunther. I told her that he had been present during the Gestapo raid and had offered to help me.

Unfortunately, this turned out to be the lull before the storm. The next day, I heard from one of our men that the group had been arrested just beyond the bridge as they left the village. A German detachment had been unexpectedly patrolling the area with a dog and had intercepted and arrested them. Only their son, Salomon, and the guide had managed to escape. All our efforts to save this family from deportation had been in vain, and the guilt was phenomenal. I was in shock. Kohler seemed as distraught as I was.

That evening, shortly after dinner, we heard a stone hit the kitchen window. Although faint, the noise could only have come from something being thrown at the shutter. I went and opened it slightly and saw Salomon hiding behind a hedge. I signalled at him to come around to the front door. When I opened the door and prepared to take him in my arms, so delighted was I to see that he had escaped, he shoved me aside violently.

"Which one of you talked?!" he shouted.

I urged him to lower his voice, as Ernestine was in her bedroom on the second floor.

"What do you mean? Nobody betrayed you!" I said, astonished at his words.

"Was it Kohler? Or you? Or your wife?"

"Salomon, are you crazy? Do you think we'd hide you all this time just to denounce you?"

"We heard you and your wife talking the other night. We can hear everything through the chimney, even from the cellar!"

"That's enough, Salomon! What would we gain from having you arrested? Your father is a friend, why would I do that to him?"

"I don't believe you," he snarled.

The pure look of hatred twisting the features of his fifteen-year-old face made him look at least twice his age.

"Salomon, come on, be reasonable. Go back downstairs and wait for the war to end," I pleaded.

"What? Just so you can hand me over to them again?!"

I drew closer to him to try to make him see reason. Noemie came out of the kitchen and joined us. Solomon glared at her.

"Was it you? Or your Kraut?"

Noemie looked at him, dumbfounded. I began to lose my patience.

"He's not Noemie's Kraut any more than he is mine, so please calm down and go back downstairs," I said, desperately trying to defuse the situation.

"You're all fake! The lot of you! You take Jews in, pretending to save them and buying yourselves a conscience in the process, but you're even worse than the Nazis!"

"I beg you, Salomon, the war is almost over! If you don't go back to the cellar, you'll be arrested like your parents!"

When Kohler heard the shouting, he came down to see what was going on. As soon as he caught sight of the German, Salomon rushed at him. Kohler gripped the teenager in his strong arms and managed to restrain him. Salomon then turned and ran to the front door which I had carefully closed behind us because of the blackout restrictions. He opened it hollering, "I hate you! All of you! You're all traitors who've sold out to the Krauts!"

Then he ran towards the gate. His hatred lingered in the hallway. This second departure plunged me further into disarray. This war has to end, for pity's sake, let it end!

To cap it all, a few days later I was reading the local newspaper and learned with horror that a dozen Resistance fighters from the Langlois troop had been arrested by the Gestapo in the forest of La Trappe. They were reportedly tortured. They would no doubt be shot within the next forty-eight hours, whether they talked or not. How was this possible? What on earth had happened? They were supposed to have left the hideout in the forest, my informant had been emphatic about that. I buried my head in my hands and wept. I'm the one responsible for the death of all those young people.

It's all my fault. Those young Resistance fighters who, like me and Noemie and countless others, were just doing their utmost to free France from the enemy. I couldn't accept that my negligence, foolish behaviour and stupidity had just sent those brave youngsters to their graves. How could I ever forgive myself? How could I go on living with that on my conscience?

31

Noemie, January 1944

The war is dragging on with no end in sight. The Allies were meant to have landed by now, but we're still waiting. No one knows where or when it'll happen. If the operation is to succeed, it must be kept top secret. The Allies must be going to great pains to ensure the Germans don't suspect anything. They'll probably also put out some false information. The only good news we have had is that the Russians are giving the Germans a hard time on the Eastern Front. The Red Army has taken back its cities one by one, completely throwing the Nazis off balance. The German army has lost thousands of men. There are even rumours that Stalin is liberating Eastern Europe so that he can secretly take over the rest of the continent. That would be the last straw! One dictator would merely be replaced with another.

Since August, the house feels empty. We haven't heard anything from the Bach family, nor from their son Salomon. We hope that he was able to locate his older brother, Jonathan, and get to safety. I often think of that dreadful, unjust scene he made when he left. But how can you blame him? He's still a child, and his nerves were on a knife-edge after spending a year underground in that tunnel. I hope that one day we'll get the chance to tell him just how wrong he was. But all that matters right now is that he is safe somewhere.

Gunther left two days after the Bachs. He was extremely vague about the reason for his departure. Without going into detail, he told me his commanders suspected him of having helped us rescue the Bachs. Apparently, he was being sent to the Eastern Front where the Reich needed reinforcements. This worried me at the time and I am still very concerned about him because we haven't heard anything from him since.

Once the Bach family and Gunther were no longer living under our roof, I had hoped that the atmosphere would become less oppressive and that we could concentrate on returning to something resembling normality in our family life. Solveig and Valentin are growing up and the war has robbed them of a good chunk of their childhood. Now that we have the house back to ourselves, I am enjoying giving them more time and attention. Curiously, the atmosphere at home has indeed changed, but not in the way I was expecting. Just as our daily lives should be more carefree, Armand seems more preoccupied than ever.

One evening, I sensed that he was almost at the end of his tether and I decided to make him talk. The last few months have been hell for me, not understanding what was going on in his head. I eventually put it down to a form of depression induced by the war, and the worries and strain it caused us, not to mention living permanently in fear and learning of the Bachs' arrest. At the same time, I was convinced there was something else. I knew my husband and had long admired his ability to shoulder our woes. But my goodness it was always painful trying to worm anything out of him. He always clammed up at the mere suggestion that we talk. So, after dinner, with the children in bed and Ernestine at her parents for the night, I poured us each a small glass of brandy to calm our nerves and prepared myself for the task of persuading him to open up.

Little did I suspect what he was about to tell me. When he finally blurted out why he was so unhappy, I was truly shocked. It turns out that, unbeknown to him, he had denounced the Langlois Resistance fighters. He had genuinely believed they had changed the hideout location, but the result was the same. I was devastated by this news. I wept for him, and for us. Carrying such a burden is too much for anyone to bear. I knew then that our lives would be forever marred by this fatal error. He used words like "carelessness" and "foolishness", but I preferred to call it a mistake. It had been a mistake in the worst possible combination of circumstances. His intentions had been entirely honourable; he had believed he was doing the right thing by diverting the Gestapo's attention away from our house until the Bachs had escaped. The worst thing of all was that despite all his efforts, he hadn't been able to save the Bachs.

Since his confession, Armand seems less gloomy, as if sharing his anguish has lightened his emotional burden. It will still take him a long time to recover though. As far as I'm aware, no one knows that he was the informant. Even I didn't know. Maybe the fact the Resistance don't know it was him, is adding to his depression? Maybe he should explain what happened to the representatives of the Notre-Dame network? But the choice must be his and I don't wish to influence him. The time will undoubtedly come when he will feel the need to make a public apology. I made him promise to confide in me in future, insofar as the confidential nature of his mission allows.

That same evening, something unexpected happened. After the emotional tumult of our conversation, Armand and I put on Radio-Londres. For a few days now we have been waiting for a message which would confirm a weapons and ammunition drop on a site not far from Lignon. Sitting on the sofa in the small drawing room, we listened attentively to the wireless. Then the announcer's nasal voice said loud and clear, "Father Christmas will be coming early this year, I repeat, Father Christmas will be coming early this year." We smiled at each other in joy and simultaneously lifted our fists in a victory salute.

I don't know how or why it happened, whether we were just overwhelmed by emotion or the fact that the horrors of the war had brought us closer together, but the fact is, after the broadcast, we threw ourselves into each other's arms and embraced madly like two young lovers discovering their first kiss. Our desire for each other was palpable. I had a sudden urge to show my husband just how much I loved him in spite of everything. I undid his trouser buttons one by one as his penis strained against the fabric. My mouth left his lips and moved downwards, something I had never dared do before. As I caressed him and kissed his body in places I had never previously explored, I felt Armand relax. After managing to restrain himself for a few minutes, he gave in and gently pushed me back onto the carpet. He pulled up my skirt as I frantically tore aside my undergarments. Our lovemaking was fast and sensuous as we reached new heights of passion never before experienced together. After the final climax, we lay back, panting like teenagers. Then we started to laugh hysterically. We didn't seem able to stop. What we had just done did not resemble our normal relations in any way. I had dared to do things with Gunther that I had never done with my own husband. Until now. It was as if our sex life had been straitjacketed all this time, consistent with my moral upbringing which forbade taking any initiative in such carnal pleasures. It wasn't even as if we—or rather I—had not already felt the thrill of challenging conventions and breaking the rules. I could see just how much I had changed during the war. Once we managed to stop laughing, we stood up. Armand cupped my face in his hands and kissed me again. We looked into each other's eyes and knew that our lovemaking would never be the same again.

I was relieved when Gunther had gone, but curiously I missed him too. He had been living with us—almost constantly—for three years. My feelings for him had subsided with time, but it felt good to know he loved me. Our farewells were rather hasty, as his commanders didn't allow him any time for such niceties. That evening, as he was packing his few belongings, I went up to his room. I wanted to thank him for helping us with the Bachs and say goodbye. I also wanted to tell him that even though our relationship had changed, he meant a lot to me. That's when he told me he was going to the Eastern Front. He took me in his arms and we were both overcome by emotion. I felt sorry for him.

One day, shortly after confiding in me, Armand told me about his last conversation with Gunther and the dilemma he faced because he was half Jewish. You could have knocked me for six! In hindsight it made sense that his fiancée's name was Hannah. I wished he had told me while he was still living with us; it would have saved me a lot of worry.

"How did you find out?" I asked Armand.

"He told me the day before the Bachs left."

"But why did he tell you?" I insisted.

"Because the Wehrmacht had discovered he was half Jewish and wanted him out of the army. They had him cornered. The Gestapo suspected that we were hiding Jews, and since he lived with us, they offered him a deal: either denounce us or face being sent to one of the OT forced labour camps."

"This is unbelievable! I thought he had gone to fight on the Eastern Front and that he may even be dead by now!"

"The OT isn't exactly the safest place to be either . . ." Armand reminded me.

"But it's less dangerous than fighting on the front line isn't it?"

"Yes, no doubt."

"So he chose to do hard labour rather than betray us. Why didn't you tell me any of this at the time?"

"Because he asked me not to."

Well, well, so my husband and my lover had been secretly colluding behind my back. I smiled and tried to imagine poor Gunther, with his long, slim musician's hands and his impeccable nails, labouring to build infrastructure and weapons so that the Third Reich could win the war.

"When I think back to how terrified we were the whole time the Bachs were in our cellar . . . And to think he wouldn't have betrayed them after all . . . By the way, how did the Gestapo guess the Bachs were here?"

"I wish I knew . . . I hope it wasn't one of the staff. We must have been careless at some point and one blunder easily leads to another. Someone was bound to find out sooner or later."

"And report us . . ." I added.

"Yes . . . what an unbearable thought."

"Who could hate us that much?"

"Oh, I don't think it was aimed against us, I think whoever did it loathed Jews."

"Even so, our heads were on the block too! The Germans have shot people for less! What abominable times we live in!"

"This is precisely why we have to be extra vigilant."

I didn't hear his last words. I was too shaken by what I had just learned.

"His answers to Solveig's questions about Jews make sense now too. How ironic!"

Why hadn't Gunther told me he was partly Jewish? I suddenly remembered something he had said when we broke up, some private affair he couldn't tell anyone. At the time, I had felt offended that he didn't trust me. In hindsight, I realize that he must have been petrified of the consequences should he share his secret.

32

Solveig, September 2011

In 1971, I had a surprise visit at the bookshop. It was near the end of the day and I was tidying up the shelves and tables. The shop was almost empty. The few remaining customers were enjoying a slow, last-minute stroll along the narrow aisles, grabbing a book, reading the back cover, only to put it down again. Many came in not knowing exactly what they were looking for. They browsed, got ideas, and finally settled on a title. With so many books to choose from, it wasn't an easy task. I knew most of my customers well. So when they couldn't decide, I would suggest an author I thought they would enjoy.

It was raining cats and dogs that day. Salengro Square was awash with umbrellas that the Toulouse inhabitants had resigned themselves to carrying. Everyone was rushing to be somewhere. Those who came through the door and made the shop bell tinkle, were only too happy to talk about the weather. It hadn't rained for weeks and the torrential downpour that had been falling since early morning was a godsend. The farmland would be well watered, and everyone was delighted, except for those perpetual grumblers who are always moaning about something or other. They would never be satisfied, no matter what. I was lucky that my customers were rather cheerful on the whole, which helped raise my spirits that day. It was my mother's birthday, and every year on this day, I am filled with sadness. Today was just one of several landmark days for me. You know . . . the sort of dates you don't need to mark on the calendar as you couldn't forget them if you tried. Some customers who knew me well respected my dark days and sometimes left the shop only to return with a small box of chocolates, a flower, or even a simple joke. Nothing over the top, just empathy and human kindness. No one else knew the source of my unhappiness, but the regulars understood that I was consumed by a deep-rooted pain, despite the cheerful disposition I tried to maintain. My changing mood sometimes forced me to fake it if I didn't want to scare all my customers away. I was amazed by the power of a smile. Just starting the day with a fake smile, meant that the smile would spread to my thoughts and turn into a real smile by the evening.

It had been a tiring day and if it weren't for my customers' thoughtfulness, I would have closed the bookshop early to cry my eyes out in the back room. I had been holding my tears back all day and could feel the emotion welling up inside me as the hours dragged by. My chest was getting tighter and tighter and I could hardly breathe. Shortly before closing time, the bell over the door tinkled again. A middle-aged gentleman walked in and apologized for the water dripping off his raincoat. I reassured him that he wasn't the first person that day to enter the shop soaking wet. As I said this, I tried to place his accent. He wasn't a native French speaker. Curiosity pulled me out of my melancholy.

"Can I help you, sir?"

He seemed very embarrassed, as if he had entered my bookshop by mistake.

"Would you be Solveig? Solveig Lenoir?"

"Yes," I said, surprised to hear my maiden name.

"You probably don't recognize me, but we knew each other when you were a child, in Lignon."

The sadness I had been feeling all day suddenly engulfed me. Why did this stranger have to come and find me and bring up my childhood today of all days? I wanted to scream at him that it was a bad time. Why should I have to listen to what he had to say? I supposed he had come a long way, judging by his accent. And who knows, maybe he would provide some of the missing links to my shadowy past, links I still haven't found after all these years. So many questions remain unanswered. Now an opportunity had walked right in which might help me find some semblance of peace. I didn't have the luxury of pushing it away. I had forgotten all about the book still grasped between my sweaty palms.

"My name is Gunther Kohler."

I dropped the book. He bent down to pick it up, leaving me frozen to the spot, stranded between two display tables.

"Do you remember me?" he asked gently, seemingly aware of the effect his presence was having on me.

There was no beating around the bush. He probably thought I had been too young at the time to remember him. I may have suffered from amnesia in my childhood, but all my memories had long since come back and I recognized him straight away as the UG who had spent three years in our house. He was part of that unfortunate and unhappy episode of my life. Fragmented sentences came back to haunt me; snippets I had read in the file that Justin had compiled for me for "when you grow up":

"But how did you expect to get away with it after you freed them?"

"We thought we could blackmail them into silence, threatening to rat on Armand Lenoir as the one who betrayed the Langlois Resistance, and denouncing Noemie Lenoir for sleeping with a Kraut."

Justin gave me this file when I turned eighteen, deeming me to be old enough by then to know the truth. He had put it together using elements from the official investigation: the indictments, the testimonies, the announcement of the verdict, a few photographs, and everything he had been able to record that would one day allow me to understand exactly what had happened. He knew that even when I came of age, the law would not allow me to access the court documents. So he copied and transcribed them from memory, noting point by point, step by step, everything I needed to know to give me closure on this chapter of my life. Or at least to help me vanquish my demons and come to terms with my past.

I needed to find out and understand, to be able to put this mental torture behind me. An answer to my eternal question: Why? A few days after Justin had given me the envelope and explained what was in it, I immersed myself in the bundle of documents he had compiled for me. The moment had come. I had to feel ready to face and accept my past and be able to come to terms with it. Up to then, I just had a few snippets to work with, the sort of details you could tell a child. With Justin's notes, the bits of information I possessed had a common thread, a link from A to B. In other words, my misfortune now had a beginning, a middle, and an end, as well as a why and a how. The hardest thing to accept was that this tragic course of events was all down to circumstances. The unpredictable had sneaked into the real, tangible and controllable part of life. If the whole episode hadn't been so appallingly horrific, you could have just put it down to "rotten luck". Of course, they told me at the time who the perpetrator was, but they spared me anything that would taint the memory I had of my parents, so as not to sully them in my eyes. They didn't want to inflict additional trauma on a young girl whose short life had already sorely tested her.

Justin had done the right thing. He had given the envelope to me when I had been old enough to understand. Understand that my mother could fall in love with another man yet continue to love my father. Nationality didn't come into it. She fell in love, full stop. Such things are out of our control.

Even in wartime. Or should I say, *especially* in wartime, when daily life is one big repetitive helping of gloom, deprivation and restrictions. Okay, he was German, so what? As an adult, I could almost understand, if I compared their love with my own love for Justin, who as it happened, was much older, and had been like a father to me. I couldn't have given Justin up. I also learned that my father had been accused of being a traitor only then to find out that he wasn't. But I'm getting ahead of myself.

One answer I had not found in Justin's envelope and one which has been nagging at me all this time was whether my father knew about my mother's affair with the German. In other words, had he suffered? I needed closure and wouldn't get it until I had this missing element. I could forgive my mother for falling in love with another man, even a Nazi, but not for causing my father pain. As I gazed at the man standing in front of me, I knew that if anyone could answer my question, it was him.

"Yes, I remember you," I whispered, nodding. "I've often thought about that conversation we had about Jews, do you remember?" I added, to reassure him that I really did recall who he was.

I could see from his expression that he did.

"You were such an extraordinary child! At the time, I thought that if ever I had a daughter, I would want her to be just like you. But alas it wasn't meant to be."

"You're not married then?"

"I was married, briefly."

"With the young lady from the photograph in your room?" I asked.

His face dropped. "You remember her too? No . . . Unfortunately, I didn't marry Hannah. She died during the bombing of Cologne in May 1942. In fact, I lost my whole family in that bombing. I only found out at the end of the war. It's tragic and ironic in some ways because up to then they had managed to escape the clutches of the Gestapo . . . only to die in the Allied bombings."

"I'm so sorry . . ." I muttered. "But I don't understand. Why would your family be hiding from the Gestapo?"

"Because they were Jewish on my mother's side. They were arrested during the roundups in the autumn of 1941 and released several months later. Probably because my father was what they called 'a good German'. After that scare, they decided to go into hiding at a friend's house, to avoid being rounded up again. The Nazis are very temperamental, one day it's black and the next it's white. Hannah's family was in hiding too but they all perished in the bombings."

"I'm sorry . . . So you're also half Jewish then?" I asked.

"You could say that."

This conversation threw me. So the German living under our roof for three years had been Jewish all along?

"I have a very clear memory of asking you what you thought of Jews at the time."

"Yes, me too. I remember how it unsettled me, especially coming from someone your age. I suspect I evaded the question?"

"No, you didn't, you said in no uncertain terms that you liked Jews, which unsettled *me*, because I wasn't expecting to hear that. I realized at that moment that not all Germans were the same. And this was an important lesson for a child during the war . . . You said that your marriage didn't last?" I went on after a pause.

"Let's just say my wife couldn't cope with living in the shadow of another woman."

"Another woman?"

"Your mother, Noemie. I thought that when I returned to Germany I could forget her . . ."

My heart sank.

"You do know about us, don't you?"

He nodded.

"But I could never forget her. And I have never felt for another woman what I felt for your mother."

"And did she love you?" I asked, looking him in the eye.

"I believe so, yes. At least at the beginning. We slowly fell in love, without really wanting to."

From the inside pocket of his overcoat, he pulled out an old book. It was a beautiful anthology of French poetry from the 1930s. A bookmark poked out from the middle. He let me turn to that page and I read the title: "Tomorrow at Dawn". It was one of Victor Hugo's most famous poems and desperately sad as it had been written after the tragic death of his daughter, Léopoldine.

"We both liked this poem a lot . . . We both loved alexandrines."

Then he leafed back through the book to the title page where there was an anonymous, handwritten dedication: "For G in memory of the good times. N". I recognized the handwriting immediately. My eyes filled with tears and my throat tightened.

"To answer your question properly," he continued, "your mother wanted to end our relationship while I was still living at the manor. It was the sensible thing to do I suppose, but I couldn't accept it. I was very much in love with her . . . and very lonely too."

"Do you think my father knew about . . . about your affair?" I asked, looking up at him and finally asking the question that had tormented me for so long.

He hesitated before answering. "I doubt it. I think he would have said or done something if he had. In front of your mother and me, he always acted as if our relationship were just a forced living arrangement. Your father was a good man.

Although I suspect he got a thrill from seeing me screaming in pain the day I arrived in his surgery badly injured and he treated my head wounds without anesthetic!"

He smiled at the memory. "All's fair in love and war. Isn't that the expression? Your parents used to call me the UG, you know."

"Yes, I remember that," I said, smiling too.

"But in 1943, my relationship with your father changed. I can explain why if you wish. But as far as Noemie and I were concerned, I don't think he knew anything about it. He was always holed up in his surgery with patients coming and going all day."

I plucked up all my courage and asked him outright, "I suppose you heard about . . .?"

He nodded and looked down. "I'm sorry. I received a long letter one day telling me what had happened."

I looked at him in surprise. "A letter? From whom? Who could have written to tell you about that?"

"A policeman who had investigated the case."

"Justin? Justin Mayol?"

"Yes, that's right. We even met up in Paris one day. He wanted me to tell him about your family. He suspected that if Armand had denounced the Resistance there must have been a reason for it, and he had to find out why. He wanted you to have the whole story, the good and the bad bits, so you would have no doubts about your parents' true characters."

That's Justin all over. He always had a compelling need to get to the bottom of things. The case could only be closed if everyone involved knew where they stood. He had tracked down the German with the chocolate bar name. It couldn't have been simple. What surprised me was that the letter Gunther mentioned was not in the file Justin had given me. Was it an oversight? Or did he think it unnecessary to dwell on this part of the story, not wishing to add to my pain as it concerned my mother's feelings towards a man other than my father?

"I'm about to close up," I said as I dealt with the last customer's money. "But do stay awhile. I suggest you take off your overcoat, it's soaking."

I showed him the coat rack I had installed at the entrance so that my regulars could explore the shop unencumbered. Then I locked up, leaving him to roam among the shelves like a customer.

Alone now in the bookshop, we resumed our conversation.

"You were saying that your relationship with my father changed in 1943?"

"Let's just say that one day we spoke to one another for the first time ever simply as 'men' and not as enemy citizens of rival countries."

He then related the terrible dilemma he had faced and everything that had happened afterwards with my father. There was something touching about this man. I could sense his vulnerability beneath his solid Teutonic features. I could gather from what he revealed, just how much he had suffered. He had lived in fear of the Wehrmacht or anyone else discovering his Jewish origins, his political opinions had differed from those of the very regime he was supposed to serve, and he had been heartbroken by his illicit relationship with my mother. His entire life had been a lie for the three years he had spent under our roof.

"And then where did the Wehrmacht send you?" I asked, curiously.

"I had to join the Organization Todt. It was a kind of prison where we were subjected to forced labour and built all sorts of civil and military infrastructure such as buildings, bridges, and the famous V-2 rockets. I was sent to help construct the Atlantic Wall in Le Havre at first and then to other locations where they feared an Allied landing might take place. What I dreaded the most was being sent to work in the V-2 factories, but I was somehow spared that. I must have been 'born under a lucky star' as the French say. I was the luckiest German soldier alive. Many died at the front, and even working for the OT. Others perished in the camps too, of course; anyone who didn't fit the mould of the 'perfect' German."

"So you had no more news of my mother?"

"No, of course not. She ended our relationship several months earlier, leaving me heartbroken."

"And how did Justin find you?"

"He wrote a letter to the German army asking for the information as part of an investigation. This wasn't entirely true but his status as a police officer probably helped."

"Your French is very good, Mr Kohler . . . Or Gunther, if I may?"

"Yes, I prefer Gunther too. Thank you, that's kind of you to say. My mother was a Francophile, and raised me with a love of French culture, so I started learning the language from a young age. After that, I was more than happy to carry on her tradition, though I could never get rid of my accent!"

I had always kept my blue notebook at the bookshop. This was the exercise book I had started writing in as a child at the suggestion of my school teacher to keep myself out of mischief. I then carried on writing in it throughout my childhood, enjoying the simple pleasure of noting down anything I thought to be of importance. It was lying in a drawer behind the counter. I can't remember how it ended up there. To be honest, I never opened it any more. I was too scared to delve into those memories. I had even thought of getting rid of it, to make a symbolic break with my toxic past.

"Here, I've got something to show you too, Gunther," I said, taking out the faded notebook. "You're in there too, you'll see, written from a child's perspective of course. Take it, please."

His eyes went as big as saucers at the sight of it. "This is incredible! I remember that notebook very well. You had it with you all the time! It was more important to you than your toys. Thank you for entrusting it to me. I'm honoured. I shall of course return it to you."

"There's no need. I'm trying to remove anything painful from my life," I said, looking down and placing the exercise book on the counter in front of Gunther.

There was a momentary lull in the conversation. We chatted a bit more about my family, then he said he had to go. I saw him out. Outside on the street he held his arms out and we hugged each other. Those were the same arms he had wrapped around my mother. That thought alone brought me closer to her. I could tell from the way he was holding me that he sensed my emotion. Then he stepped back and took one last look at me before turning around to leave. He had already walked away when I called out to him.

"Gunther?"

"Yes?" he said, turning around.

I saw the tears in his eyes, and he could see mine.

"Can I be rather forward and ask you something?"

"Of course, go ahead, Solveig."

"Why did you come to see me?"

"I don't know exactly . . . Curiosity, probably. And above all, I needed to know that you had come out on the other side of all this and that you were all right. And from what I can see, you have and you are." He looked at my window display. "You have a delightful bookshop here. Your mother would have loved it."

After a pause, he said softly, "It was her birthday today . . ." Then he nodded goodbye and had soon blended into the evening bustle of the Toulouse streets. Meanwhile, the rain had stopped, and the wet pavements sparkled in the city lights.

We had promised to write to each other, but neither of us did. Too daunting I suppose. A few days afterwards, I realized just how important that meeting had been for us both. In a way Gunther was my missing link. And he had found solace in meeting the adult I had become. We both knew that pursuing our relationship would inevitably lead to more pain.

That was forty years ago. I doubt he is alive now but I have always been grateful to him for coming to see me that day.

33

Justin, end of June 1946

Once Ernestine had been questioned, we used our lunch break to go to the manor. When we arrived in front of the Lenoir property, I noticed the park was in bad shape. I watched Solveig out of the corner of my eye, hoping to gauge her reaction. As soon as we were through the gate, she ran to the pavilion. She turned round to look at us and we could tell by her smile that she recognized the place. I should have insisted from the beginning that we cast the net a little wider. God I regret this and can't get it out of my mind. Visiting the house where she lived clearly evoked more memories for her than meeting the people from her past. We had wasted precious time in our search for her family by sticking to our arbitrary thirty-mile limit.

"Is this your house, Solveig?" I asked, to encourage her to talk.

She nodded.

"Do you recognize it?"

"Yes!"

"Will you show us around?"

She took me by the hand and led us around the building to the park behind. A big grey cat came to meet us.

"Figaro! Oh, my gorgeous Figaro! You're so handsome! Do you recognize me?"

"Your cat is beautiful, Solveig," I said.

"Do you know why he's called Figaro?"

I had an inkling but wanted her to have the pleasure of telling me herself. The cat was rubbing up against her legs now. She tried to pick him up, but he was too heavy for her.

"Think about it, Justin. Figaro! Doesn't that name ring a bell?"

"I don't know . . . the opera . . . 'The Barber of Seville'?"

"No, *silly*! It's Pinocchio's cat, how could you not know that!" She looked at me with pride. The slightest connection to her former life was a victory for her.

"Come on, Figaro," she said, turning to the cat. "Let's continue our tour."

Sergeant Rousseau and Dr Bertin watched her in amusement as we walked down the long path to the pavilion.

"Mother loves coming here to do the flowers and to read."

As we strolled along the path, I tried to imagine what life was like for the owners of this beautiful but overgrown estate.

"And this is Germain's vegetable garden," announced Solveig. Her smile faded for a moment, as she blinked. I was about to ask her if anything was bothering her, but she went on her way as if nothing had happened.

The vegetable patch was in a deplorable state. Most of the plants had died, shrivelled up from dehydration and lack of care. There had been a few attempts to salvage the plot; some weeds had been pulled up and thrown into a pile and wet patches showed recent watering, although this appeared to be too little, too late. Only the hardiest varieties had survived. Sergeant Rousseau rubbed his chin and frowned as if something was puzzling him.

"Something wrong, Rousseau?" I asked.

"I don't know . . . This vegetable garden is in a pitiful state . . . I'm surprised at Germain."

We carried on walking, accompanied by our young guide.

"And this is Germain's potting shed!" Solveig said eagerly.

Hearing this, Rousseau and I glanced at each other. We smiled as we pictured Ernestine and the gardener in the throes of passion among the garden tools.

Once we had explored the park, we went inside the house. Dust was beginning to settle on the furniture, and the spiders had come out of hiding. Solveig hiccupped and began to cry. Her house was strangely empty which served to remind her how alone and lost she was. She remembered every room, telling us a little anecdote about each one. In the living room, she even showed me the "console of the dead" that she had told me about the day she saw me put a candle in front of my mother's photograph. But these were all memories from further in the past. Nothing came back to her about more recent events. She took my hand to lead me upstairs and asked me to come with her as she was afraid to go up alone. Rousseau stayed on the ground floor to look for any signs of an argument, a violent break-in, or other clues.

In her bedroom, Solveig went straight to her little desk, opened the drawer and took out a blue school notebook. She clutched it tightly and then handed it to me. She obviously knew what was inside. I opened it and to my amazement discovered that it was her diary. In beautiful, neat handwriting, the text was written through the eyes of a little girl; how she saw the world and the people around her. She had started it back in May 1943 but had not written every day, and the paragraphs were short. On the last page I read, "8th May 1946: surprise outing!" Then nothing.

"Don't you remember this 'surprise outing', Solveig?" I asked, shaken by discovering this direct connection with her disappearance. I showed her the page, despite knowing the answer.

She shook her head, embarrassed. The smile she had had on her face since we got here had disappeared.

"Don't worry, sweetheart, we'll find out. I'm going to read this and maybe there'll be some clues."

Once we were back downstairs, I held out the diary to Rousseau so he could see the last entry.

"Apparently, they left of their own free will. Looks like they had planned an outing," I said.

"Good grief! 8th May . . . What day did she arrive in Bournelin?"

"On the 15th. That means she was with her parents for seven days, but we don't know where . . ."

"So they left of their own accord for a few days, just as their note suggests," he said to sum up.

After lunch, we returned to the station to continue our interviews. We had invited the Lenoirs' gardener in for questioning but he was keeping us waiting by being rather late.

"So you know Germain Gachet?" I asked Rousseau, to pass the time.

"Oh, just a little. We were in the same class at school, but we lost touch after that. From time to time, I received news of him from my parents when our two families happened to bump into each other."

"Tell me about him, so I can get a feel for the man," I said.

"You know, there's not a lot to say. Their lives are rather uneventful, really. They're simple, hard-working folk. They weren't born with a silver spoon in their mouths, that's for sure. The family was distraught at the loss of one of their sons during the war. He was a member of the Resistance. He had been a child prodigy, the brightest child in the family and the first to go to university, you get the picture . . . Very early on, he joined the Resistance and managed to mobilize several hundred people in the area. He led a very active branch of the Notre-Dame network. He was high up in the BCRA[1] and close to Colonel Rémy, do you remember who he was?"

---

1 Bureau central de renseignements et d'action, the Central Intelligence and Action Bureau of the Free France movement, created in July 1940 by General de Gaulle.

"Yes, of course, it wasn't that long ago . . ."

"Somebody talked to the Germans and told them the location of one of their camps. All of those who were in it at the time, including Germain's brother, Etienne, were tortured and then shot. But none of them talked. They were a brave bunch."

"There were only men there?" I asked.

"Yes, I think so. Etienne wasn't even supposed to be there. He had just come to do some training with them. He wasn't out in the field much, you know, with him being a leader and that. He mostly coordinated action between the local *maquis* and the central Resistance network. It's been very hard for their parents."

"When was all this?" I asked.

"I would say . . . about three years ago. I remember that it was just after the STO was brought in and many of the guys who refused to go to Germany joined the Resistance instead. So they had a lot of new recruits. Hence the need for organization on the ground. So it must have been around the summer of 1943."

In the meantime, Germain Gachet had finally arrived. A man of average height and build, and rather rough looking, entered the office. He had the sort of sympathetic, ruddy face that people who love nature and live a simple outdoor life usually have. We sat him down and introduced ourselves. This time, it was Rousseau who would conduct the interview.

"Why did you call me back?" asked Germain.

"Because since our last interview, a colleague from the Bournelin station has arrived to give us a hand. He has brought fresh evidence to the inquiry that we didn't have the other day."

Germain looked surprised. "Bournelin? What kind of evidence?"

"We're the ones asking the questions, Germain, if you don't mind. Tell us again about what you've been doing since the Lenoirs disappeared."

"Well, when I saw the note they left, I went to help a cousin out with wheat threshing down south. I told myself that there was no point hanging around here, since they were away."

"What, there's no work to do in the park in May? I heard that you had planted a superb vegetable garden?"

"I did indeed! It helped the Lenoirs out a lot during the war and it's very useful even now! I mean, until they left."

"And all that went untended for how long?"

Germain paused to think. "Err . . . I'm not sure . . ."

"Germain, it was last month, you must remember!"

"I don't know. About three weeks maybe . . ."

"That's not very precise . . . And weren't you only supposed to be gone for a few days? How did you get to where you were going down south?"

"By train."

"Did you keep your tickets?"

"Well, no, I had no reason to keep them."

"That's a shame. You know, we went to the manor. And we saw the park. And the vegetable garden."

He nodded, looking sheepish.

"It hasn't been tended to for more than a month, everything is dry and wilting," prodded Rousseau.

"It's just that . . . I had to stay longer at my cousin's as . . . there was a lot of work to do in the fields! I decided to take the leave due to me at the same time. I even asked my mother to tell the Lenoirs that I would be away for a while, but they weren't home."

"There's a good reason for that! So you just let the plants in your employers' beautiful park wither and die?"

Rousseau's remark visibly upset him. The sergeant had explained to me, during our visit to the Lenoirs, that Germain was very fussy and exacting in his work. He was reputed to be the best gardener in the area. Many people came to him for advice. Hence Rousseau's surprise when he saw the state the garden was in.

"I'm sorry, Germain, but this just doesn't add up . . . It doesn't sound like you."

Beads of sweat broke out on Germain's forehead. He wrung his hands until his knuckles turned white.

"If the police visit your cousins, can they confirm that you were there with them?"

". . ."

"Germain? You weren't down south at all, were you?"

Our deliberate silence after this question prompted Germain to fill it.

"You're right. I was in hospital," he mumbled.

"In hospital? What were you doing in hospital?"

"I had an accident."

"What kind of accident?"

"I fell out of a tree."

"A tree?"

"I was pruning it and slipped off the branch. Mr Lenoir had forbidden me from pruning the trees on my own so I was afraid I would be yelled at."

"How long were you in hospital?"

"A month. But I haven't been quite right since the accident. I've been suffering from the after-effects of my injuries and couldn't go back to work. I still can't bend my knees properly."

As he spoke, he stood up to show us his disability. Sensing that we were making headway and that this could be the turning point, I took over from Rousseau. I continued to use Germain's first name so as not to disrupt the flow of his questioning.

"Say, Germain, are you not sending us on a bit of a wild goose chase here? Staying in hospital for a month implies you were seriously injured. Yet you fell from the tree, went home and *then* went to hospital for a month?"

"Well, no, it wasn't quite like that . . ."

"Who found you after you fell?"

"My brother. He comes to see me from time to time at the manor."

"And he just happened to drop by that day . . ."

"Yes, it was a real stroke of luck."

"Which hospital were you in?"

"Bordeaux."

This nitwit was beginning to annoy me, trying to fob us off like this. I whispered in Rousseau's ear that I was going to make a telephone call. When I returned, Germain had turned crimson and sweat was dripping down his face. I sat down again and slapped both hands down hard on the desk in front of him, as if to say, "That's enough, you can't fool us". I looked at my colleague.

"What have you learned in my absence?"

"Not much. I was waiting for you."

"Well, I learned something very interesting . . ." I said, turning to Germain. "I phoned the hospital in Bordeaux."

" . . . "

"And you know what they told me?"

Germain was sinking lower and lower in his chair.

"They told me you were in there for five weeks, not three, and that you had a car accident. Can you confirm that?"

He was hunched over now and just nodded.

"What's more, you weren't alone. Your brother, George, was with you. And he's still in pretty bad shape."

I was trying to push him over the edge to get him to tell us the truth. And it appeared to be working. His shoulders started to shake with spasms that he could barely control.

"Do you still stand by your version of events?"

"Yes," he murmured.

"So what does that mean? Why are you lying to us?"

"Because it was me who was driving . . ." he whispered suddenly, letting out a sob.

"And?"

"I don't have a license."

"Is that all?"

"I can't bear the fact that I did that to my brother. You can understand, can't you? Plus, I could go to jail for injuring someone while driving without a license! And I can hardly imagine what—"

"Where exactly did the accident take place?" I cut in.

"Near Girac, on the big bend. The steering just went."

"Near Girac? That's very close to Bournelin . . . What were you doing there?"

"We were going to have a picnic in the woods."

"Just the two of you?"

"Yes. Why, is that against the law?"

"So, one day, you just fancy going for a little picnic with your brother, thirty miles from here, despite the fact that petrol costs an arm and a leg at the moment?"

I was hoping to provoke him enough that he would fly off the handle but my intimidation tactics failed on this occasion.

"Where exactly did you have your picnic?" I asked then.

"I don't know, it's usually George who drives."

"Please stop taking the piss!" I shouted.

"I don't know! We never go to the same place."

"Could you drive us there?"

He shook his head.

"You're even stupider than I thought then!" I retorted.

"But I have no sense of direction! I don't know where we went that day!"

"What if I told you a girl was found in Bournelin?" I said next, deciding to play my trump card. I was careful not to reveal whether she was alive.

He looked up suddenly. All the blood had drained from his face. "A girl? Which girl?"

"It's funny that you ask which girl rather than asking what that's got to do with you!" I said.

"It's because you know who the girl in question is, don't you?" added Rousseau.

"No, I don't! I swear! I don't know what you're talking about!" he protested.

I stood up suddenly and banged my fists on the desk again. It was obvious the guy knew something. I went out to look for Dr Bertin and Solveig. When I told Bertin that I wanted Solveig and Germain to meet face to face, he categorically refused.

"If this is the guy that kidnapped Solveig's family, it could have a devastating effect on her . . . We have to tread carefully . . . If this man tortured her and her family, imagine what the shock could do to her. If you really want them to meet, you should ask a professional, such as a psychiatrist, to be present and take responsibility."

"What are the risks?"

"She could relive her trauma . . . The risk is also that the whole episode will come back to her, and as we don't know exactly what happened, we don't know the extent of the horrors she experienced."

"What if we show her a picture of Germain?" I suggested.

"Why not. That gives us more distance than if she were to see him face to face."

"I've got an even better idea. We'll show her photographs of several men, including Germain. If she recognizes him, we'll be able to observe her reaction."

"That's fine by me," the doctor replied. I returned to the interview room where Rousseau was still grilling the gardener.

"Do we have a picture of him?" I asked Rousseau, pointing at Germain.

"Not yet, but we can take one."

While Germain was having his picture taken, Rousseau and I took stock of the situation and shared our theories.

"Assuming it's him . . ." I pondered aloud, "he doesn't know that Solveig is alive. If she had been able to tell us what happened, she would have led us directly to him. But that's not the case. He suspects that she hasn't said anything, though he doesn't know *why* she hasn't, and he also suspects we don't have enough evidence to charge him . . ."

"Your analysis makes sense . . ." Rousseau agreed. "We'll have to find something else."

"Let's be logical . . ." I said then. "Why would someone go for a picnic so far from home?"

"Well, you would have to have a pretty good reason for going. Maybe you like it there because you've been before . . . Or you're meeting someone. Or because you own the land and need to do some maintenance. Or quite simply because you feel an attachment to a particular place and want to connect with your memories. Though I don't see the Gachet brothers as being the sentimental type!" said Rousseau dryly.

"But if you were planning on doing something stupid, and I mean something *really* stupid, you wouldn't do it on your own doorstep would you, unless you want to become the prime suspect . . ." I said.

"Of course," he replied. "Unless it's not premeditated and happens by accident . . ."

"The car accident . . ." I mused. "It's still strange that he had an accident and was hospitalized for so long at the exact same time his employers disappeared, don't you think?"

"Yes, I agree," said Rousseau. "But I don't see the connection. Why would he want to bump off his employers? It doesn't make sense to me. You know what, I think I'll drop by the notary's office to find out if the Gachets own a plot of land over there."

I went outside and requested a cigarette from the policeman who was standing there on his break. I hadn't smoked since the war but now felt a sudden craving to do so. We were getting closer to the truth and I was becoming increasingly nervous. Germain was lying a lot and lying badly. He was hiding something. His story about the driving license was designed to throw us off the scent. But I had a gut feeling that we were getting closer to the truth.

Rousseau returned from the notary's office half an hour later in a state of excitement. In the meantime, Germain had been brought back into the interview room. While we were waiting for the photograph, we picked up the interrogation where we had left off.

"The forest of La Trappe, does that mean anything to you?" Rousseau asked him.

"Well, yes, it's the *maquis* where they arrested some Resistance fighters during the war," he replied.

"It's the *maquis* where your brother, Etienne, was arrested! And where exactly is this camp?"

". . ."

"It's funny because the notary has just told me that the plot of land where the *maquis* was located belongs to your family!"

"Well, yes, that's why Etienne set up part of his network there. He knew the area well."

"Is that where you and George went on the day of the accident?"

"Yes. We wanted to pay our respects."

"It's strange you should want to pay your respects there when your brother was actually shot by the Gestapo at the Souge camp near Bordeaux . . ."

"Yes, but there in the woods was where he was taken prisoner. We've been going there every year since 1943. Plus, it was VE day."

"It was 8th May?" I cut in. In my mind's eye I could see Solveig's diary entry: "8th May 1946: surprise outing!"

"Why didn't you tell us the truth?" Rousseau went on. "Why didn't you want us to know that you had gone there of all places? Why? Did you hide something there? Or someone?"

He shook his head and began to cry. "It's because it's a sacred place for me and my brother."

"My heart bleeds for you! You really think that we are going to fall for your sentimental bullshit? You took the Lenoirs there, didn't you?" I said as I held up Solveig's blue notebook and showed him the last entry.

"Why would I have done that?"

"If you don't tell us, we'll find out . . . I assure you; we'll find out!" I shouted. Then I decided to change tack. "What about Ernestine? Was she an accomplice?"

"No, Ernestine had nothing to do with what happened!"

"So what exactly *did* happen, Germain?"

34
Armand, September 1944

The long-awaited Allied landings finally took place in June! Since then, the Allies have been liberating the country, little by little. Or should I say, *we've* been liberating the country, as the Resistance has been more active than ever to ensure the Germans are driven out. Numerous battles still have to be won. The Germans are not giving up. In mid-August, another landing took place in Provence to open up a second front and corner the enemy in a pincer movement. At the end of July, Hitler miraculously escaped an attack masterminded by opponents of the Nazi regime who were determined to take power and negotiate with the Allies to wage a joint fight against communism. Hitler was saved by his heavy oak map table . . . It just goes to show that all life hangs by a thread. In the meantime, he's alive and well. He will neither admit defeat nor burden himself with a conscience, it seems. He even flouts the basic rules of warfare and attacks civilian targets. In June, the SS cowardly massacred the inhabitants of a village in the Limousin. After the battle of Normandy, Germany aimed its V-1s and then its deadly V-2s towards England, causing considerable damage and appalling loss of life. The war is far from over. The fighting continues with greater intensity than ever before as Hitler clings to power. His troops are in despair, however, and their morale is flagging. The Allies are marching towards Berlin, the Russians are advancing from the east, and the British and American troops are arriving from the west. But at what cost? So many lives could have been spared if the Führer had not been so stubborn and conceded defeat.

Over the past few months, Noemie and I have been very active with our clandestine activities, but more cautious than ever as the reprisals are absolutely ruthless. Anything is permitted now, on both sides, in utter contempt of the Geneva Convention, which was heralded as a safeguard against such barbaric acts. This year has been particularly hard on our network as some of our leaders were suspected of conspiring with the enemy. Many of us were arrested and much information got leaked. This often came down to simple negligence: documents not being concealed properly or envelopes getting lost, idle chatter and so on. Stupid mistakes that could have been avoided.

Since last March, all Resistance fighters have been regrouped into a single unit, the French Forces of the Interior. This has only exacerbated rivalries, however. In the southwest, there was a devious and deadly battle between leaders. As a result, deep distrust has taken root within the ranks, and sometimes even executions have been carried out. In the so-called name of security, people have committed outrageous acts, even killing each other within their own camp. Noemie has had a hard time accepting all this. I must say I am amazed at the courage she has shown in completing each of her missions. Especially after our discussion about the risks we were taking and the possible impact on our family. My wife has been a gallant soldier in the shadows. Who would have thought it before the war?

Bordeaux was liberated on 29th August. Last week, General de Gaulle visited the city. We all hope that his intervention will bring some order to the mess that the Resistance leaders have created in the region. But since that fateful day in May 1943 when the Langlois camp in the forest of La Trappe was raided and seized because of my negligence, I am not the same man. It took me a long time to be able to open up to Noemie about it. I am ashamed and horrified at my carelessness. The final blow came when I learned that the son of Aurelia Blasco, that dutiful, fragile woman, as well as Etienne, our gardener's brother, were both at the Trappe *maquis* that day. Once again, I sank into an abyss of guilt. Etienne was the Gachet family's favourite. Everyone admired him for having made something of his life and for successfully completing his studies, as well as his unconditional faith in his political commitments and France's victory. And now a dire misunderstanding had destroyed all those lives. Young lives reared on the milk of courage, altruism and tenacity.

I feel a little better now that I have told Noemie why I've been so despondent. It's as if I have offloaded part of the burden. For now, nobody seems to be aware that the dreadful "leak"—I cannot bring myself to use the word "denunciation" as it wasn't one—came from me. Maybe I would feel better if I told them? But how could I prove it was simply a blunder, a prodigious and excruciating blunder, and not a betrayal? If I were to make amends, would my sheer commitment to the Resistance be enough to clear my name? Publicly perhaps, but it wouldn't erase the guilt. I wouldn't loathe myself any less.

Because of this black cloud hanging over me, I am unable to join others in their rejoicing that the war is ending. I'll be relieved, but I won't be celebrating. We have seen so many of our people die. It's too painful. Five years of frustration, persecution, restrictions, fear, violence and death. Millions of deaths . . . Sometimes I wish I could put an end to it all. Crazy ideas run through my head. They often say that violence begets violence. Only a barbaric act could put an end to the mental torture I'm experiencing. Sometimes I think of finishing things for good. What worries me, however, is that I don't just envisage it for myself. I can't bear the idea of leaving my family behind. I must banish such thoughts! I must! My conscience is tormenting me and I am torn between two conflicting desires.

35

Noemie, beginning of May 1946

We were so relieved when the war ended. This last year has been particularly agonizing. The Allied landings were long overdue and just when we thought the war was going to end, 1945 hit us extremely hard. The Germans wouldn't give up and we lost so many lives both in the *maquis* and in the bombings. But all of this is over now. Rationing is still the norm, but we are holding out. Germain continues to cultivate our vegetable garden. He produces more than we can eat, so I have started to give some to those in need, like Aurelia Blasco. She is still recovering from the loss of her son, Pablo. He helped her raise her four other children, all much younger. He became the man of the house after his father died under Franco's regime. Giving her a few vegetables is the least we can do.

Armand is slowly recovering from his depressive spell. He still feels terrible guilt at what happened. I'm not sure if he will ever get over it to be honest. If only we knew what has become of the Bachs, it would help him a bit. Especially if they survived. But the end of the war merely exposed the horrors and reality of that deadly regime, including the existence of concentration camps in Germany and Poland for the mass murder of Europe's Jews. Hitler's public speeches during which he ranted and raved like a crazy puppet meant people's attention was riveted on him, while his relentless murder machine was silently working away in the background, slaughtering entire families with horrifying meticulousness and efficacy. Were the Bachs among them I wonder? Did Salomon manage to slip through the net? We are desperately waiting for news from them.

Armand and I agreed not to talk about what had happened to the Langlois *maquis* until a few days ago. I get the feeling that he needs to make amends. Germain doesn't know the exact circumstances that led to his brother's death and Armand can't stomach the hypocrisy any longer.

"I'm going to tell him," he told me a few days ago. "You'll see, Germain is a good sort, and he is fond of us. He'll understand that I never wanted such an atrocity to occur."

I was sceptical, however. Germain is a model employee, kind and helpful, but he is also rather crude and tactless, and he has not shown himself to be very discerning. God only knows how he'll react when he learns that his brother's death could have been avoided and, worse still, that his employer, whom he interacts with on a daily basis and serves loyally, was the perpetrator.

Since his confession, Armand has started opening up to me. In fact, a short while ago, he unburdened himself of another secret which had been playing on his conscience. He told me about a young woman who had consulted him a little over a year before. She had been pregnant and had asked him for an abortion. Although Armand had explained to her that he couldn't do it, she wouldn't take no for an answer and came back several times, begging for his help. Yet Armand steadfastly refused to play any part in the termination of this unborn life. An abortion would also have put the young mother's own life at risk, and Armand wasn't willing to assume the responsibility for this. The grief-stricken young girl had become pregnant after being gang raped. I didn't know about it at the time, but she regularly pestered Armand, venting her fury and frustration at him for refusing his aid. In desperation, he advised her to give up the child if she really couldn't bear the thought of keeping and raising it. He also warned her that she should stop harassing him and that if she failed to do so, he would get the police involved.

Armand had been in disarray after these encounters because he had sent away a young woman in distress. But there was nothing he could do for her. She was a mere adolescent faced with the horror of having to give birth to a child conceived through suffering, violence and hatred.

"Do you realize," he confided in me, "I advised her to give up her child . . . It's an abominable piece of advice to give to an expectant mother."

"You didn't exactly have a choice. It was either that or put her life in danger," I said to soothe him.

"She didn't care about that. She said she would rather die than give birth to that child."

"She didn't realize what *you* were risking too . . ." I added.

"I think her misery blinded her to any predicament other than her own."

"You have done nothing wrong; you did what anyone would do!" I said comfortingly.

"I know, but it's constantly on my mind. It haunts me. She was so young. I wonder if she had the child after all. I just hope she didn't do anything foolish."

"You mean take her life? Or the child's?"

"One or the other, or both . . . Either way, it's abysmal. Sometimes I have this urge to go and check the orphanages to see if the child is there."

"And what would you do then?"

"I don't know. Just to find out, that's all," he said pensively.

"But it would just cause you more pain," I argued. "You would feel so helpless afterwards."

The conversation ended there, but I could tell Armand was very affected by what he had just told me. It's funny because before the war, I used to think I was married to a cold stoic man, who was as tough as old boots. Yet as the years went by and events unfolded, I discovered just how fragile the man I had been married to for ten years really was, despite his hard exterior.

The war caused its share of monstrosities. All this is behind us now. We need to rebuild, look to the future, live life to the full, and watch our children grow. As it happens, Germain has invited us all to go for a drive out in the country with him on 8th May to celebrate "Victory Day", as he puts it, in his brother's new car. I wasn't convinced but Armand said it was a genuinely kind offer and it would be rude to refuse. On the contrary, he saw it as a sign that it was time to tell Germain what really happened. He tried to convince me with his arguments, and I could see that he was also trying to convince himself.

"Germain probably doesn't even know that I was in the Resistance. Our two networks worked in parallel and their paths never crossed. After all, think about how we endangered our lives hiding Jews! He didn't know about that either. And I didn't talk when I found those weapons he was hiding in our cellar . . . That proves that we were on the same side. We're not monsters—he needs to know that."

"I'm sorry, but I still have my doubts . . . But do whatever you wish, Armand. If it eases your conscience . . . But bear in mind that whatever you tell him will spread like wildfire through Lignon. Are you ready for your confession to go public?"

"I think so, because I have lots of people who can testify to the fact that I was an active Resistance fighter. And it's high time I took responsibility for my deed. I'll tell him at the end of the day, when we're back and he'll be in a good mood after the outing."

Despite all this, I'm sure we'll have a fabulous day out in the country next Wednesday. The children will love it. After a trip in a cabriolet, they'll probably start pestering us to buy one too. And maybe we should consider it. Imagine the freedom of being able go wherever you want!

36

Justin, end of June 1946

The day after Germain's interrogation, we went to the forest of La Trappe at dawn with the dogs. We took Germain with us, wearing handcuffs. We hesitated about bringing Solveig along too. The urgency of the situation tipped the balance in favour of this solution, and we decided she would come along and wait with one of us in a police van while the others conducted the search. She had recognized Germain in the photograph, but only as her parents' gardener, nothing more. We were convinced that the terrible crime had been committed in this wood. On the way there, I asked her if she recognized the road from a recent walk. She couldn't answer me. She seemed agitated and confused and didn't seem to be making much sense.

Once we got there, the forest was almost inaccessible. We needed a pickaxe to clear the way, despite seeing that someone had left recent tracks. The little house referred to by the notary was more like a simple shack or wood cabin. The door was wide open. A crack had split it in two. Germain was brought right up to the cabin, his wrists still handcuffed behind his back.

"Is that where you had your picnic?" I asked.

He nodded.

"Show me where you sat."

He pointed to a clearing in the vegetation near a small stream. Sergeant Rousseau and I entered the cabin. The stench of urine and faeces assaulted our senses. Yet we found no trace of animal activity; only a few dark spots on the wooden floor.

Rousseau asked two colleagues to look carefully inside and around the cabin, and two others to walk around the plot to look for any clues. The place was quiet and deserted. Birds were warbling happily away on this summer morning. *One of them had probably witnessed the scene.* We found nothing after a quick scout of the area. I could see Germain out of the corner of my eye. He was standing between two policemen, looking dazed. Then one of the police in charge of searching the house called out from inside.

"Come and see this!"

We rushed in. Our colleague had made a surprising discovery. Someone had etched a message into the wood. It wasn't very deep, but you could see the inscription clearly enough with a well-aimed torch. The person must have carved the letters in the dark, as there would have been no light in the cabin. You could read a "C", followed by a short horizontal line. Then two slashes, with a space between them, the tops of which seemed to join, and what looked like another "C". Then an "I" was followed by another crossed-out "I" and a third "I" was followed by three short horizontal lines, stacked as two equals symbols on top of each other. Another "I" accompanied by a horizontal line completed the word. The lines were small. The person etching these letters was obviously trying to conserve their energy and the tool they were using. No matter how hard we looked at the inscription, we could not decipher it. One of my colleagues eventually had the bright idea of stepping back to read it from a distance. As he pointed his flashlight at the inscription again, he gaped in amazement.

We all stood back to read C- /\ C I Ɨ I ≡I-. At this distance, our brains were able to assimilate and render comprehensible what they hadn't been able to decipher close up: G A C H E T.

Our initial reaction was to assume that was it, that the investigation was over. We had found the culprit. I then realized we were getting ahead of ourselves, so I brought everyone back down to earth.

"This land and the shack belong to the Gachet family . . . One of their children could easily have carved their name here."

The policeman with the torch wasn't buying it. According to him, the engravings were pretty recent. "Besides, kids would have done it in daylight, more legibly. This looks more like the desperate scratches of a victim . . ." he said, pointing to the marks. He approached the wall and crouched down. He ran his finger over the floor. Fine sawdust had accumulated beneath the inscription.

"We'd have to find the tool that was used. It might still be here. Given how the inscription was made, it must have had a sharp point."

We looked under our feet. In the halo of the torch, we noticed a tiny nail stuck between two floorboards. Its size and bluntness made it possible to assume that this was the tool they had used.

"If the Lenoirs were kept prisoner here, then where are they now?" I asked.

We all went outside to find our suspect standing there hanging his head. One of our guys had been searching around the hut and had found a small metal comb under some leaves; the sort women use to keep their hair in place. He showed it to me.

"Germain, the Lenoirs were kept prisoner here, and we have the proof inside," I said. "Plus we found this," I added, holding up the comb. "You didn't do a very good job at cleaning up after yourselves."

He looked up. His hair was a mess from his night at the station, his eyes were bloodshot from lack of sleep, and his unkempt and unshaven face gave him a strange, haggard appearance.

"Where did you take them?" I asked.

". . ."

"Gachet, talk! You're just making it worse for yourself by keeping silent. If we can still help them, you'll get a lesser sentence. At least tell us if they're alive?"

Germain collapsed. His weak knees could no longer support him. The two policemen on either side of him had trouble holding up his bulky body.

"Gachet!" I shouted. "Are they alive at least?"

The dogs were agitated now and had started sniffing around in a corner of the plot. They were clawing at the earth, which seemed softer and more malleable there than in the rest of the woods where it had hardened during the recent drought. With their noses to the ground, the dogs started to scratch and dig with increasing intensity. Then, all at once, we realized.

Germain was crying and nodding, kneeling on the ground, his shoulders held back by the two policemen. His cries turned into moans.

"Now you're going to tell us what happened!" I shouted.

"I didn't mean to . . . I didn't mean to . . . It's because of the accident . . ." he wailed, catching his breath between two hiccups. "We just wanted to scare them . . . to punish them . . ." He sniffed loudly and swallowed his phlegm.

"Punish them for *what*, damn it?!"

"For denouncing my brother's *maquis*!"

"Did Lenoir tell you that?"

"No! For a long time we thought that one of the group had denounced them, so that the Krauts would release his wife who they were holding prisoner."

"So who told you?" I asked again.

"A Kraut from the Gestapo told me just before he left Lignon after the Liberation."

"And you believed him?"

"Why else would he tell me that?"

"Out of spite, of course! To destroy more lives and leave as much chaos as possible behind! So why didn't you confront Lenoir then?"

"I had no proof. It was my word against his. Besides, I wanted to get my revenge on him, and punish him. He had to pay for what he did, damn traitor!"

"But you knew that the Lenoirs were actively involved in the Resistance, didn't you, you imbecile? We checked them out. They belonged to the Civil and Military Organization, a large and very active Resistance network operating out of the Bordeaux region. Did you not know that?"

"Eleventh hour rebels, those bastards!" he spat, releasing his long-suppressed venom. "Saving their skin at the last minute!"

"You're wrong!" I shouted. "He and his wife joined the Resistance right at the start of the war! Your informant got it wrong!"

"That bastard was way too friendly with the Krauts!" he protested.

"Did you never stop to think it was maybe a strategy of his to humour them and stop them from getting suspicious?"

"He was friends with the local police commissioner. All that lot were Vichy brown nosers, everyone knew that."

"You've got it all wrong, you filthy bastard!"

"They housed a Kraut, and that whore of a wife of his was having it away with him!"

"You know very well that people who had the space were ordered to take in German soldiers. You're not that thick are you?"

"Yes, I know, I'm not stupid. But it didn't seem to bother them at all. They were quite happy to take all the extras the Kraut gave them. But his wife didn't have to sleep with him, did she?! So I wanted her to pay for what she did too. And it was Lenoir who denounced the Langlois *maquis*, I swear!"

"Assuming you are right, was that reason enough to assassinate them and their children?"

"We didn't want them to die! We just wanted to punish them and let them stew for a few days, then release them. We did leave them some food and water."

"And you think they wouldn't have told the police about you afterwards?"

"We had enough on them to keep them quiet."

"What do you mean?" I asked, intrigued.

". . ."

"Speak, for God's sake!"

"We would have threatened to tell the whole of Lignon that it was Lenoir who betrayed the *maquis*, and that his wife, Noemie, had been sleeping with the Kraut living under their roof."

"My God, you really are a pair of scumbags, both of you! Do you know how they actually died?"

"What about my brother? It was horrible what happened to him, and for my family too," he mumbled, his face tense.

"Did you at least tell them why you were locking them up?"

He shook his head.

"So you didn't even give him a chance to explain? Or let him tell you why he did it?"

"I didn't have to; I knew why he did it!"

"Except that you got it all wrong, you idiot! Because we checked it out. Lenoir was indeed a first-rate Resistance fighter. Something unexpected must have cropped up, something out of his control. He would never knowingly have denounced a *maquis*, just like that, for fun. But don't worry, we're going to get to the truth, while you spend the rest of your days rotting away in jail!"

My hatred for this man drove me into an indescribable rage. A whole family wiped out for the sake of a bungled revenge! It was too absurd, too unfair, and beyond belief! And as if that wasn't enough, he was the source of Solveig's misfortune. He had stolen the happy, carefree childhood she was entitled to. This monster had destroyed her life. She would never be happy or have peace of mind after this. Because of Germain, she would drag this terrible burden around with her all her life, weighed down by the guilt at having lost her memory and not being able to save her parents and little brother. I pulled myself together, trying to calm down. I clenched my jaw and went on, although I was unable to bring myself to look him in the face.

"When did you come back to bury them?"

"After I got out of hospital. Three weeks ago."

"Were you alone?"

"I wasn't about to get all of Lignon involved and brag about what I'd done now, was I?!"

"Why didn't you send someone to free them while you were in hospital?"

"I was scared. And they were injecting me with painkillers that put me to sleep and made it hard for me to think straight. But even when I was clearheaded, there was no one I could ask to help me. I didn't trust anyone. I wanted to deal with it myself right to the end. I was afraid of the Lenoirs' reaction. They would have told the police who would have come straight to the hospital and I wouldn't have had time to make sure they kept their mouths shut."

"And when you realized that your plan had gone awry, did you not think it was better to cut your losses and save their lives? That it might cost you more in the long run to leave them here to perish?"

His eyes were riveted firmly on the ground and he was shaking his head as if he didn't believe the scene that was playing out before him.

"The note that was left in the hallway; was it you who wrote it when you all left the house? Did you imitate the doctor's handwriting?"

He nodded.

"I see, you didn't want Ernestine or other people who knew them to get suspicious . . . If it wasn't so serious, I'd say that was rather clever . . . And which car did you use to drive back from the hospital?"

"I borrowed one."

"How did you manage to dig with your injured knees?"

"I had to. I had no choice."

"Did you bring a shovel with you?"

"Yes, I did."

"You thought of everything, didn't you? You knew what you were coming back to, didn't you? And how did you react when you saw that the girl was gone?"

"I panicked. I thought she was going to turn me in. I tried to look for her, but I quickly gave up because I didn't even really know what I would do with her if I found her."

"Oh we can believe that all right! In the realm of horrors, you have well and truly proved yourself! The poor girl was so traumatized by what you did to them that she lost her memory. She doesn't remember a thing. We're not even sure she'll recognize you. Anyway, I don't want her to see you. You're too much of a monster; you destroy everything you cast your evil eyes on. We had a hard time figuring out that she was from Lignon. And we nearly didn't see it. It was your tomato plants that gave you away!"

We took the dogs, who were still sniffing around in the freshly turned earth and headed back to Lignon. The next day, a van carrying three coffins, including a small white one, went to the site. The police exhumed the bodies of Noemie and Armand Lenoir, as well as that of little Valentin.

37

Solveig, the same day

I waited ages, sat in the van parked on the roadside with the doors open. A policeman stayed with me. He would probably have preferred to go into the woods with his colleagues than sit here minding a child. He was nice but hardly spoke to me. And he was really big and strong, which made the van sway every time he got out to stretch his legs or sat down again. Sometimes I got out too, as it was hot inside. I watched the butterflies fluttering around in the bushes on the side of the road. How I wished I was as light as them. I felt as if a lead weight was hanging from my neck.

I didn't feel very well either. Maybe it was because I knew this was the end. I would soon find out. And then I would have to leave Justin's house. There were just two possibilities now. Either I would go back home to my parents, or I would go to an orphanage, for good this time. My life with Justin was over. It would have to be filed away under "memories". I remembered an expression I'd heard recently: "It's a blessing in disguise". At the time, I remember thinking how true it was because I had recently fallen over in the police station yard and grazed my knees. And while I was on the ground, writhing in pain, I suddenly spied all the marbles I had lost up to then, under the cistern. They had gathered there as there was a slight slope. So if I hadn't fallen over, I would never have found my marbles. But now it will be one extreme or the other. Either they find my parents and I go back to my old life, which is *good*. Or I lose my parents and Justin, which is *bad*.

We could hear dogs barking in the distance, muffled by the forest. They must have been a long way from the road. Sometimes, shrill voices reached us too, the sound swallowed up by the trees. Then nothing . . . After what seemed like an eternity, I saw Justin coming out of the bushes. His face had changed. I hardly recognized him. From a distance, I knew it was him from the way he walked. The closer he got, the more I could see how wrinkled his forehead was as if he was in pain. His jaw was clenched, and his face looked shiny. It was weird, but as he got closer, I realized that his face was wet from crying. My chest tightened. I got out of the van and went to meet him. I could hardly breathe. I felt faint and had to stop and close my eyes. When the dizziness passed, I opened them again. Meanwhile, Justin had come a little closer. I threw myself into his arms and he picked me up. He carried me away, grasping me tightly.

Once I was in his arms I screamed. I had been holding it in for so long and now I wanted to let it all out. I clutched Justin, while he rocked me like a baby, crying with me. The other policemen came out of the woods with a man in handcuffs. They didn't dare come near, probably because they didn't want to disturb us. I felt like I was wrapped up in cotton wool, like I was looking at the scene around me from the outside. As if it wasn't me and this wasn't my life. It was another very unhappy little girl. And I felt so sorry for her. On the way home, Justin and I stayed wrapped in each other's arms. I was so exhausted that eventually my head dropped onto his legs and I fell asleep.

38

Solveig, September 2011

To this day, I still find it very difficult to talk about it all. My whole life I have had to carry the burden of my parents' death, convinced that they wouldn't have died if I hadn't stupidly lost my memory. I had been lucky enough to escape. But I hadn't been able to do what my parents expected of me and get help so we could go back to our quiet life at home and prevent Germain from carrying out his deadly plan. All the years of counselling and therapy I received from a very young age made little difference. Not to mention the sheer grief and agony of my loss. Living without my parents left me feeling like a plant without roots or support, at the utter mercy of the elements or the slightest gust of wind.

In spite of it all, I found a form of happiness with my husband, Antoine. Thanks to Antoine and Justin I was able to live my adult life. I became Mrs Lenoir-Moustier on 29th December 1957. I kept my maiden name along with my married name as a tribute to my family. I was twenty-one years old, and he was thirteen years my senior. He was my philosophy teacher from school. All the girls fancied him and used to vie for his attention, but he only had eyes for me. At that time, Justin was still the man of my dreams, and it was only later on that I realized my teacher had a crush on me and how much I actually liked him myself. After I completed my Baccalaureate, he started pursuing me. Freed from the confused feelings I thought I had for my substitute father, I let myself be swept away by a new love of an entirely different kind.

I wasn't interested in boys of my age. I found them superficial. I needed someone to lean on. I was still fragile and I would buckle under the slightest knock that life sent my way. I realized that I needed a father figure by my side whom I could rely on, to help me cope with the harsh reality of the adult world. Antoine embodied this role perfectly and our love story lasted fifty years.

After that fateful day on 30th June 1946, on which I simultaneously found and lost my family, I had to learn how to live with my identity and my past, large swaths of which had started coming back to me. It was as if the outcome had opened up the floodgates of a memory that had deliberately stalled to protect me from the horrors of it all. Everything came back in fits and starts. The cabin, my parents, my brother, all chained up. I was the only one who was free to move around because the Gachet brothers wanted to make sure that someone was able to feed the others. They had left a bucket of water, a bowl, some fruit and bread, and locked the door with a wooden bar on the outside. I was the one who had scratched away at the crack in the door for days with the little metal hair comb that Mother wore, till it was big enough for me to slip through. By a stroke of luck, the wood at the bottom of the door was rotten so it came away easily. And then the mad race, the fall. I can still feel the thorns and dense vegetation I had to run through, scratching my skin. I have no precise idea when my amnesia kicked in but it must have been at some point between escaping from the cabin and arriving in Bournelin, because by the time I approached the town square, I didn't know who I was, or that I was meant to get help for my family. When I left my parents, I had a clear sense of panic and urgency. I had to act fast. Valentin was very weak. He wouldn't last long, and neither would my parents. We had no food left. By asking me to go for help, they were sending away the only person who could feed them.

But not knowing how long the Gachets intended to keep us prisoner there, they took the risk. I ran at first, but after my fall I could only stagger, dazed, not thinking or even knowing where I was going. Had the shock of my fall triggered my memory loss? Or was the burden I bore simply too heavy for a little girl like me?

The police estimated that I had walked about six miles. I arrived in Bournelin utterly exhausted. For a long time I had to live with the appalling contradiction of never knowing whether my amnesia had protected or betrayed me. Would I have been able to locate my parents and my little brother if my memory had remained intact? Would we have arrived in time to save them? Nothing is certain, given the distance I had covered and the fact I had to scramble through woods and fields. And we only had limited time to act. The amnesia had freed me from a huge responsibility. So, yes, in some ways you could say my amnesia protected me in the short term. But it also betrayed me by preventing me from providing the investigators with the clues necessary to find my parents quickly enough to save them.

In hindsight, the amnesia gave me an excuse, a semblance of an alibi, but my conscience has always rejected it. What would the course of my life have been if I had got my family back? Would I have been happy? These questions are as futile as they are inescapable. Justin would probably not have featured in my life for long and Antoine would not even have entered it. Everything could have been very different. I had the distinct impression that right from the beginning, misunderstandings, hasty judgments, and unverified assumptions had led events to unfold in this implacable, unstoppable way. I had been the unwilling protagonist of an adult drama. And part of the script involved my childhood being snatched away from me. My little brother's too. Looking back, I miss him the most. As a child, I mourned him, of course, but I found it crueller still to be robbed of my parents. As an adult, I realized that he had suffered most from the dire injustice of it all. A seven-year-old child who hadn't asked anyone for anything and whose incomprehension at what was happening to him was met by silence. He, the most innocent of all, had died of thirst and hunger; a slow, painful death. In addition to accepting the actual tragedy itself, I had to cope with the visions, the nightmares and the endless questions. Who died first? Did they suffer? Were they scared? Did they worry about me when I didn't come back? Did they call out for help? Did they call out to me, Solveig, who was supposed to rescue them?

The death of my parents made me an orphan. I was only able to cope with this thanks to Justin. Even when the threat of being discovered by the family's kidnapper had passed, I carried on living with him. The thought of going back to any kind of orphanage was intolerable. I didn't want to be just another orphan in the welfare system. Justin decided to adopt me. Of course, he had to convince Eliette, who finally softened in the face of my misfortune and agreed. But the country was full of war orphans, so the process was long and tortuous. I was not a member of his family, which complicated things. Justin and I were always worried that someone would come looking for me. In the end, the process never came to fruition. My file got lost in the meanders of an administration overwhelmed by the implementation of the new post-war regime, and I was forgotten. Justin did, however, belatedly obtain my guardianship so that he could manage my affairs. And that's where we left things. On a symbolic level, I preferred that he didn't become my father. Even as a child, I understood what was involved. It was only after I got married that he was finally able to legally adopt me and make me his daughter. I can't tell you how happy I was when I signed the papers.

In the years that followed, Justin did his best to try and find out exactly what had happened that day in May 1946, the start of this whole tragedy. My blue notebook was of no use to him for the investigation, but it helped him get to know the child I was before that cursed day. He went to see Germain in prison to talk to him. At first I was angry at him for this, but one day he explained it to me.

"It's important, Solveig, to understand what happened. You've got to banish hatred and judgment to get peace of mind. Germain didn't want them to die. He just wanted to teach them a good lesson, because he thought your father had betrayed them, which wasn't the case. He needs to know this. I'm searching for evidence to show him."

"Have you found anything?" I asked.

"I think so. While talking with the surviving members of the Langlois *maquis*, they explained to me that the day they were arrested, they weren't supposed to be there."

"I don't understand . . ."

"Apparently, your father wanted to divert the Wehrmacht's attention away from your house. Your parents were hiding a Jewish family in the cellar and the Gestapo were getting suspicious. He had to distract them for a few days while he organized the Jewish family's escape. For the Germans, taking down a local Resistance group was an even greater prize than capturing a family of Jews. Your father supplied this information believing it to be erroneous. The *maquis* was supposed to have changed location to the other side of the hill, a few miles away. Sadly, your father learned afterwards that that hadn't happened due to the weather. The river separating the two hillsides had flooded preventing them from crossing to the other side. So they stayed put. Alas, it was too late, and all the Resistance fighters present that day were arrested.

"My parents weren't traitors then?"

"No, on the contrary, they were good people. They were true patriots who were actively involved in the Resistance and hid Jews in danger. Do you know what your mother's codename was?"

I shook my head.

"Grieg."

"Grieg?"

"Do you see why?"

"As in Grieg . . . who composed 'Solveig's Song'?" I asked, before bursting into tears. Minute details such as these reminded me how much my mother had loved me, and how much of a void she had left.

Germain's trial sent me to a dark place. Even though he was convicted of a triple homicide, the reasons for his revenge were never examined. His accident was not deemed reason enough to qualify for involuntary manslaughter, as he had had ample time in hospital to inform the police and have my family released. For the judiciary, he had sought revenge on his employer who had denounced his brother's *maquis*, full stop. The investigation stopped there since the betrayal had been proven: the *maquis* had indeed been denounced by someone. We then learned with astonishment that it was Dr Lenoir who had talked. Then nothing more. Nothing that could justify his deed. That's what Justin tried to establish afterwards, since the judiciary wouldn't do it. For instance, *why* had my father denounced them? Luckily, Justin had found the answer.

I learned much later that the German with the chocolate bar name had helped clarify many points. He was notably able to confirm the presence of the Bachs in our house and his help in evacuating them, the information my father had given about the *maquis*, and of course his love affair with my mother, which Germain had described as some cheap sexual encounter. After Gunther's visit to the bookshop in the

1970s, Justin told me that he had met up with him. He had kept this from me deliberately because Gunther had been my mother's lover. He didn't want to rub salt in my wounds. His intentions were good but he hadn't stopped to think that the most painful thing for me wasn't the fact that my mother had fallen in love with a German, but that she was no longer there to see me grow up.

All these factors cast a dark cloud over my young existence. I had been led to believe for a long time that my parents had been mere opportunists who had paid for their betrayal with their lives. But Justin's investigation ultimately brought them justice. As for Germain, he was a man in distress, a victim of his desire for vengeance and his own poor judgement, who had limited himself to what he saw on the surface without trying to understand what was really going on. Every missing piece of the jigsaw that Justin found regarding my family's death soothed my troubled conscience and above all made me stronger. Events could have unfolded differently, but that's how it was. Nothing more nothing less. We couldn't do anything about it, except deplore the terrible and unfortunate combination of circumstances. At some point in our lives, I think we all wish we could just hit rewind and replay certain scenes.

Justin also strived to find out what had happened to the Bachs. At first, he couldn't find any official trace of them. Then he decided to look for their sons, Salomon and Jonathan. Their surname was very common, and he had no idea where they could have fled. He was unable to find them. But one day, about five years after the tragedy, the Lignon notary informed us that a letter had arrived in my parents' name. He passed it on to us. It was from Salomon Bach. He informed my parents that Gabriel, Mélanie and Ethel had died during the deportation but he himself had gone into hiding by changing his name and identity until the end of the war.

He had tracked down his brother, Jonathan, in Bordeaux in the neighbourhood where they used to live before the conflict. They both had the foresight to get in touch with their mother's best friend who lived not far from their home on the Allées de Tourny. While describing their stay in the cellar of our home to his brother, Salomon finally accepted that my parents had not betrayed them but had on the contrary tried to save them. Grief-stricken by the disappearance of his family, he needed to let a few years elapse before making contact with my parents and expressing his gratitude. He had put an address on the back of the envelope. I couldn't bring myself to leave his letter unanswered. I was fifteen years old at the time, which was about the same age as Salomon had been when we hid him and his family in 1942–1943. I thanked him for taking the trouble to give us news, expressing my sorrow at the death of his parents. I also took the opportunity to inform him of the loss of my family in May 1946, without going into any detail.

In the early 1950s, we were told that Germain had hanged himself in his prison cell. After his brother had succumbed to his injuries, he had fallen into a deep depression. Germain's death left me indifferent, as the information Justin had gathered had helped quieten my emotional turmoil by then. By this time, a form of resignation had taken over and I had banished hatred and judgement from my thoughts. These were the seeds of ultimate acceptance, a small step towards healing.

After I got married, I decided to sell the manor. It hadn't been lived in for nine years and the idea of moving there filled me with dread. Antoine and I were already thinking of moving to Toulouse, to put some distance between us and my past. One morning, we received a call from the Lignon notary. He told us that a Parisian couple had asked if the uninhabited manor house in the Vaillant district was for sale.

I didn't even discuss the price they were offering and the deal was swiftly done. The building was just four haunted walls to me and getting rid of it would be part of my healing process. Against Justin's advice, I donated the entire proceeds from the sale to an orphans' charity. Antoine didn't attempt to influence me. Justin thought that the money should have enabled us to build ourselves a beautiful home with all the material comforts which would help ease my pain and start afresh. I, on the other hand, didn't care much about material comforts and I felt a strange sense of purification in getting rid of the manor. I felt like I was washing away the horrors that had been clinging to my skin like leeches all this time. I had to get rid of the old, the soiled, the terror of the past, to rebuild a new life on a clean and solid foundation. We got married, moved to Toulouse, and I purchased the bookshop.

There is one point I still need to clarify . . . It concerns the hastily scribbled note left by Lucille, my friend Sylvette's mother, just before she committed suicide. Had my father received a distraught Lucille in his surgery? Was my father the doctor who had refused to perform the abortion? Had she really ended her life because of him?

I decided to keep very few of my parents' belongings. Just a few personal affairs so I could connect with them when I needed to. I was still young, barely twenty, when I made these choices. They probably wouldn't have been the same ten years later, or another ten years after that. We don't give the same importance to things throughout the course of our lives. In addition to the small gold Occitan cross that my mother wore around her neck every day, which I now wear in her place, I kept a piece of jewellery that came from my mother's grandmother. It was an enamelled pendant of the Virgin Mary, very ordinary, but which had intrigued me as a child as it could be opened to reveal a small secret cavity. It was this little detail that I had liked at the time. Today I find it rather ugly. I don't think it is worth very much and it has taken on an awkward sentimental value. If I could do this all over again, I would have kept the painting that my mother loved so much, painted by an artist friend of hers. It depicted an old man lighting his pipe against a background reminiscent of the paintings of Georges de La Tour. This painting made an impact on me at the time as the man in the picture seemed to be enjoying this simple pleasure of lighting his pipe despite being engulfed by clouds of smoke. As a child, I remember always being surprised that it didn't seem to sting his eyes! I sold the painting to an art dealer who evaluated everything in the manor. I have always regretted doing so. Instead of the painting, I now just have an ugly pendant. I kept Valentin's favourite cuddly toy, a little bear with rough hair and glass eyes, called Prosper. Absolutely no one was allowed to touch this toy apart from him, otherwise they risked provoking Valentin's screams followed by my mother's hollering.

I didn't have the heart to part with the famous "console of the dead". It served as a bridge between before and after. I continued the ritual and sadly completed it with my parents' wedding photograph and a picture of Valentine, proudly perched on a carousel horse. I placed Prosper the bear next to it. He looked older and tattier but sat there faithfully. Finally, as a reminder of my father, I decided to keep his appointment books. There was one for each year he practised. Their beautiful leather binding captivated me. I couldn't bring myself to throw them away. Sadly, I don't have anything personal from him, which is tough. But these notebooks feel like an extension of my father somehow, as he had one to hand at all times.

After talking to Sylvette about her mother, I retrieved my father's 1945 appointment book to see if her mother's name featured anywhere. I knew my friend's date of birth and so also knew that her mother must have consulted a doctor at the beginning of the year. I flipped through the pages of my father's appointment book trying to decipher his handwriting. I searched for the name Lucille Lelièvre—Sylvette had the same surname as she had never married. My father only noted his patients' surnames, preceded by Mr, Miss or Mrs, and the fees charged. There were no patients registered under the name Lelièvre. There was a Lefèvre, but it was a man. Then I remembered that Lucille had been very young at the time and that he may have just noted her first name. I scoured the months that interested me but still found nothing. I was about to close the appointment book when a thought struck me. The young woman had come for an abortion. Maybe she had wanted to remain anonymous. Or maybe my father had chosen not to record her name deliberately? If that was the case, I would never know. Having said that, my father must have noted the appointment somehow, even in code form. I looked through the appointment book again, and instead of scanning the pages for a specific person, I looked closer at the columns of names. And indeed, on Wednesday 14th March 1945, a Miss LL. had consulted my father. She also came back a week later, then twice more on 27th March and 3rd April. So it could well have been her.

I told Sylvette all this sometime later and even showed her the appointment books. We agreed that neither of us were responsible for our parents' actions and that in the end, if my father had performed the abortion, we wouldn't be standing here talking about it today. Our friendship was made of stronger stuff. Besides, we were more convinced that my father had actually saved Sylvette's life rather than caused her mother's suicide. We still had doubts, however, about how to interpret Lucille's last words. Sylvette clung to the idea that Lucille's fatal act had been driven by her extreme youth and despair, not by her lack of feelings towards her child. If that had been the case, she would have chosen to have her adopted or put in an orphanage. What we did know, however, was that she had been unable to accept this child's existence, a cruel living reminder of the outrage she had suffered, and had preferred to bring down the curtain for good.

Sylvette is still my friend today. She couldn't bring herself to start a family. She had the opportunity but had absolutely no desire to. She said she was too tough, too mean. This was in complete contrast to me as I desperately wanted to have a family and become a mother. I felt a strong need to draw on the abundance of love my parents had given me and had never lavished on anyone. No one except Justin of course, but he had never been interested in me romantically.

Justin . . . He died about ten years ago of a heart attack. I was absolutely devastated by his death. Eliette also had a very hard time overcoming her grief and has since chosen to live in a retirement home. Apparently, she is happy there. I sometimes visit her.

So now you know my story. You may think it's pretty awful, or you may think I've come through it pretty well. Both are true in fact. After all, I could have perished in that cabin too. People judge things according to their own personal setbacks. The little girl inside of me lives on though, still reeling with guilt at losing her memory at such a crucial time. She only got through this because of the support and kindness of those around her who helped her with her innermost struggles. Nevertheless, the need to be punished for not being able to save her parents and little brother never left her despite years of therapy. No doubt a remnant of her religious education. Penance that serves no purpose other than to prevent people from enjoying life. Despite such tragic circumstances, Solveig accepted the cards she was dealt and grew up to find relative happiness. My husband was wonderful, ours was a love story in the truest sense of the word, and my children gave me everything a mother could dream of. But in the end, it was down to me. "I took the bull by the horns", as little Solveig would say, determined to vanquish my demons and not let this episode destroy the rest of my life. This is how I was able to face my destiny and ultimately accept the course my life had taken. It didn't take me long to realize that only I, and I alone, had the power to transform my suffering into a form of happiness. Yes, those were the cards I was dealt. I could have shown my hand and pulled out of the game. But I had a zest for life and decided that not only would I play the game, but I would play to win. You can take a horse to water but you can't make it drink. The difference being, I *wanted* to drink. I had a thirst for life, for myself and for my loved ones, including my family, who hadn't been as lucky as me. I couldn't change past events, but I could change my perception of them. I could observe things from a different perspective, without judgment and hatred. I owe the happiness I have found in my life to Justin who was a father to me, and to Antoine, the love of my life, my only love. Both crossed my path at the precise moment I needed them. They are my saviours, they lit up my life. And I know that when we meet again, and we will, they will light up my way to eternity.

Author's Note

This story and its characters are entirely fictitious. As for the historical parts of the novel, I did a lot of research and reading and have tried to stay as close to the facts as possible. Although I have tried to render historical details accurately, I hope my readers will forgive any errors or approximations that remain.

Acknowledgements

To write this novel, I drew on help from many people and I wish to express my sincere thanks to all of them. Here they are "in order of appearance" as they say in the film business: Angèle Benoît, Monia Tamarelle, Christophe Arnaud, Franck Roncaglia, Christine Rodière, Nathalie Pican, Charlotte Polivka, Clément Hubin-Andrieu, Nelly Pillon.

I also wish to say a huge, hearty and just as sincere thank-you to the people who encouraged, reassured and supported me in one way or another throughout this journey. Here, I'm referring to my family and friends, of course, but also to strangers who expressed interest in my work not knowing how much this meant to me.

Special thanks also go to François Juncker, Antoine Guilloppé, Anne-Gaëlle Huon, and the teams at Kobo-Fnac, Babelio and Préludes who placed their trust in me.

Finally, I wish to thank Pascal, Salomé, Clément and Maéva, my "tribe", who support me unconditionally and are, as the heroine of this novel puts it, "my haven of peace".